CLARA
A Divine Comedy

CLARA
A Divine Comedy
Eia von der Flur

UNITED WRITERS
Cornwall

UNITED WRITERS PUBLICATIONS LTD
Ailsa, Castle Gate, Penzance, Cornwall.

British Library Cataloguing in Publication Data:

A catalogue record for this book is
available from the British Library.

ISBN 1 85200 067 8

Printed in Great Britain by
United Writers Publications Ltd.,
Cornwall.

This story is
dedicated to Roo,
and is a thanksgiving
to Mary McNelis
and Loraine Borg.

For Jeannot Keith
with Love, Eia.

Eia von der fleur.

Munich on 12th of february 1998.

Acknowledgements

Thanks are due to the following sources:

The kind permission of A.P. Watt Ltd., on behalf of Michael Yeats, for the inclusion of an extract from *The Stolen Child* by W.B. Yeats.

EMI Music Publishing Ltd., for the inclusion of part of the song *Side by Side* by Harry Woods - Lawrence Wright Music Co. Ltd.

Suhrkamp Verlag of Frankfurt am Main, for permission to reproduce two verses from R.M. Rilke.

R. Piper and Co. of Verlag, München, for the use of *Von den heimlichen Rosen* by Christian Morgenstern. In: Margareta Morgenstern (Hrsg.), Meine Liebe ist groß wie die weite Welt. Ausgewählte Gedichte, 1936.

Poet Philip Elston for the translations of German Poems into English.

Letters to Beatriz

The Letters to Beatriz, instead of being the story, became an overture in which are touched lightly the themes that are become the stories of the Story.

1st Letter
Last Quarter Moon. Wednesday 14th October 1987.

This is the story. Gradually, it will unfold. Slowly, intricately, it will unravel the ravelled skeins of my life. - And yet, there is already a tapestry woven. Thread upon colourful thread, a shine of gold here and there, a light of silver, image upon image, grown out of deep dark depths, dark, dark deepnesses of me, through-lighted by the shine of my daylight-eyes and woven by my clear strong hands into this tapestry. - It is terrible and it is beautiful.

It is my adventure.

It is my journey to the within from hence it was begun, unwittingly.

There will be so many letters, my love. I don't know how many. Many. They do not need answering.

This morning, I have been born: like spring upon spring out of the earth of me, I am happening!

I am the seed; for every time when you die, all is gathered in, all life is in-gathered and becomes the seed, the egg, waiting for its new befruiting.

I am the befruited seed *and* the tree bearing red-golden apples. For I am the woman who died this morning and who is born this morning from her own ashes. All in an unspeakable moment.

All the many faces of hers have become the one face: open, clear, light. True.

All time has become the one time, inner time, *my inner time*, as uniquely mine as the wise writing on the soles of my feet or in the palms of my hands. These were given from the beginning, that was received.

I am the woman who died this morning, and this morning is been born. All the many faces by which she was known and unknown to herself are the one face: open, clear, light. Known.

And her being is Love.

There is a task to be done. And I will take off my ankle-long velvet gown shot through with gold thread, and I will put on my work-dress.

I know my task.

You said it, Beatriz, when you interpreted my last dream: 'Put two and two together and make five.' (Just as my Mother used to say.)

It is my own life now, mine. There is at once a fulfilment and a beginning.

Insightful and aware in a new consciousness, I can draw from the full well that is my life and each draught will be a gift to myself and to you, my love.

And may by this doing be stilled the thirst of all Womankind and no woman's heart be in a drought, not ever more.

There is a threefoldness in these 'Letters to Beatriz': Letters to an actual person, that is you, Beatriz, as a tangible, alive focus, meaningful in my life in a many-fold way; Beatrice as an inner guide and lastly, not leastly, Beatrice as that which innerly has always been and which now has become the inner being out of which *I* can say:

The Key is in my hand
and there is Love.

So, now, my right hand holds the key and in my left hand is the lantern that is love, and with these I shall delve into the deep of me and bring to light. And all the while by invisible hands invisibly, the tapestry of my life will be woven.

The Story is of my descent into ever darker realms, fearful, terrible, satanic, and of my flight in the blazing laser-beam light of my mind, which I came to call Lucifer's light, frightful and seemingly destructive to others, a masterful magicianship to myself.

My Story is of my descent and my flight and my redemption by love, by becoming love.

As inner happening, all is tangible, real; without, in the outer 'real world', it is known as mental illness, madness.

But oh, the grace of it, when the invisible guardian and guide is Beatrice: Maria, Sophia and Lucia in one, the trice-beautiful, trice times trice gone through the fire: the through-spirited love.

Beatrice, the inner woman, innerly and outerly as love become.

I am love become. I am wakeful.

I am in a wakefulness that is in a dimension of aliveness, where it is understood, that the unconscious - the well-spring of my being - is the highest conscious, when it has become knowledge through-lighted with spirit and through-warmed with love.

In my letters to you Beatriz, my love, I will trace this journey of my descent and my flight and my homecoming. It is a woman's Odyssey.

It is my Divine Comedy.

2nd Letter
Porth Enys, 15th October 1987.

There was no sleep last night. A wind faster than a gale and wilder was tearing all night and in the early light, I saw the spray from the tossed sea fly over the highest of the rooftops, which I look over from my eastern windows seaward.

There was talk of this, or of some such imminent happening, in the strange grave conversation of a couple of jackdaws that, on my neighbour's rooftop, always seem to sum up the news, that the seagulls fly in silent circles - that is always a foreboding and days before it happens - or shout to one another or in raucous chorus together from over the tops of the roofs.

Later, I found a grave crowd round the harbour looking out and a sunken feeling returned like the one of the morning after our lifeboat went down. Later yet, I heard of deaths and devastation that a wind of hurricane force had caused in many places farther afield and that we had been in a blessing down here and well preserved.

Some people I met were innocent of it all and had slept like children through the night and were wide-eyed to see the waves high and wild in our harbour and many men labouring to secure their boats.

An atmosphere of family, of a belonging together was in the village. I felt exhilarated by it.

The wind exhilarates. The wild huge sea uncovers and let's loose in me a wildness. The taste both of sharp and sweet, that it brings onto my lips, I lick it and fierce sensuousness flames through my body. Ha! this is my Self, brand new, elemental. And yet, bespirited element and only a few days ago is the other one, now a shed skin, blown and torn and gone.

The one that said to Susi only on Monday: "I am in pieces; I go to bed in pieces and I wake up in pieces." She stopped her chanting at once and came down to her kitchen and made me a cup of tea. I did not feel sorry for myself, but I was bewildered and lost and that feeling was in the stomach pit, that is a nameless weight. Susi invited me to the Buddhist chanting that evening.

"It is mostly women, it is in Laura's beautiful home. I feel something will happen for you just being there."

"I can't, Susi, you know I can't join anything and this is so alien to me anyway."

But she persuaded me, that some weight-shifting will surely come about. And I gave in.

Indeed, I was given to know once more and deeply and clearly:

Follow your own Heart.

I came away grateful and strengthened and slept wonderfully well, and I woke into the morning with the prayer more direct now: 'Let me be clear and strong in all my doing and all my being and oh, free me from the bondage and the shackles of myself. *'I am ready.'*

There was a strength in this prayer, it had become the gesture.

In a sudden spell of sun in the early afternoon, I took myself to

12

the sea below the Gurnick and sat on the rock which I had long called 'mine', but a cold wind blew through me and a chattering couple came and spoilt the peace I sought. And then I found *the rock*. It is part of the south face of the ancient harbour wall; I had noticed it before many times, but not seen it and known it like now: *my seat!*

The movement of the tide was towards its lowest and I was close by it. It is a splendid place, for in front of the rock that makes the seat is one that makes a foot rest in just such a way, that made me belong. As the wind was up and quite cold and coming easterly, I covered my left side with my cloak, while the right side and front of me were warmed through by the sun. I closed my eyes - the morning prayer in my heart - and I listened to the choral of the stones, as they are singing in the to and fro, to and fro of the sea's ebb and flow.

My eyes are closed. Listen - let's listen together! Is it not a sound, that a woman knows, deep innerly knows and then quickly is one with it and quickened by it? Is it not like a love-making, oh, such a love-making! All one's being exalted in the moment of penetration . . .

I opened my eyes and threw my arms wide and high and dissolved in tears I shouted: "Thank you for giving me this." So much given and so much let loose . . . I knew I could write again and that the form should be 'Letters to Beatriz.' I then fell into a doze: was it I or the sea or the sea was I . . .

You had come in the morning, Beatriz, remember? for the woman that you had carved in a piece of slate was now created and there to touch with eyes and hands. I said on seeing her, "The woman born of water; when Michael makes the metal base, let him make it so she is visibly from the water."

You smiled and said, "You always say it so clearly and directly, Clara, the way the work happens."

Well, I felt immediately, that this woman figure is born from the water and lo, in the afternoon *at 3 O'Clock, I was water-born!*

Touching thus is lovemaking. Love is invisibly and mightily made. How far do the ripples reach, the circles draw themselves from this one stone thrown . . . How much love happens, how far, how wide, how deep, from the one gesture of love . . .

It is truly wonderful to have been given the gift of the form of the vessel that is to carry the words that need to be said. For by

13

these Letters, everything becomes now, a timeless time. The vision back and forward, down and up, this way and that way becomes this moment, a reality into which the everyday enters easily and *is* part of. This way, too, there is a flow, a movement, an aliveness in which we all have a part *and* partake, both, and it all becomes actual and present. A current.

Sitting on my sea wall rock, this also was given to me: that every drop of sea *is* sea, but sea is not aware of this, but I am to be aware that every bit of me is only me awaredly and alive, when I build each moment of me with wakeful hands.

I died and I was born again in a fast, immeasurable movement.

3rd Letter
17th October 1987

With so much already happened and given and received, I went to see Susi to have dinner à deux and later to have her update and reinterpret my star-chart.

In Susi's hands, Astrology becomes Astrosophy.

She carried a bright lantern and lovingly took me by the hand and led me into the mansion of me, and the one key that she had put into my hand opened all the doors. In each room there were things never noticed before, and I could see them now with one glance, for my eyes were clear. And the clarity of all senses grew with each room and my openness at each turning of the key became more glad. And the dread that had been on me vanished, for in each room everything was in its own place and no other. Twelve rooms had thus been opened and entered, and I felt enriched and in a flow, as I stood in the midst of the twelfth, the largest with many large windows, and I realised: *This is my mansion.*

So much had been given. So much had been done. So much received. And each thing in each room was seen in its own place and that it could be in no other. Each room was stepped out of in greater wonderment at how this ground-plan is given. A living force, impulsed by living forces of dark and light; and how it is all laid into your hands and no other, for you to build your mansion. *Your own mansion. And it is a wonderment to realise, how a hell of you can become a hail of you by your own hands, your very own.*

There was a thirteenth room, the most beautiful, its door was wide open, an immediate invitation to enter. The light was falling through alabaster - and stained glass windows and the largest one, arched and of clear glass, was looking out onto a day-lit landscape. The high and vaulted ceiling gave this room a spaciousness and there on the wide-planked shining wood floor lay the pieces of me, a double-image, reflected in the high shine of the polished floor. I recognised them at once. There was nothing else in this room.

I took one piece after another and put it in its place. And each gesture was the only one. And lo and behold, a stark-naked new whole Self is standing there, indwelling me as insight. Awed at how it happened and warmed through with love, I found myself on the threshold of the mansion and about to step out. And in my vision now was a new road, a whole new world. For such light had been shed into every room of the mansion that *is my Self*, that the very forces, that seemed to have been retarding, destructive, hindering and darkening, could now be recognised as the builders, that helped most essentially in the process of becoming; in the creation of the new seeing.

A moment ago, it was so many pieces, and now it is this mansion with many rooms, where not one thing is not in its place. Where everything *is* in its place and could be in no other. And then this sudden understanding: *I am this mansion and the one who built it and the one who dwells in it and the one that has to go across the threshold now with this insight and go forth and bring forth.*

The light that Susi carried is in my hand now.

It is an overwhelming gift *to know* that it is in your hands to create your life. And yet, at once, as you respond to this knowing, in accepting it as your task, a living force fills you. - I see now, that it is this accepting that my Mother meant, when she said 'Put it into His hands.' - My life is then at once fed by the source of all life and thus becomes a stream. The conflict falls away and life itself is the dynamic force: as challenge, as adventure, as quest. As vocation: I am being called upon. In the same moment the sacrifice of an old life and the receiving of a new one.

I stepped out of Susi's place, light-footed. I could have flown. And I wanted to embrace the forlorn huddle of people that were waiting for the last bus.

Later, as I sat at my candlelit midnight kitchen table cheering smilingly my lovely transformation with a glass of spring water, Albert Einstein appeared - lovingly known to me as Zweistein-Einstein - (hush, now, it is a secret, but we have been one minute-after-midnight lovers for sometime, on and off). With the warm smile shining his grave face and the dark eyes asparkle, through the halo of the candle light, he said:

"Alles liegt in der Einfachheit.

Guck mal! Clara, wie ein-fach alles ist."

And with a peal of laughter, he vanished.

I lifted my glass of spring water smilingly and through the halo of the lit candle I blew a kiss after him. Zweistein-Einstein . . .

Next morning, I woke into the happening which is told in my first letter to you, my love. And you and Michael had just entered my morning kitchen, when, with tear streamed face, I lifted my teacup to my new born Self in Hallelujah. And we wept, the three of us, together for joy.

But such birth is terrible *and* glorious. To awaken thus, to be given this clarity, to see thus! Lord, Lord have mercy and give me the strength to see what comes in sight. And let all be through-warmed with love and born in it. *And let my love for myself never falter, for it is the beginning of all loving. Amen.*

4th Letter
Monday, 19th October 1987. Porth Enys.

I have become at once an explorer and a pilgrim. I have been given provisions and the vehicle of transport to explore the outer-space of innerspace and simultaneously, the journeying will be a pilgrimage to the shrine of my Inner Self. I shall build cairns on my path and tie silk ribbons onto twigs and branches and I shall listen to my feet and heed my Little-finger. Thus gifted with insight and understanding and enriched with love, I know, I shall not fail.

Already this morning, my feet took me where they were ought to. I had made a pact with myself that whenever there was a sum of money visibly to spare, I should carry it to the Key Bookshop, to create what I call a 'Higher Purchase in reverse', so that books on order or about to be purchased would hopefully already be paid for. That's the idea, anyway. So this was my errand and to pick up a book that was waiting.

I then made my way to Susi, keen to report on the happenings since I last saw her, but I found her door locked. So into Penmare Park, I thought, to see what the storm had left of autumn gold. But by Penmare House, where you turn right into the park proper or left to the main gate into Penmare Avenue, my feet turned left and my Little-finger said 'down 'Adam's Lane' to see the Sun-and-Moon door-knocker and stained glass window that Michael had recently made for Adam's home! I found myself just approaching the door, when Adam stepped out of it, stopped, then made a few hasty steps down the lane. I was about to call his name, when he turned abruptly. There was astonishment in him and great joy in me. And he said, "How wonderful you look, Clara. You look wonderful, Clara."

All along the Promenade and wherever I had walked, people had smiled at me and greeted me and I had wondered 'maybe I am shining my joy.' It is lovely, when one so infects people, strangers, anybody.

I said, "I feel wonderful," and what joy to meet him in this spontaneous way as I had a message for him. I was invited in. The table was laid for three.

His mother was to arrive shortly for her 87th birthday celebration. I was asked to partake in the lunch and accepted. We were alone just long enough for me to tell Adam the joyous news of all that had been given me that morning a few days ago. And how instantly all ill feeling, all anger, all fear had fallen away. And that, as I can say 'I love myself,' so I can say 'I love you, Adam'. And that I had felt at once, how I would want to meet him in just such a way to tell him. And how, at the moment it all happened, I said aloud that I "wished that something real and earthquaking might happen to Adam at this very moment also."

So, I was able to tell him all this and that I was writing again, and that I had already written the first letter and was well into the second one. Here I was, in Adam's own space, telling him all this, when only a week earlier I could not hear his name spoken or have him come to mind without being roused in one way or another, ill feelings hindering me from my Self.

Nothing had happened to him. No spark had shot to him nor a

ray of that light that was on me had hit him in the way that I witnessed one evening a day or so ago, when after the sun had gone down behind us a long time, there was the whole last light asparkle like the Star of Bethlehem in the one window across the Bay. Nothing else was lit up. I had stood at my window here in my Hermitage and witnessed it with a great joy coming into me. It is with me now.

But Adam had not received anything. He sat like one numbed. The air around him without breath.

But my love *is*, and I shall be ever wakeful and pray. It is as though there was one imprisoned there, self-imprisoned in that man. He wants out, but is afraid, terribly afraid. There is a perfection in the beauty by which he surrounds himself. I hear no singing.

But my love is. And this is my ennobling and his also. A gift and a grace from the moment of my birth of seeing. The story of my descent would have been a horror story of a descent only, now, illumined by love, it will be the story of my healing.

I cannot live my life for another, nor can I live the life of another. The way I live, I can darken or lighten another life, other lives. A man can be less at the end of his day than at his beginning. But now and then, there is this spark that leaps from one grace given and lights fires of what seemed the ashes. Consider, Beatriz, my love, the one window pane of plain glass far across the Bay become a bright star . . .

When you have been given to see in such a way, everything becomes yours. There is no more judgement or transference, in the clarity of your new seeing, the one without is the one within, your twin-brother, your twin-sister. *But this love become is not a sweetness, but rather a force.* When Mother put a healing salve on a wound, she might say 'it will hurt far more for a bit than it ever did; but then it will heal and there will not even be a scar.'

Not a sweetness, but a force. And when it gets hold of you, there is no other way than total surrender. That is the victory.

The healed becomes the Healer.

The healed becomes the healer. And my feet say and inner and inner and inner space. Evermore. Ever deeper in. And ground and grow your love so it illumines everything it looks upon and responds to it and recognises it. Not the limelight is for you, nor the stage of the big world, but the inner, the inner, and your words will be healers, and your words will irradiate.

I cannot go any other way but to the interior. The space to which they are flying in their ships, let me discover it in my within. For there it is, real, terrible and wonders full.

My surrender is my victory. To have no more choice but to be chosen. Free! in the bond with the love of my Self, which *is* the love of God.

The inner creates the outer. Each is given to us, to create or to destroy. We are capable of both. *I am all Mankind.* I am you and you and you. The story is written in my within, word for word. All lived life, all unlived life is there, real.

To recognise this is to be of a sudden in a oneness, for you are in the flow of the life given to you.

I am now at the beginning of my own life. It is a mighty recognition, a powerful gift. And for the first time I understand:

Be wakeful and pray.

How good to have seen your work place, Beatriz. Sometime ago, when it was an overgrown ruin, it seemed not just to need a huge effort but well nay a miracle to make it into a studio. And here it is, your very own Hermitage! And I wonder, what will emerge from those speechless lumps of wood and silent stones and the formless mass of clay by which it is now populated . . .

I can jot down notes in any old place, but I cannot work my writing but here in this smallest room. As soon as I enter, I am in the space of the silence out of which the words emerge. I know full well, how important and necessary it is, to have this place of one's own, however small.

So, I am glad and grateful for you, my love.

5th Letter.
Porth Enys, 4th of November

It is Roo's birthday today, eleven years. I imagined her looking into the mirror you and Michael made and I imagined her wanting for something magical to happen. Wonderfully, the most beautiful rose in my yard started to unfold yesterday, Fragrant Cloud is its name. I cut it and brought it in and this morning my kitchen is filled with its sweet fragrance. It is the most rose of red roses and in my heart I saw Roo standing there holding it. I had asked it to bloom again after cutting the last rose from it in September, for it to bring joy to a beloved one. Each day, I carried the tea leaves to it and whispered, "You'll bloom once more and make a glorious rose for Roo, won't you . . ."

And then the bud appeared one day and it grew, but it seemed the heavy rain and fast winds would damage it. Then this unfolding for the very day - for Roo, my first grandchild, on her eleventh birthday. I telephoned Wales this evening, Roo seemed quite overwhelmed by the gifts received, and said 'Oh' in a wonderful astonishment, when I told her the miracle of the red rose.

Sometimes, lives touch more deeply by the glance of an eye, or a voice rings your heart, or the back of one walking in front of you moves you, or the movement of a hand reaches another within, or this little word 'oh' with such wonderment in it fills you like music and it becomes flow and the one, known or unknown, is in the other. - To be awake to one's Self so, to be awake so, one to the other.

All Souls Night (31st 10th), or as I like to call it 'The Lord Death's Feast night', I must tell you of, Beatriz, for curiously, you got into it. I sat with my last 90 pence worth of paté and a bottle of Hungarian wine given me by Rose for the occasion of the celebration and was waiting for the many knocks of the trick-and-treaters. But not a single child appeared, and I had a whole bowl full of colourful jelly sweets ready!

I had everything in two on my table, just in case His Majesty came in person or His impersonator! No one came at all, and I listened to the evening's play called 'All Souls Night' by Joseph Tomelty. The scene a village in Northern Ireland, 1949. A family bereaved of one by the sea, this same night, a year ago. Very well played. A deep play and by its poetry transporting and still stirring, now.

While sitting thus in the candle-light, I disentangled a small basket full of handspun wool. I love doing it. As I love undoing knots, mending tears and darning holes. Somehow, this kind of simplest doing rightens me inside and brings about silence and makes me receptive. Later, as there did not seem any readiness to write, I read through a scatter of notes, small pieces of cardboard cut from candle-and-tissue paper boxes or old envelopes, some proper sheets from note-pads, but so often serving also as shopping lists and sounding very funny: '5.25 or 5.30 20th X, early morning, last slither of moon in the east, open armed, small seed, ready for impregnation and in the pure west radiant in balance Venus and Orion just South, Garlic, Vecon, Paprika, do not forget to call the dentist'. - So, I can laugh at myself.

Just before midnight, I had another little sup, the same, paté, rye biscuits and a cup of red wine. I filled the second cup for His Majesty, tended the AGA, wished everyone a good night, left the rest of the food on the table for Him that might yet come, and bedded in.

Lord Death might not have been at my table, but He came into my dream. He carried an armful of sheets of white paper and introducing Himself as 'I am the Lord of Death', he scattered these sheets as a wind would and each fell with a klirr to where it fell, like the Virginia-Vine leaves from the walls of The Lobster-Pot Hotel. In a sonorous voice He said, "Here are written all the words you need to grow your Life-tree of words with. NO tree can grow without me." And with that, the last sheet floated from His graciously gestured hand and klirr klirr, faster and faster, it somersaulted down the lane. I went after it, but it blew into the sea, which was huge. Suddenly, you were there, Beatriz, on the one wave, on that fast movement and waving the sheet, you stepped out of the wild sea, your body jewelled with the drops of water and laughing, you handed the dry, blank white sheet to me.

Then, in an instant, I was standing in the kitchen astonished, gazing at the blank white sheet of paper, when you came with your arms full of white sheets. And you laughed and laughed. Such hilarity. And I said, "Come, enter, and fill my house with laughter." And we laughed together. - What a healer laughter is!

I was so surprised on coming down in the morning to find the second cup untouched. The dream had been so vivid.

The next night, He appeared again. He unslung from his shoulder a linen bag of seeds, the kind my father used for hand sowing. And he hung it on me saying, "Hold my hand and trust." And He led me out into a vast landscape of many freshly tilled fields and He said, "Go now and scatter these seeds from which

21

will grow the trees that will bear the healing fruits for your fellow women to reap." And gone was He. And I stepped out and remembering the gestures from my father, I scattered the seeds so each should fall in its place. It is a wonderfully fulfilling movement, this: the delving into the seed filled bag, the filling of your hand with seed, the throwing of the seed in a gesture of a pure half-circle from your heart-side, the step in harmony with it, the heart singing with it. - In this way, field after field was sown, for the seed bag was being invisibly and magically refilled, until the last throw of seed.

At this moment, I stood on a horizon gazing down into a valley in the last, golden light of a sun already gone down, and from behind me sounded a huge chanting. Turning, I found I was holding a flowering tree in my hands with its roots and fully turned, I looked on a vastness of women walking towards me, each carrying a flowering tree with its roots and chanting.

These two dreams are more actual than my sitting here. The motive of the tree was the first of a series of recent dreams, that have made it seem that I was more fully awake in my dreaming than in my waking, for there is a might in their reality. And it must be so, that both my heart and my soul are more utterly wakeful in a sleep that brings such dreams.

I have written down these dreams, for by them I have been guided and am being led, as though a bright Angel was holding my hand. They are helping me to affirm my destiny and firm myself in it. For it is not a matter of taking this road or that one, but only the path that is inevitable, which I do not choose but am chosen for to go on.

I receive these dreams as rich gifts for my journeying, as helpers and guides and nourishment. They are with me like Angels: holding my faith, keeping my courage, warming my love.

I feel so blessed, Beatriz, all through my life dreams have thus been given me for the enrichment of the trust in my Self and my understanding of my life.

It is a rich and wonderful life that is given me and I am glad, that in these letters, I will share with you, my love, some of the wealth of it.

6th Letter
Martinmas, 11th of November 1987.

This day always rings in me, there are so many childhood memories piled into it and around it. The Last-Quarter Fair came with it: the round-abouts so exciting with their magnificent horses, lions, elephants and swans to ride on and just seeing them going round and round was being transported into Magic-Land. The chestnut-roasters, the Big Woman with the huge upside-down umbrellas full of silk ribbons and herself bedecked with them looking in deep Autumn like the Goddess of Spring.

Meanwhile, Remembrance Sunday has come and gone. I listened to the reading of 'Letters of a Friendship', which was formed in the trenches in the First World War, 'The Great War'. These letters were discovered at the bottom of a wardrobe after the death of Frank Cocker who had written them to his fiancée. Beautifully, movingly and well written letters. I quote just this following bit to show you, Beatriz, my love, a little of the depth of these letters by an ordinary man:

'Evelyn, darling, I don't think anyone can replace Charlie or ever will. It is a very peculiar thing and a very sacred thing is the friendship which binds two men, heart and soul together. And Charlie is the only friend (in this sense) I have ever had in my life . . . However, I have still got you, sweetheart, and the tie between our two hearts remains strong, and grows stronger by day and year by year.'

And I had the five minutes of poems by Wilfred Owen (one of the young poets who also died in the same war) out of a programme on Radio 3 that lasted 1 hour and 30 minutes! I would have loved to listen to the songs that made up the rest of the time, but I love voices, that haven't in their learnedness lost the singing, and the singers are so rarely of this kind.

However, this kind of celebration is always so painful to me, for it would seem, that the Dead are being most remembered by remembering and respecting the Living and by the way each one lives and respects and loves his own life. It is even more painful, when you see, what wasteland of violence and bewilderment Life itself has become.

And this is the pain, this waste, that is made into the illusion of sacrifice, and thus glorified.

- Did the great big heart of life and joy grow out of those wars, did grow from all that blood spilt even one daisy?

Yes, there is a brave heart once in a while, a courageous life here and there, but people as mass are so gullible, so easily led and so forgetful. 'When will they ever learn, when will they ever learn?' The song with this refrain was sung so much by the young in the USA in the 60s. By the mass, the wolf in the sheep skin will ever be mistaken for the lamb. - There is more wisdom in the Tawny Owl than in any man. Aeons of owlhood are ever present as instinct in every moment of Owl's life, and she and her spouse will not have a brood, if the territory chosen is likely not to yield the food needed to rear them. Owl is owl from the beginning and is always owl. But I am the maker of my Self. Aeons and aeons of Mankind bring me but to my beginning at every morning of my Self. And I must build myself with the Stones, that I have hewn myself. I fail, lest it be my labour of love, lest I am in the grace of my own love.

And it is this, that differs me from all creation, that I am given the human form and all the potentials to be human, but my *human* being, I have to make with the tools crafted by myself. So help me God.

This terrible and awesome gift of being human, impulsed by a force of life that has its source deeper in the darkness, than anyone can fathom and empowered by this other force, that needs to bring to light and then see, see that which is brought forth. See it. God help me, that I am made in the image of this creative God, that this God indwells me, that I am gifted with this terrible gift of this spirit, this energy, which by my own hands brings forth evil or good, by my own words heals or hurts; by my own gestures destroys or redeems. God, it is terrible, God it is wonderful, that my own heart is a dungeon and a well. That for the joy in this hand, the sorrow is in the other. That for what burdens me, is that which lightens me.

Mass of people never learns. Mass will be led and will, always being in the grip of a fear, be mislead. I quote here from a poem by Siegfried Sassoon who did not lose his life in the war but whose life was profoundly affected by the experience and says here so well, what I am trying to express:

> *"For you, our battles shine*
> *With triumph half divine.*
> *And the glory of the dead*
> *Kindles in each eye.*
> *But a curse is on my head,*
> *That shall not be unsaid*
> *And the wounds in my heart are red,*
> *For I have watched them die . . .*

So here and there, a single life is lit and sparks and radiates. And this one is in a great aloneness, for it is not, that he sees the light, but the darkness. And he has to bring forth from there, he alone, from that place, where everyone likes to hide in.

He alone has to bring that to light, which in all time of Mankind has been destructive and evil and still is so and has prevented Mankind from becoming Humankind. And has made it to mistake itself again and again.

Mass of people cannot be responsible. Mass of people will follow and will worship this God or that God instead of suffering. - Suffering is to accept my human kindness. Suffering is to make by my own hands all that is given into the livingness of my own life. A singular task. May God help me.

To worship is to transfer, to reject this sensible response, to avoid it. And so ever to increase the errors that harden and violate and suffocate life. This life of each one, that is.

Life, Life, Life and Life again should have been grown from all that blood so horribly spilt, not greater fear and more horrific slaughter. And this slow, this very slow, this insidiously accurate suffocation of the human heart that we are now witnessing the world over.

Yet always and again, everyman goes limping and out of breath, mutilated in body and spirit, bent, gnarled, blind, deaf, with the last spark in his heart, he goes and worships one God or another, dances round the Golden Calf and is led by the nose by the one who disguises his misguidance most cunningly. And he never listens to the voice of his own heart and in the end does neither know of or remember his own voice.

And the ignorance multiplies and the power of destruction grows.

b

Yet here and there is the lone one, seldom and rare. The one who knows that God is indwelling him as a creative force, which dwells in the dark of him and *must* be brought forth. He knows, that the journey is hazardous and perilous and dangerous. He has no security and no assurance. But he has accepted his task. And in this lies the affirmation of his love for himself, which is, as faith in himself, the light.

It is our own light we fear, not the darkness. For once lit, we have to see!

Lit by the love of my Self, I am in touch with my innermost, my wholeness. I am at once in the flow of love itself, which is the source of life-energy. And thus, wonderfully, in my seeing, the one that surely *was* the Beast is *now* The Prince.

Fear shone on by the light of love, becomes a creative force. With the light of my love, I shine The Beast - all that I have shunned, depressed, suppressed, rejected, transferred, violated, hated - and lo, beside me, within me, is The Prince.

"Love is the only thing", the Beatles sung it.

Love is the only thing: The Great Transformer

But he who does know love thus and is alive thus in it and with it and by it he does not dish it there in front of you and say: 'eat! drink!' But rather, it is in all things he says and does. And he may break bread with you and share his cup of wine with you and laugh with you and offer his arm when you are panting up the hill and take a child by the hand and dance with it to the music of the Organ Grinder in the High Street. And he may quietly weep, that you'd rather stay ignorant than be knowing.

This quiet-being is a force that radiates, for at every moment of itself it *is* itself and *alive*.

And who will count the buds, that were about to perish, but that have become the full fragrant roses . . . What measure for that which is measureless . . .

7th Letter
25th November 1987. Porth Enys.

The golden crescent of a New Moon this evening. Always, the sight of it lifts and joys. Always, it is promiseful, all the more so, when it hangs in the young evening sky. And there was the gift of blue sky and a balmy sun today.

At this time, with its passage so low and short, the sun comes walking right into the house through the windows and doorless doorways into the kitchen, and it makes pure gold wherever it goes and touches. And it lingers in a place here and there, and lifts out and alivens a utensil, a piece of bare wall or a picture. One is then, of a sudden, in a small lit-up silence, yet, it is like music . . . And it is as though one was being given a message, or one was being affirmed in one's silence, in one's singing, in one's simple doing. - One is in a communion.

What an unfathomable flowing-together of what a myriad of diverse forces becomes this order from which in wonderful measure grow day and night, wanes and waxes moon, tides the sea, happen the seasons . . . Pray, let us never ever not be aware of the intricate web of relations that life is, and that if only *one* finest, *finest* thread is torn, that all life is injured by this tear. Let us never ever not be awake to this: that by this one tear, all flow is rent and the current cut. The Godly-knot, by which my life, all life, has been tied, is undone, *I* am severed.

Always, I have loved sewing by hand and always the sudden knot in the thread! As a child I would say 'Mother, there is this knot again, this very most knot, from nowhere sudden in the thread, here it is look, so knot a knot!' And Mother's answer would be 'Like the Godly-knot - or Heavenly knot,' she called it sometimes - 'that holds all together, it is a mystery.'

This mysterious knot! my nimblest fingers cannot undo it, yet, I am known as the one to whom everyone comes to have the knots undone, any kind of knot. But this knot, in my own thread, I can never undo. So then, the thread is cut at the knot and the very same knot, that stopped the flow of the sewing, now becomes the anchoring knot at the end of the left-over thread, and the sewing continues.

Ach! the contrary! the paradox: the knot, this *and* that. *Always, this and that!* Yet, in the contrary, in the paradox is the most force, *dynamis* itself. When they meet and twine, they become a dynamic whole, the nucleus: bearer of life force and healer.

I am based in the same order that has grown like a tree by an inspired relating of infinite - seemingly - contrary forces. Thus I am alive and life is alive by the interplay, by the playing together of a multitude of contraries. A vast network of relating and interrelating forces.

Inextricably, all is linked. And the destruction of the infinitely small is the first deathblow to the all. The balance is disturbed, instantly. - How can I grasp the precision of this balance, where the infinitesimal is of the same weight as the gigantic . . . This equilibrium of forces, how could I grasp it . . .

My love, I am wonderfully turned on by all this. Seeing my journey in the light of this Godly-Ungodly game, I feel quickened and pray for deepening of insight, for inspired looking and listening. Above all, listening! And that in discovering, my heart be bold and I be without fear.

There was a great dream given last night, and I will tell it here: I am sitting with friends round an oval-shaped large table in a festive room, in a festive atmosphere. And the table is laid as for a celebration meal and lit with tree-like candelabras. Through the open door, Selina enters, carrying a very large oval silver dish with on it what seems a snake dressed with lemon - and orange slices and sprigs of parsley, but it is an eel. "For the Feast of Life", she proclaims in her exuberance. But all the guests utter 'uuh' in horror as though Selina had said, 'For the Feast of Death'. And they flee the table and vanish, their fearful 'uuuh' filling the air for a while like an ominous wind. - I am alone at the table. The dish with the eel is in front of me and *I know* instantly, that I have to cut off the fish's head and eat it whole - swallow it, as a seagull does. At the very same moment that I know this, a magnificent kingly man appears in the doorway dressed in a robe in the bright and beautiful colours of the Kingfisher-bird, and he says 'I caught it, I am the Fisher-King.' No sooner said, a snake or eel slithers out of the room by the same doorway, and for a moment, I am in a space of golden light and then in a young and green paradisal countryside.

The dream is with me strong and real, like a deep inner happening. And again, so it seems, that in the dreaming I am in more of a wakefulness as in my day waking.

I receive this dream as meaningful for my journey. And I am grateful for such guidance.

28

8th Letter
St David's Day. 1st of March 1988.

The fallow days are past, Christmas truly belongs to last year, and only today I feel I am in the New Year. And I would I'd be plucked at top of my head and be carried there into those heights where the Aspens whisper ever to the stark immensely tall silent Pines: up above Taos, New Mexico. Oh, to fly to there, where the air is so light, you need hardly breath for you *are* the breath *and* winged.

Just these few words transport me there, to this particular place, light-filled and potent with vibrant magical force. Where every step carries you weightless to the centre. Where, wherever you stand *is* the centre, in which the might of the Heavenly and the force of the Earth are in an embrace as it were, become as one, ...cleus of highest potency. ...urably small and fast, that it ...happens and the kernel is ...e immediate moment after, the ...on of their flowing polarity, ...changing form manifests. We ...moment. We cannot conceive ...makes it. We see a form ever ...g, ever transforming, and we ...of the transcendent forces that ...t of me, a photograph of St ...a field on the tiny Isle of Iona ...before St Columba in AD 563 ...ere sent out his missionaries), ...just been trying to say. It is a ...d upper vertical are held in a flowing movement by a ring, that moves through the arms, thus, the flow of the symbols cut into the long vertical becomes a spinning mandala in the cross centre and flows upward and, as it were, out of itself, so that a tree of life is born, for in the reflection of it, the full flow of the forces is being perceived. It is a powerful symbol, and although only a postcard picture, its presence is so strong and immediate, that its moving force flows into me, and a most wonderful enlivening is experienced, so much like the one in that lofty place in New Mexico. Within the movement of the two intertwining snakes up the cross appears the four-petalled rose which becomes highest form in the cross-centre as mandala. The two snakes encircle another rose in the centre of the head-vertical, touch imperceptibly just above it and move in a lightning zig-zag each out into the corners and out of the cross into ones imagination. This creates an amazing force of movement in oneself and one is carried back into the foot of the cross. In this way, the powerful movement in the cross and the movement created in you becomes one flowing force.

You are deeply unwell, Beatriz, my love. Learn my love, what you are in, learn it as a journey. Put your feet on the road, try, and allow not your eyes to set themselves onto the horizon, but let them be your good companions at every step. Go slowly. Let your eyes receive image upon image. Let them fall silently into your heart, like dew does onto the morning leaves. There, in their own time, they will become vision. Listen! Listen! Listen! There is a music, that wants and needs to be heard.

Let us learn illness as a journey. Let us welcome the dis-ease as a guest, who brings good tidings to the home of ourselves. To welcome this, that has been - known or unknown to ourselves - rejected again and again, is already healing.

The dis-ease comes from the deep of you and wants to guide you to the deep of you. It is forcing upon you a time and a space to slowly, with ever growing insight, come to the wholeness that you are.

You will want to be, again and again, anyone among your friends and acquaintances rather than yourself. For everything for them, in your tarnished eyes, seems so effortless, so perfect, so secure. But do not compare yourself, their world will never be your world, for you are meant *to live your life, your own.*

Oh, let's brim the cup of our lives! Oh, let's live our lives to the brim and over!

Candlemas, 2nd February 1989
The Story

"Don't you know, this is Golgotha, Mountain of Skulls? They whipped me and spat at me and threw stones, and the cross was a terrible weight. All these miles, these endless miles of cross."

"Your body is very badly bruised, what happened?"

"The journey up here, the godless journey, Doctor, Sir. This journey up here, this god-abandoned journey up here, it had to be. I have to die on this forsaken Mount of Sculls."

"All these awful bruises on your body, how did they happen?"

"I have to hang tonight to redeem It, The Feminine, that was crucified 2000 years ago as Him and every moment of human time and history since. Do not leave me now."

"I need to know, where the bruises come from, were you beaten?"

"The Cross, Sir, the cross and the stones and the spit, Sir Doctor. Why are *you* here, where are my Sisters, no one is weeping. Lord God, thou hast forsaken me worse, no one is weeping this time."

"Look, I can't sit here all night," holding my hands in his now, "tell me about the severe bruises, your body is blue, black and purple. How *did* it happen?"

The Doctor's face is very close to mine. The 'on-looking self', that is always present, answers, "Baby-Boy mine, you should never have married this woman, I told you right at the start, she's always been mad. Get her down and out of here and see, she is never coming back. There my Baby, there, the suffering you have to go through, there, get her down, force her down and out of the house and away with her!"

The screeching in an acquired American accent entered the innermost of me. Vortex of vortex of me was being penetrated by this voice, which had Adam's in it, too, and so much of hating. A homeless voice. It never was rooted in a Mother-tongue nor in a Fatherland. It did not know itself and never would do. The bearer of it was dead to life and living, had been so for a long time.

The crime of the cutting of the Mother-tongue, roots are severed, roots of rhythm and rhyme and sound. The song, that is this life, this unique new life, can never find its voice. The feet in which the life-story is engraved, how will they dance, what dance will they dance without that music?

Oh, the pity of unlived life!
Oh, the pity of unsung song!
Oh, the pity of dance not danced!
If I have roots, I can wander anywhere and feel at home. If I have my Mother tongue all the ten thousand tongues of mankind sound like home in my echo chamber and my heart and my feet will go where they must ought to, the compass is in my blood.

"You don't seem to understand, I am your doctor, I have come to examine you."

"O, I have got my degree, flying colours, Sir, passed all my examinations years ago."

"Once and for all, I need an explanation for the bruises on your body, how did they get there?"

"And then he tore me once more off the balustrade onto which I had held with all my dear life and might, and I fell flat on my back and was dragged thus down the stairs. All the while, the mother's tongue wagged gleefully, 'well done, my boy, action my boy'. Thus I was pushed and bullied through the living room, shoved out into the granite-flagged hall and out through the main door into the street and there I was banged and shoved with feet and knees and fists into the waiting car.

"By my Beloved. My Beloved. My Beloved. My Beloved. Adam, my Beloved. Can't you hear, Doctor? Love is what's done it. The blue and the black and the purple. Love is a many splendoured thing. Examination passed with flying colours once more, eh, doctor?"

I didn't want to leave. Deep inside me it said 'they are trying to put you away for good.' And a terrible terror took hold of me. For that voice is true. It always is. Since Childhood, I have always known so much in advance of what is in store and how it will happen. Who's put what in which drawer and where. A terrible burden.

I am supposed to be mad. Out of my mind. But on the contrary,

I am deep in my mind. Too deep in my mind. I am treated like a leper. I have to be removed.

'In sickness and in health, I promise you, Clara, not only in health but in sickness, too, Darling.'

Words, words. They ring in my echo-chamber, but the bell is split and the sound is wounding.

"Doctor," I am screaming it, "I am not out of my mind, I am in it, deep in it and in pain of my wounds. They are open and sore. I don't belong here. Get me out of here! Get me out of here!"

"Now, now, take this, Clara and go to sleep. This will make you sleep."

Inside me, I am sinking into such a lonely lostness, sinking into a sinking lonely lostness seeing myself in this establishment for mentally sick. And farther and farther away into an unreachable distance are vanishing faces loved and voices cherished.

I hear you ask, my love, but why did Adam put you away? That time, I fear, not like the first time some years earlier 'for my best'. This time I had to be gotten rid of. I was a hindrance to peace. With my behaviour - what was this behaviour? - I smirched the image that Adam had of me. The man could never face and accept reality, it was always made into something else. Cats and dogs could hail from the sky and he would call it 'a lovely day'. My state of being, in which at any given moment *I was* whatever took hold of me, for I could not help myself, brought unease. Adam could not pretend that it was not so. It brought dark unease, fearful unease to a man, who after a life time of never really facing a situation as it was, suddenly again and yet again, was confronted with a wife who was out of her mind. Insane. Mad. He could not any more hide behind his sweet kindness. For this mad woman stirred the old melting pot inside him that was to over-flowing full of unacknowledged hatred, resentment, anger, guilt, fear, cruelty, the lot!

So, Clara had to be gotten out of the way.

"Of course, my Darling, I will stand by you whatever changes may happen to you, whatever the consequences of the operation, we shall face it all together."

"I am afeared, even if I shall be a female Eunuch, you will be with me still?"

"But, Darling, Darling, you must not doubt."

Words! But they are all substance in my blood and there they

33

ring like a split bell. Day and night.

"If you don't behave, I shall call the ambulance and then you will lose your chance of going willingly and being a voluntary patient. Pack your things and get ready. You have messed me about the whole night and the whole morning."

LOVE

Loooooooooooooooooooooooooooooooooooooooooooooooooooove

"In sickness and in health. Come what may . . ."

I rummage through one drawer after another, open the wardrobe door. I take out one pair of knickers or a vest or a petticoat or a dress. I hold each one up in the air. I look at each one. I do not know what to do with these things. It doesn't click. The mind is absent in connection to what should be put into the suitcase. But it is ringing and tolling words. Broken words of love and promise.

I cannot weep. I cannot laugh. I cannot even shout. But inside, inside deep, there is a life. Me, the woman, experiencing broken hearted this horror of the man loved become a violent hater, using brutal force to get me out of his way and his sight.

I was three persons in the one. One manifest and tangible as the 'mad-one'. One the invisible wounded vulnerable one living in the deep inside absorbing everything that was happening with a hyper-sensitive intensity; and the third one, the aware and conscious one looking on, observing. That is how, after all this time, I have such clear recall. - I was not out of my mind, but deep in it and watchful and wakeful.

You may seem to be in an enclosure, insulated and isolated, immune to the happenings around you, but on the contrary, the banned life hidden in the deep within is of heightened perception and utterly vulnerable. Things are being said in your presence, which are thought not to be understood by you, but how gravely mistaken are those that say them.

The removal of myself from the 'real' world, the world of functioning as wife, householder and housekeeper and all the worlds that these arts entail, I had not done consciously. No, I had not removed myself awaredly from this world of responsibility, not, as one time it was said by some, deliberately, to have a strange power over everyone and to take revenge on husband and children. Good Lord, no! But I had always been on this journey to the Castle of the Holy Grail. This fateful journey to the Heart of Love started with a sudden knowing early in my childhood. And it did so with a frightful clarity and an inevitable surety.

Madness, thus, as mask and disguise, not chosen consciously, but rather inflicted by fate, or as I now in retrospect love to call it, by 'The Helper', removes the obstacles in the journey, namely the burden of responsibility in the world. *In the deep within, you must of necessity journey your journey, for there is no other.*

I do not know, my love, if you will understand then when I say, that in my journeying this world did not exist. Or rather, it did, but as an alien place, of which I had no knowing how to live in it. Hence, my behaviour must have caused irritation, consternation and fear, when after all, once I had stood full square in it and had run the whole blooming show with ease and know-how. And everyone was relying on this efficiency: place clean, food on the table, tasty and beautifully presented always and on time; clothes washed and ironed . . . A daily unquestioned and taken for granted performance.

Now, the whole structure is undermined by this woman Clara, who has retreated and is wandering in a state of absence in what place, what world . . .

That night, well placed in my memory, before I was taken away the next day, I had at last reached the Castle of the Holy Grail. My light and its light were of the same measure. And I walked straight in and the radiance was the Holy Grail and I was in it and of it. And I knew of God-become-Man. And I understood. And I became a wholeness with the Being of Godlikeness. And I was in the space of the Mother. The All-Mother. In whom all and everything is contained. And I saw the Holy Trinity as holy, when it is within The Mother. The Triangle within the Square within the Circle. And I drew this image again and again. And by so doing, I experienced matter as mater as spirit as light as music. A force. Me, myself, being it.

Then, all of a sudden, I heard my name being called. Loud and clear. 'Clara!' And there was this urgency, that I was not allowed to see and know and understand all these wondrous things, without a sacrifice.

I was to hang like Christ hung and to be stoned and spat on and ridiculed like Him. Also, it seemed suddenly most terribly urgent to be christened, now, immediately, to re-confirm my name Clara. Which had come to me to mean 'She, who sees clearly and understands.' My name must be confirmed in Christ to affirm truly my God-likeness.

So, I leapt out on to the landing - it was in the deep night, possibly very early morning - and I dialled the Vicar of Zed's number. The only Vicar I knew.

He had at the beginning of my illness often come to the house to lay on his long fingered gentle hands to dispel the one who possessed me, and he prayed with his congregation in healing services for my recovery.

I spoke in urgency: that my journey to Golgotha was imminent and that a Baptism here and now was of the greatest necessity. That the re-Christening of my name Clara, the meaning of which had just been revealed to me, was the only way by which I could, after my crucifixion, re-enter the All Mother's womb and be reborn. My Vicar did not want to hear it. He could not and would not do it. That I was not well, and that, of course, I would not have to go to the Cross. But I was terribly urgent. For me, all was real and I saw myself hung in the agony of no baptism.

'I am in the power of giving you the power to baptise me, Vicar. I have just been born into my name and this has to be confirmed at once for the price to pay is to give my life. Hurry, the hangmen are already surrounding my house.' - And I screamed into the telephone all sorts of names and curses. But in an ever more calm and kindly voice, the Vicar of Zed told me that I was not well and that I should go to bed.

In my desperation, I smashed the phone and this woke Adam, who rushed out of the house, obviously to call the doctor.

It is a wondrous thing, that alongside with the growing awareness of oneself grows guilt - Schuld. The awareness, that we owe something for that which we have been given.

I had but for a moment looked upon the essence of me and seen and known and understood it as being my Self: a wholeness. God, the spiritual father, His son as God incarnate in Man, shone through and through by Spirit and all held within the All Mother, making a wholeness, my essential Being. Such gift of seeing asks for sacrifice, Opfer. I become die Schuldige, the sinner, the transgressor of the divine law. No less than my life must be given in return for having received my individual essential being.

God help me, how the poor Vicar was brought into it all. Well, perhaps, here was a brand new Clara, a new born Clara and this *must* be confirmed in baptism by an appointed person, who else but the Vicar! Heaven forbid!

Had I not been on this pilgrimage a life-time already? Had it not been my most innermost destined journey? Mine. My own. Urged from within. And utterly inevitable . . .

This journey had to be made, foot in front of foot. Chosen by myself to follow my heart. This journey and no other. Chosen by myself, this forsaken, lonely road and yet compelled, and yet appointed and yet destined.

The freedom is to choose that which is destined. In my case, the hazardous and tormented road of the heart. The quest for the realisation of the Self, of becoming a conscious and aware human being.

So I can never separate myself from life. At its source, I daily fill my bucket, what's in the bucket, that I must accept and transform it into substance for my life to maintain the flow from life-source to life-stream.

I cannot flee into or get lost in or identify with concepts, creeds or philosophies. That would not do, not in this life given me. No, I have to go the whole hog. This journey is for real.

The adventuring into the Self, *down* to your God-likeness, is a descent. And you go it alone. There is a might and a power there, which have to be conquered and overcome and so to become yours. Your weapon is your awareness, your shield is your love.

You are alone. The Third is invisibly present as the guiding force.

This morning, Sunday, I came running down the stairs wondering if the first Arum Lily blossom was opening and found, instead, the whole plant whipped to a pulp. Most savagely done! - How it had stood there, only last night, some five feet high and so vigorous, a gentle undulating movement in its large arrow-head shaped luscious green leaves. The Arum-Lily, like no other plant I know, shows so intimately the metamorphosis of the leaf into the flower. Each leaf grows on its own long succulent stem out of the same sheaf, and the stem, that finally bears the flower comes from it, too. Out of the very most top of the tubular stem shoots this six, seven inches long spear, paler green than the stem or the leaves, and at the moment of the first unfolding, which is a whirling motion, appears an arrow-head shaped candle-white tip of the blossom. And when you look again, there is this flower, a waxen white chalice. From within it thrust stamen and stigma like a phallus of iridescent butter-yellow, which later becomes the amazing ovary-like fruit: a bright cluster, big as a man's fist, of small pure round deep yellow eggs. This Arum-Lily was brought to me as a gift. A former neighbour had nurtured it in a pot, so that it could be planted out at a given time and be strong already. I was to understand, that each garden *must* have an Arum Lily, but that never must the blossoms be cut and taken into the house. So, when the sharp, salt-laden winds had abated, I planted it in the space, that I had at once destined for it. Where it could be seen from all my front windows and would be joying everyone approaching from the main road, and indeed greet like a flag everyone that came down the road. I nurtured it well, put handfuls of deep loam around it and leftover tea-leaves. And we had many a silent communion.

Encouraged thus, although it is still early February, it had grown into a full beauty ready to open its first blossom.

I stood out there, in front of my home, in my small triangular garden, helplessly picking up the scattered slimy bits of stems and slashed leaves, tears streaming down and saying over and over 'I am feeling sick.' Then I came inside and wept.

Suddenly, I became still as in front of me rose this image of an encounter, long years ago, with a Mexican-Indian Flower-man. Just where he was, on the very steep slope of a dusty road, so that he looked stooped, the deep blue sky reached right down behind him. He had, to my eyes, stepped at that very moment out of all that immensity of blue with his over-flowing basket of Arum-Lilies, that he carried on his broad back, tied over his chest with a wide band like a ribbon, and that were like a vast halo over his raven-black head.

*   *   *   *

38

I was supposed not to be in my right senses, well then, I was in my wrong ones and with these, I experienced my journey laden with the unbearably heavy cross, scorned, spat on and stoned by faces I recognised and loved. - The loneliest journey. Abandoned by everyone.

The woman Clara went to the Mount of Death to redeem the feminine, that 2000 years ago quaked Western Mankind, rocked and split its hard and fast foundation as Him: God become Man. The old God of judgement and fear, eye for eye, and thou shalt-not, is incarnate in Man as Love. - Die Liebe - Love -

God is in Man. God as Love is in Man.

Love thyself and you love the God within you.

Love thyself, so that you may love your neighbour and forgive him, that has harmed you.

Thus, like lightning, awareness strikes. The gift of the awareness of your Godlikeness.

God incarnate in Man is speaking: I and my father are one and the same. We are one in love. You man, you woman: Godlike. God within you, one with you.

Love thyself and so you will love me and life eternal.

That is God as plain man speaking.

That is my own heart speaking, when my name has been called.

Suddenly, wonderfully, you recognise your responsibility for the life given you.

Suddenly, wonderfully, you respond to the life given you and you understand it as a gift.

Heavy stuff! frightening! Die Liebe! Love! Murder it! Be quick! Before it spreads.

And so, they murdered Him.

Clara was deprived of death on the cross, her life was snuffed by a sleeping pill.

Next morning, I woke up in this narrow room with a thick head not used to sleeping pills and with three more pills after breakfast, a senseless body was shuffling its feet hour after hour up and down the barren corridor. - How many times did I drag my feet round the world . . . Most people haven't got the spunk of a cabbage, I therefore don't want to say, I was a vegetable, for that would, indeed, have been something.

What *was* it, that was shuffling up and down, up and down that corridor from 7 in the morning till 11 at night? Day in, day out.

If sanity is to give the go-ahead to a 90 million research programme into lethally destructive tanks, what is *madness?*

Is this woman mad, who deprived of vision and fantasy, flattened in all her being, stiffened in her limbs, with no stride in her legs and her shuffling feet, with arms arrested in pitifully bent elbows, that are held stiffly in front of her chest? This woman, that moves like a grotesque shadow up and down the corridor, is she mad?

Is this humanless creature mad, this pitiful pulp, made senseless by drugs?

Was that one, full of bright vision and blazing fantasy, was she mad?

Who decides these things . . .

I was not dangerous to anyone or anything nor to myself. Merely, I lived in an inner world, which was more real than that which is acclaimed to be reality.

I was in a world of my own, as a child might be, and I had a sense of belonging in it and being of it. While in the 'real' world, I was unloved and rejected by the very ones that ought to have given me love and the one in whose promise of love I had thought I was.

'The on-looking-Self' looks on, disbelieving: Clara, the husk, the empty husk.

There was a sudden dreadful darkening this evening. The sky looked grim and the sea a forbidding slate-grey. Then, a flash of lightning that lit everything sharply. Then one single thunder clap. All the windows clattered. No doubt, there will be late snow. 'When it lightens into the naked wood, it will snow into the leaves.' I have never known this saying not come true. - Snow in March, eh? - A small rose which I broke from the old rambler early this morning is opening and its sweet fragrance joys me sitting here. The bud was rose, but once open, it is a yellow rose. Every time I lift my eyes, it is a little more open and when I gaze at it, its as though there is movement visible, like a tender breathing.

*   *   *   *

Clara's descent was violently cut short, her journeying
abruptly broken.

*If only it could be understood, that you have to get out of your
mind in order to get into it. And above all, that each one of us has
His Story. His and his alone. His myth, as I like to call it. And that
this story is sacred, for it is this unique person's unique life.*

My song. My music. My dance. - May be out of tune. May be
out of step and balance. Still mine. Mine alone.

Swinging in disharmony, allow it me. Allow me to sing out of
tune. Let me dance my wild dance. Let me go my journey to
Hades. My tormented exploration, leave it me.

No tree grows into Heaven lest its roots are in Hell.

Had Adam stood still and listened! Had he reached out and
held hands! Touched: palm to palm (sounds like a hymn). Had he
danced with me a crazy whirl this way and a crazy whirl that way!
Had he looked! I could have let him partake in that which I had
seen and been in. But his sleep was disturbed. And this mad,
deranged woman had to be gotten out of the way.

Little man, who always spoke from on high of facts and reality.
Poor Little Man, rattled out of his sleep.

Reality! I say 'welcome to you, Reality, you unfathomable
one! Be welcome in all your one-thousand-and-one dimensions!'

Welcome into my realm, Reality! And never let me be able to
grasp you, but let me float with you like the boat with the stream.

To kill pain, to wipe out disease, to make level insanity:
Leitmotiv of our conventional well established medicine. Done
by kindness and often with caring and in every absence of the
understanding, that this life which is trusted into their hands is
holy. Thus, a verdict is reached, a name is given, one chosen from
a long column of possible mental disorders, and drugs that match

41

this assumed name are being prescribed.

Henceforth, this holy life is a case. And this case produces a case-history. Daily observations that nurses make, or on a rare occasion a psychiatrist, are noted down. Sometimes something that this case happens to say is taken in account. But the story, that this case has to tell, its own story, is never asked for.

Is there really not the haziest notion, that I might have a story to tell? Not even the slightest awareness, although my mind, my soul is called dis-eased, that I am a *unique human being with my story?* Psychiatrist - healer of the soul - whenever, so very rarely, I am allowed five or ten minutes of your time and I want to share my torment and the lostness of my innermost with you, how come, that you have no time to listen, no interest in me at all?

You, for whom I am a case with a definitive name, will never ever know, that the terror in my eyes is my soul: a butterfly flying desperately against a sunlit window pane and there is no opening for it to fly sunward. Could I but tell you this, or were you able to read it from my eyes, how healing for my utter loneliness.

Alas, I am a case, dear Doctor. And a case is a case. And no doubt, you mean well and are doing your best with the knowledge that you possess, the time you have available and the place you occupy within the establishment that you are functioning in. And there is no doubt, that you have added up responsibly the bits and pieces of information that was given you. And it is, I expect, understood in good faith, that the next-of-kin or whoever hands the patient in and makes the telling is deeply concerned with the welfare and well-being of his. - But, how biased might this story be . . .

However, that is of no avail and a name is given to fit the conclusion and drugs and treatment are prescribed. - They should, in time, bring normality.

This is absurd and above all immoral. It is a violation of the right to this life. And a grave violation of the rite of passage of this singular life.

Deep, deepest injury caused my mind to absent itself from the set norm of reality. My soul is soundless to the world and peoples of the normal and accustomed surroundings. But what volume of sound in the innermost of my within! What show of images there!

What dimensions of reality in that immense space that my life has fled into.

Who measures normality? What is normality measured by? What tool is applied to measure normality with? What the hell is normality? Sweet kindness, that pretends it doesn't rain cats and dogs when it does, is this it, this normality? Yes Sir, no Sir, thank you Sir, perhaps that's it, eh . . . All sewn and packaged and smooth, never causing a stir or a moments trouble, that's it. Yes, that must be it. Normality!

Normality! Deader than a door nail, for a door nail spins. Quite fast. I have seen it spin.

So, according to the measurements of normality, your measurements, Clara, are totally out of norm, therefore, we, the appointed authority, declare you insane.

Not sound in mind.

Sound or not sound, each has something to do with listening.

Don't give me drugs, but listen to me instead. I have a story to tell. You are acting from ignorance of my right to my life as a human being and out of a measure of arrogance in your assumption, that because you are versed in the science of the human soul and you think you have the right measurements, that therefore you know me instantly sufficiently to judge my state of being accurately. You add up a few things, the story given you by whoever put me in your hands, a few questions answered by me, perhaps, the way I stand or sit there on the other side of your large desk, and you - supposed healer of the sick soul - become the judge of my life. Your summary sentence is a sentence for life or a death sentence. The way you look at it, either or, each way it is a kind of damnation. There it lies, black on white on a sheet of paper, there it is, imprinted on my being.

Clara is now a case with a distinct name to be treated with drugs accordingly. Clara has been most severely judged. She may never ever hear the verdict, most likely not, but she knows that it is heavy. *That name given* will be colouring every gesture she makes, every word she speaks, her silences, her movements, the way she eats. Every aspect of her life within her confinement.

Such a name is a heavy sentence indeed and it will be for the rest of her life!

Can you see, my love, that the order that we can measure and seem to understand, must be thrown into chaos, now and then, if life is to be and to evolve and to be renewed? Can you imagine, that this chaos, too, has its own structure, its own order and that innate in this is the new order, creation, life? That in the eye of the Tornado is the heart of the earth's spring? - That's where God comes in. The Immeasurable. The Mystery.

That's the Dance.

Let's dance.

To measure, to grasp, to name! - You put your net over the butterfly, and you got it. You got the butterfly! - Today, this morning, yesterday, tomorrow, someone somewhere far away caught this butterfly in his net and he got it. Today, Sunday, February 26th 1989, round eight a.m., there was a lightning flash and an enormous thundering rumble rolled over the village. Down-pourings of sunshine and hail, sunshine and lashings of rain followed one another, all day like this - and he got it, the butterfly, safely in his net, thousands of miles away . . .

You say 'God' and you think you got Him and you forget, that you have to create Him in every breathing moment of your life.

Jonathan came visiting me once a week after his teaching. He'd take me close to one of the large windows of the modern clinic I was in at the time, where men and women were together. A gently sloping hillside with spring flowers was spread outside. He'd sit very close to me and hold hands with me and point to the nature outside and say, "Clara, can you see the beauty out there, oh, *do* see it, my love, it is real, it is right there, look. Look, all that there is real."

It was not so much, that he might be speaking in an incomprehensible foreign tongue, but that his world could not impress itself on mine. I can see, how well he meant to want so eagerly to carry his world of beauty into my world of horror.

*   *   *   *

Clara was kept in a deep narrow valley that had no way into it and no way out of it. The steep endlessly high mountains on either side were of wombs and breasts and babies. And they were alive. Clara was forced to walk non-stop up and down in this eerily lit chasm and listen to the story that each one of these 'beings' screeched or howled or shouted. And her ears grew to an enormous size and the volume of sound inside her so huge and unbearable, that she became a scream. Somewhere inside her, Clara understood, that these discarded bits and pieces cut off or taken from living women and all these aborted babies had here become living fear. Terribly, horribly alive fear of these women and that they called for help. There was no night in this valley, no sleep, nor day either. And no exit.

In the ward, Clara tried to wash off the guilt of her helplessness by opting to wash up and dry the huge mountains of plates and pots and cutlery used by all the patients at the main meal. She did this for days and scrubbed the large scullery floor afterwards immaculately, only to be thrown deeper into this chasm of fear and horror.

The Angels departed. All the Helpers departed. There is no one to turn to. Nothing to hold on to. There is an entity that is horror and fear, that somewhere knows of Clara and Adam and their children, of sunshine and meadows and curlews, but cannot move towards itself or these things faintly known.

It is rigid. Fixed. This is Hell, when your being is thus held within a rigid state of fear and horror.

No movement.

No flow.

No one asked, 'Clara, where are you?' 'Clara, why are you so afraid?' 'Clara, what is the terror in your eyes?' 'Clara, my love, tell me. Speak slowly, Clara, take your time my love.'

One time, I sat in the row of the patients waiting to see the psychiatrist. My name was called: 'Come in', he said: 'Sit down,' he said. I did not want to sit down. 'Sit down', he said. I did not want to sit down. 'Sit down', he said. I was terrified to sit down on the other side of the vast desk. I was terrified. Why? No one asked.

I was given a new lot of drugs after tea that day.

45

*   *   *   *

To hold hands. Palm in palm. A hymn. Let's sing it. Feel the flow of warmth. Feel the sap rising through the sole of your feet. Weep.

Somewhere a voice said 'drop the drugs down inside your dress, don't swallow them, you'll land in worse of a hell.' I tried. But the nurses saw; and they were put into my mouth and my hand was being held that poured the water after them.

The nurses mean well. They do their duty. They do their best.

No one asked: 'The anguish in your eyes, Clara, how come, tell me . . . dear Soul, what is it that torments you so?'

The drugs did naught to prevent Clara from falling from chasm to chasm. On the contrary, it was as though her being was being shrunk and banned into the most abominable regions of sub-human state. And again, it was as though her eyes and ears were outsize and her nose too, so that all the vile atrocities, that happened there, froze her to stand and to witness and to watch.

Clara could not feel. The drugs had numbed the senses and the emotions. - But, you see, my love, somewhere she was living. Somewhere, however tiny a dot her being had shrunk into, there was vital partaking, storing and noting and an anxious, dreadful helplessness.

And Fear.

Fear.

Here, in this God-forlorn space, Clara witnessed women being raped, mutilated, cut up. And wombs and breasts and foetuses and babies devoured by monstrous men, who were to gain eternal life, for in the female, the foetus and the baby was the essence of life to be found. Man here was a mindless, soulless, heartless monstrosity, removed from humankind and yet, born of the Mother.

The Mother.

The mothers bore and gave birth to these monsters.

Help me, someone, help . . .

In the ward, Clara went up to the food counter and waved a

46

hand over the assembled patients, who, ready in a queue, were waiting to be served. And she said, "We are starving, all of us, we need more food."

This was the only way she could express her suffocating Angst.

From then on, Clara hardly finished one enormous helping, when one of the nurses came for her plate to fill it with a new enormous helping. And she stuffed and crammed it all down. - Nobody grasped, that her asking for more food was like a cry from the space of terror, which she innerly dwelt in. The world of Angst.

From this incident, the nurses assumed, that Clara had obviously been in a concentration camp, where she had experienced severe starvation, and she became known as 'The poor Soul.' - And at every meal 'the poor Soul' was stuffed to overflowing with heaps of food.

Through this misunderstanding, Clara fell into deepest isolation and her dwelling was the anguish of her soul. Images of happiness and times of joy would appear, of peoples she loved, and landscapes and places she was fond of, but they receded into an endless distance as fast as they appeared and made her isolation a measureless separateness.

Her soul became frozen scream and fear.

Suddenly, Hugo comes to mind. He was just five years old, when he joined 'my family' to make up the seven boys in my special care. They were to be under my observation in the Observation Station for the Department of Child-Psychiatry of this particular University. The Head of the Station held the only and fairly newly created Chair for Child Psychiatry at that time.

'His soul is frozen scream and fear,' might well have been the first entry in my notes of observation. The only way that this five-year-old pale, thin, love-starved child could let himself be known, was either in stony silence or violence. And when his banished and anguished soul thus broke out, it did so with such ferocious force, that he could topple over a wardrobe full of clothes, turn the fully made wooden beds upside down and attack an adult with the strength of a man ready to strangle.

It was a terrible unhealed scar to be an unmarried mother in those days; how society judged you and especially, how you were judged by the other 'proper' mothers. Under such pressures, Hugo's mother, who had to earn her living as a housekeeper, had handed her son out for fostering. And he went from foster-parents to foster-parents. Finally, no one was able to handle him.

After the allocated three months observation time, I begged in my report to prolong Hugo's time for another three months. Although the tests made by the Assistant Psychiatrist and the Psychologist came to a condemning verdict, I was granted my wish.

Hugo's violence had well neigh ceased and his silence was broken. We had a relationship and he was beginning to relate to others. And in my report, I had been able to say, that there was a deeply sensitive and highly intelligent child emerging. A beautiful looking boy, too.

Although, after the additional three months, I was able to speak in my report of this boy fully emerged, no sign now of the battered, fearful, violated soul, but on the contrary, a bright child, full of laughter and thoroughly able to communicate with everyone now, the psychiatrists and the psychologists needed their case. My report was ignored and the verdict given: psychopath. Hugo should be put into a suitable institution.

I got hold of Hugo's mother, showed her a copy of my report and urged her to ignore the Psychiatrists' findings, which were all based on very doubtful tests, and to heed my recommendation, which was born out of close encounter and grasp of Hugo's true being. - Namely, that she must accept her unmarried motherhood gladly and proudly and take a job as a housekeeper only, where they will accept her status and will have her with her child. This would at once make of her rejected child a child accepted and loved and return to herself the motherhood that she had denied. A necessary becoming and flowering for both mother and child. A healing.

Six years later, a small parcel reached me, wherever I was at the time. Enclosed was a thanksgiving letter by Hugo's mother, a long and wonderful story of Hugo's development and a necklace of fifty-five hand cut mother-of-pearl beads, five for each of Hugo's life-years. The gift was sent on Hugo's eleventh birthday.

*   *   *   *

Having been made aware so early in my life of the many fold splendour of everything and the divine order underlying all life and of the aliveness of everything - that even a speck of dust, each one a world, is dancing a magical dance - I have been shaken again and again at the lack of understanding of this and the absence of respect for life. Especially among those, that because of their learning, are being put above and before others.

It alarms me, how science, any science, needs to pin down, name, frame, consolidate whatever the findings are and there-by instantly losing or killing whatever it is, that might have been found. Or depriving it of the possibility of its otherness, its trans-formation or mutation, regression or progression, disordering and reordering anew.

It is not Death, that Western Mankind is afraid of, but Life.

You see, dear Sirs, your yardstick, your intellect, is a measure or two short. How much does the spirit weigh?

Palm Sunday 1989: over 30 wars are being fought all over the world. Many of them in the name of a God or Jesus the Christ. At this moment.

In the urgency to know and own and possess, the Knowers - the Apprentices of the Magician's Apprentice - dig and delve, go high and low, dissect and vivisect. And by these doings, they think they have got 'It', whatever. And then might follow that with statements like the one I found in last week's *Radio Times* that a Professor X had uttered: "Cystic fibrosis? Anaemia? Never mind, we'll soon have that replacement gene in and working; it is my belief that gene therapy will prove simpler than the horren-dous things we're doing these days with transplant surgery."

How soon will this gene therapy be called 'a horrendous thing . . .'

Meanwhile, all these horrendous things, findings, weapons, works, machines, medicaments, chemicals, philosophies, beliefs are being let loose on mankind, gullible, unthinking mankind. Which is in total enslavement and enthralment of these life under-mining, death orientated, destructive forces.

* * * *

c

A vision came into my closed eyes early this April Sunday morning: Two gold shining Angels holding between them a staff that was barren but for three rosebuds at the top of itself. Their fragrance was strong and sweet. The Angels spoke together these words: "Hold to your Heart. Never doubt it. Hold to it fast, as we, your Helpers hold this Staff of Roses. So you hold to your Heart."

The morning vision vanished, leaving my morning room filled with sweet wild-rose fragrance.

There was no music anymore. No sound. No colour either. Nothing did sing any more. The wooden spoons didn't sing anymore.

Clara stood there on one of the large slate-stone slabs, that, worn from generations of feet, sorrow and laughter and prayers, made up the kitchen floor. She held a small, egg-shell coloured teapot dangling in her right hand in front of her eyes, and she could not comprehend it: What this teapot was, what it was meant for, what she was supposed to do with it.

Later and always, she could only remember standing there holding the teapot up in the air and that she must have stood there like that for some time, but never, if she ever made a cup of tea. And very clearly that she didn't respond to anything and nothing responded to her. She was, in a sudden, without name and all the things were nameless, too.

Yesterday, there was so much meaning, and oh, how the wooden spoons had sung. And what holy communion that had been every morning with the eggshell teapot for one, that Lucie Rie had, so, so many years ago, specially crafted for her and the one cup small enough to fill it three times. It had become a daily ritual to guide Clara out of dream time into the day wakefulness.

Now, this morning, close on to Christmas 1977, shattered, all of it. With one blow. Everything shattered and gone, as though nothing nor herself had ever been. Overnight.

There was no more meaning. And yet, it was not death, but rather, that all the threads had been cut: the ones to Earth, the ones to Heaven, the ones to Things and Beings and Humankind. And the ones to Loved Ones.

Snip, snap, snip. Cut. Cut and severed. When the memory goes, you are bereaved. What is the now without the memory and where does the future fall . . .

The memory, which encompasses not just yesteryear, but all past, the dream-time of humankind and its non-being and its becoming. Being, too, goes with memory gone. All spark is gone from the fire. Where to does life fall without the fire? Is not all state and manner of being and becoming a degree of fire . . .

This woman Clara who had - only yesterday - seemed to be gifted with the gift of all senses added to each sense, her life having dimensions of clarity and radiance. There was wisdom in her words and wholeness in her loving. And now look at her on this morning: there she stands on this worn down slate slab with not a cinder left to be kindled in the hearth of her being.

The fire's gone out.

Days passed in this way, maybe weeks, in which Clara did not relate to anything or anyone, nor to herself. Yet, she went up and down in the house, in and out of it, over the meadows along the foot path, and again and again down to the cliffs, as though she was in search of something lost.

The one that was her in a way too, observed and watched, stood there and looked on, but as it might be in a dream, not known to the dreamer, not known to Clara in her severance from life.

The strangest thing is this - and oh how terrible in retrospect - that in this state of sunken or vanished mind, there is no music anymore, nothing sings anymore, nor is there any colour. You don't respond. Your Self is not there to respond. And nothing responds to you.

Have you been in this dumb silence . . . Have you ever been in it . . . Somewhere, some thousands of miles away is your aware Self, your shrunken soul as a minute speck in a terror, that it might not ever again be partaking of this life that is Clara.

So, so strange this: Clara a manifest body, tangible, real to all eyes. Yet not inhabited by living life, yet eating and drinking and sleeping and getting up. An automaton that has no will, no need, no want, no desires? Is she a husk?

Where is the far departed one, the awareness of herself: seeing the severance, knowing the deprivation, yearning desperately to be part and partaker of this life that Clara is . . .

Yesterday and the day before and on so many other days, young women came to be in Clara's presence as in a breeze that soothes, as in a silence that sings, to break the home-made loaf together, to share the cup. They'd say, "What is it, Clara, that makes you the way you are . . ?"

"I am a woman loved. I follow my heart. I love myself. I would not want to be another."

The kitchen sink, the hearth, the cups, everything was this song. Her gestures were this song. She was in communion with the source of life through love. She was thankful for this gift. For being held so. For being guided so. For being able to build her true being so, stone by stone.

She had no secrets, but only this earliest understanding, that naught truly begins unless: I love myself. In this loving, I am responsible. I respond immediately and awaredly to the moment and in the moment. I respond spontaneously to the source of life, inspiration, God, for all the helpers are in my presence.

It is not a security, no, but an aliveness. Oh, to be alive so: now you laugh, now you weep, now you dance, now you are still, now you sing, now you are silent. Oh, to respond so, to be alive so. And then to be deprived of this flow, to be cut off this current in the small time of a few sleeping hours.

Tonight you dance, tomorrow morning your feet do not remember that there was a last night and dancing . . .

If Clara had marked that morning in her calendar, she might have found, that exactly to the day six moon-months had passed since the event of the removal of her womb and her ovaries.

The gorse had been so golden that early summer. Some of the slopes running down seaward were like floods of gorse-gold, deep summer-sun-gold, ha! and Clara drank the intoxicating fragrance cupped handfuls of it. And she had lain in vastnesses of sea pinks that poured over the cliffs. She had lain there wide, the deep blue sky her lover.

In the dark aloneness of many nights, though, she had lain

thoughtful and in pain, that the growth in her womb was growing ever bigger, that she had been bleeding for so many years now, and that her prayers to the healer within had not been heard. She had not woken up one morning miraculously healed.

Clara had seen all sorts of doctors. She had seen specialists, too. Even the doctors from alternative medicine had suggested that an operation was necessary. It had been the best part of seven years since it was confirmed that there was a growth and it was likely to become malignant if allowed to grow on. At that early time, one of the well known gynaecologists she saw put horror on top of fear with his obviously vengeful attitude towards woman and his gleeful way of saying: "Much better to cut out all these useless bits and pieces you believe make up your womanhood, imagine the fun and freedom you'll have without them." He shook with scornful laughter, while Clara fainted with the image of this inhuman man dancing in front of her eyes, sharpening his butcher's knife to cut up his own mother with.

Horror on top of many fears: fear of doctors, fear of surgeons, fear of hospital, fear of operation and the dreadful fear of losing her vital womanhood, her very Self.

On top of these fears, Clara built the faith that as the growth had been caused by herself, albeit not consciously willed, that the healer was within that self, too. Is not all healing art based in the wisdom, that the healer is within? The God who inflicts the ill is also the healing God, the redeemer?

But can you build faith on a foundation of fear . . . surely, that is kidding yourself. Clara built this faith and was shining and strong with it to herself and to everyone who met her. She did not for a moment see the cunning self deception: where fear *was*, there *is* now faith. A house built on such foundation surely cannot last long, and faith as a cover-up seems more to do with make-believe.

Clara did what deep innerly she felt she had to do. She certainly had had no notion of self-deception or was conscious at the time of avoiding to bring into her awareness her many fears. To welcome them in at last and look them straight and brightly in the face.

She followed her heart. She built her faith on fear, big and shining. She held hands with her Angel and never had an inkling - or had she - that her life and world were to fall and crumble.

End of May of that fatal 1977, Clara sat with Adam and two beloved friends by the wood burning fireside. They had just celebrated with a meal the first one-man show of Marc's sculptures, which had well-neigh overwhelmed him with the success of critical acclaim and the many works sold and commissioned. He was sitting there, his child face beaming with wonderment, recounting this most eventful happening, when Zarah, his wife, abruptly cut in and turning sharply to Clara said, "Clara, you are dying." She said it in alarm, but calmly.

Very calmly, almost laconically, Clara replied, "Yes, I am dying."

"Do you want to die?"

"No, I don't want to die".

Although it was late at night, Zarah was up and on the telephone to make an urgent early appointment for Clara with her own family doctor. Adam said, "But why, Clara, didn't you tell me that you felt so unwell?"

With tears choking her, she answered, "Because every day I expected the miracle of a sudden healing to happen." In her heart she asked, 'Why, oh why, Adam, had you not seen . . ?'

That night, Clara dreamed a dream, which she had not dreamed for more than twenty years, but which had been appearing from her early teens up to just after Adam had become truly part of her life. And it had stayed in her like a vision.

The Dream: Clara walks along a winding dusty road in Tuscany. This road is well known to her. She reaches and enters a large white mansion, that stands solitary in the landscape. Through a wide Romanesque arch, she descends wide stone steps beautifully lain in a spiral movement. She comes into a huge vaulted cellar and finds a graciously beautiful young woman there, who, dressed in a fawn brown flowing gown, is ladling liquid manure from one huge tank into another. She chants, while she does this work, "Oh, what fragrance, oh, what fragrance." And indeed, the cellar is filling with sweet fragrance. Clara is longing to be this woman, when suddenly, she hears herself saying, "remember, she is the Beautiful Woman of your within."

In the long gone past the Beautiful Woman sometimes shifted solid manure from one heap to another. But always, by the shifting, there was delicious fragrance and always, the Beautiful Woman was dressed in a fawn coloured full flowing gown, the wide sleeves lined with white. She chanted her chant, then did her task in silence, in a rhythm of joy and movements of gladness. Her face open, harmonious, beautiful like the Christ face in the Mosaics of Ravenna.

That very last time, in her late twenties, when Clara dreamed this dream, Adam was suddenly at her side as she was descending the wide steps into the cellar, and she knew instantly, that she must not go into the cellar with him, and she turned back.

There is an innermost, that belongs to one's Self and to oneself alone.

With this visionary dream having been given at this very moment like the strength of a real encounter, Clara went to see Zarah's old-fashioned country doctor the next morning. He was grave and clearly deeply upset, when he said:

"Good God, how could you let this thing go on for so long!" There was warmth and compassion in his presence and he seemed to suffer on Clara's behalf. Then and there, he arranged for her to see a gynaecologist. Sensing her fear, he assured Clara, that he knew the surgeon personally and that they had worked together for many years.

"It grieves me," said this seemingly cool, handsome man, "that an intelligent mature woman can be so irresponsible towards herself and allow such an urgent situation to happen. It is too grave to wait a moment longer, I can have a hospital bed for you immediately."

Clara said, that she was innerly not ready for an operation, and that she had to prepare herself.

"You want to go on being irresponsible, you want to die! You do not realise how grave your state is." And he pleaded fiercely with her to accept the urgency of the situation. He summoned Adam and asked him to convince Clara, that her life was in the balance.

But Clara *had* to get in touch with the Beautiful Woman of her guiding dream. And she needed to see a spiritualist healer of whom she had heard only some months earlier, perchance, through an old friend, who had suddenly turned up on Clara's doorstep, after an absence of many years. Out of the blue on a blustery February day.

Clara begged of the surgeon to allow her to get in touch with him personally as soon as she felt strong enough to face the ordeal of an operation. Also, that she could be in St Francis Hospital, a small private hospital, founded and tended by an Order of Franciscan nuns.

As Clara turned to thank the surgeon, he took her hands and said, "You are crazy," with such deep concern, that for a moment she might have changed her mind.

These two strangers, doctor and surgeon, were so personal in their partaking, while Adam was cool and distant. How she would have loved for Adam to take her into his arms and hold her there. She needed so much to sob into the warm chest of a beloved one.

But Adam was detached. Aloof.

Since last night, in a few hours, Clara's eyes had been torn open to look at herself and her relationship. Was she beloved to a loved one in her imagination only? Or worse, even: a make-believe . . ? Had she made herself believe, that she was this woman loved . . . Was the dream-vision of last night to remind her of a life-task neglected or postponed: *To make shit into manure!* A labour of love of patiently creating the innate Self, of building the Beautiful Woman that she was . . .

All healing art is based in the wisdom that the healer is within. The God who inflicts the ill is also the healing God, the redeemer. Why had Clara interpreted this to herself in so severe a way, that, literally, she was to do the healing from within herself - albeit, with the help of God . . .

The voice of the heart, is it the dictate of fate?

The soles of your feet, the palms of your hands, the map of your heaven of stars and planets, charts all of destiny? Power for-ordained?

Voice of the heart your lode star, that you *must* follow?

Fall in with fate and you become the master-builder of your life, that is predetermined from eternity. This is my freedom, then, to choose fate as my dancing partner.

Turn this way, turn that way, spin.
Turn, turn, turn with the turning point. A challenge.
Spin.
Kreis - Kreisel - Kreisen.
Crisis. Krises. Chrise.
Turn, turn. Turn with the turning point. Take the challenge.
Spin.
What makes us Master-builders, is to fall in with fate.
To choose your dancing partner.
To dance.
Dance!
Dance with Fate!

Behold the seed - the winged seed - lest it falleth into the deep dark, into the dark deep of the Earth - Behold it!

What paradox, the path to Selfhood!

This covenant between the God and myself made before my substantial entry into this earthly world, sealed with palm in palm, God's palm in mine: Pulse - for a moment of eternity - one. *My pulse and God's pulse: one pulse.*

- Lest I remember at my entry, lest I remember: The Word to be made flesh . . .

Follow your heart, your lode-star. Bear the load that comes by this voyaging.

. . . Listen! in the innermost of your own silence at this moment, the words of God's covenant with you are being spoken.

For Clara it is, as at the very beginning, *follow your heart, it is your lode-star*. Have faith. Wherever you step, you are being guided and held.

God's palm in mine. Always. All ways.

We are, all of us, in need to follow something, that both serves us and is our guide. Blessed are those, that are given to see what this thing is and recognise it in good time as the guide and servant on the inevitable road to Selfhood.

Selfhood! 'tis the meaning, is it not, for having been thrust once more into this earthly life or, perchance, having *chosen* to be thrust . . .

Gladly, maybe, unwillingly, maybe.

But remember that compact with God, you made it with him, don't forget. The agreement is binding and it is understood, that my life thus chosen is lived to its fulfilment.

If God is good, He is bad also. Good heavens, yes! You can't have one without the other. God the Trixter. Every now and then, He squeezes your hand - in memoriam of the covenant - as you are once more in a cul-de-sac or in the ice of some hell or in the blaze of a laser-beam light. He squeezes your hand, as I said and He turns His bright face on you and somewhere far away in you you know: All is well. All is well. Underneath. Above. Within. Without. This way. That way. High and low.

All manner of things is well.

And you wander on, on the God-forchosen path, that more often than not seems forsaken. As I said, you wander on. Because you remembered: it's your path.

Or mine.

When you have arrived at the arrival, which is both terminus and origin, take off your useful garments and don you with the bells and raiments of the Fool - for you have well earned these - and take your sow bladder, well blown to its limits, and run through the streets and bump the sleep-walkers over their sleepy heads and shout: wake ye . . . wake ye . . . and laugh with them and frolic and dance.

And sing. Sing. Songs of glad tidings. And let you be crowned for the day, this once in a life time, Queen of the Fools . . . and laugh. Laugh.

Can you make your heart believe? Surely, the word of your heart is true . . .

The Red Indian Shaman's voice was deep and monotone like the deep bell of Acoma Pueblo, City on the Mesa rock, Sky-City, that Clara had heard, standing lone in that immense silence of

58

endless blue sky and endless barren land and was remembering herself, long ages ago, having stood thus: "The beginning of the world, I am thinking about it. The beginning of the world I am talking about it." The bell had seemed to say these Navajo words.

Lying there, on the high bed, under the healing hands of the small little healer woman, who had now in trance become the Red Indian Shaman, Clara was listening to the story of her illness that was being told in surprising details and accuracy, and she was in a transport. It was as though she had been lifted from her physical body and, winged now, was flying backward in time and yet, what she experienced thus, was also this moment, now.

One can be, so it seems, in many dimensions all at once, when alive in the moment.

The power of the monotone, the way it summons: faces, that had only been held in a glance - in einem Augenblick - are here in an encounter with Clara.

Chihuahua, an early morning. Clara is standing by the side of the unpaved road waiting for her family. A young God, the Apollo of Chihuahua, comes down the wide road. His shining face lights the not yet sunlit street. Passing by Clara, he turns his head. Eye enters eye. They are looking into one another. Moment - so brief a space of time - and yet, such stirring happening. There was recognition. Of what? Were they lovers, once; brother and sister, once; husband and wife, twins, once? Did he call her name, did she call his? Or are we at such moment for an immediacy, in a glance that is deep, brought to the source of our own human kind - unserer eigenen Menschlichkeit - to the roots of our human experience . . .

The voice of the Shaman.

It is evening, dusk, the band plays. The teenage girls and boys of Guanajuato are dancing in opposite directions round the sacred fragrant linden tree in the town square. Their families look on in a circle around them. Clara is there, too, enjoying the high summer celebration: Lindentree, tree of young love, round which in his high bloom the girls and boys dance. The girls this way round, the boys that way round . . . and the fate of the encounter, when the music suddenly stops: who will be at your side?

Lindenblossom, scent of high summer. Clara remembers her wild dancing round the Lindentree in her native village one night, aroused by the sweet fragrance of innocent love.

As she is seeing herself thus, a head in the circle in front of her turns, an ancient beautiful face of a man, that could be a woman's, too. A face that had lived every word of its life; the story of mankind engraved in it. And large immensely dark eye-pools, both of sorrow and joy, are filling with tears as his eyes meet Clara's and a smile warms each face.

An instant of happening.

A world of happening.

The monotone voice of the Healer.

Tamazunchale, an ancient mining town, once busy and prosperous. Top of the world. Eerie. All the streets dead-silent. No one to be heard or seen. Clara, waiting for the specially cooked dinner to be ready in the Old Foundry now turned restaurant, is strolling with her two small children and Adam through the cobbled alleys and streets.

There had been no sound of doors opening and none were seen open, yet, soundlessly, a procession of women appeared and made a circle round the small family. One after the other of the women stepped out of the circle and came and laid her right hand on Clara's belly, then on her head, then on the head of each of the two fair-haired children, mumbling a prayer all the while. Then the woman, whose hand empowered by this touch and seemingly blessed, touched her own head and belly, while her left hand rested on her heart. After each of these women had thus given and received, they vanished silently and the town fell into dusk. In the foundry restaurant a feast was awaiting the overwhelmed family and the colourful Mariachis played and sang for them, the only guests.

The voice of the Shaman. The Story unfolding.

It is near noon. The sun is high and burning. Clara - sandal-footed and clad in an ankle-long white linen garment hand sewn by herself of linen grown, spun and woven on the farms of her ancestors - is walking with her family down a dust road towards Morelia. A Mexican Woman comes towards them, her arms wide in welcome. She encloses Clara in her arms and tells her in broken English: "I wait for you, you come in dream today, you bring blessing to my home and family." She then takes Clara by her hand and brings her to the silent centre of her home, where she had built a shrine for Maria, the Mother of God. Together; the two women are standing by the shrine silently. Then they kneel in

60

prayer and Clara then is asked to light from the one light at the shrine each candle in the immaculately white adobe dwelling. "Tree of Life shining now." The Mexican woman's face is a sun and everywhere is light and white as the new fallen snow, the maiden snow, the first of winter.

In the mono-tone of the Red Indian Shaman, the story is unfolding. His hands feelers, his feeling hands gliding, spread fingered, slowly from toes over the body to the head, and above the head and back. His sensing hands listening . . . the story.

Monotone, powerful, the voice. Clara's belly like a hearth warming under the Shaman's hands and his voice like a drumbeat remembered.

The huge, loud market-hall of Guadalajara, built on many levels, a labyrinth. One follows one's nose and hopes to find the open air sometimes. A maze filled with bartering voices, echoes, threads of songs, laughter, shouts of exuberance . . .

Clara and family climbed yet another rickety wooden stairs and found themselves amidst a forest of wooden spoons. All sizes and kinds, simple shapes and rudely carved, displayed in heaps or stood up in baskets. Dark wondering large eyes of a small child are gazing through these, a little baby in a crude basket by her gurgles and plays with her hands.

Clara guessed the moment: the mother had to run an errand, the little girl is left in charge. Clara seizes the moment and fills with wooden spoons the arms of her astonished family. Lots and lots of wooden spoons in all these arms, armies of them and the child's eyes growing in wonderment . . .

Lots and lots of pesos into the money tin, and in Clara's heart growing the vision of the mother returning to so many spoons sold, so many pesos in the money tin, a child in great wonder.

A little miracle. A hardship eased, maybe. A prayer of the mother answered.

These wooden spoons are magical, make magic and joy each day.

*   *   *   *

Be with me, now, O ye people, that have entered me by one look, one gesture. Whose breath and mine mingled but once, momentarily. Be with me, O ye people, as power of love, as bright light, as courage.

Heart triumphant.
Heart triumphant.
Heart triumphant.

The power of the mono-tone, the way it summons: faces that had only been held in a glance - in einem Augenblick - Am I still in the eyes of the Apollo of Chihuahua?

Clara lay calm and was still. In the short moments, in which the simple woman entered the state of trance and became the Healer, all fear had left her. Clara lay on this high couch, just high enough for the Spiritualist Healer to hold her outstretched hands over Clara's clad body. Slowly, she moved them over the body, very slowly. And to Clara it was as were these hands - now become the hands of a Red Indian Shaman - large ears listening or outsize feelers receiving radiant messages from all the bodies making up the one body visibly lying there.

The little woman, for she was not five feet, seemed now, in her transformation as Red Indian Shaman, tall in stature. And when finally her hands were arrested over Clara's belly and this deep male voice broke out of her, Clara could not help but see the spirit form that she had entered and was now being acted by. And she fell into such astonishment, when she heard the story of her illness being recounted in smallest and accurate details. All the bits, the many bits that Clara had tucked away far down into herself and hidden out of her own hearing, were all laid bare now, word for word, and with Adam listening and hearing?

Spoken thus in the Shaman's monotone voice, each word falls where it belongs and it is clear: no emotions are colouring, no judgement falls, no guilt is brought forth, no accusations are made. The events that are being recounted are in their own places, following one out of the other into another. Loop links loop links loop, on and on in this way. There is vital connection, yet seemingly so much disruption, and yet all resulting from choices made, consciously or not consciously, by the person whose story is being told.

"This life is meant for love. To this person, love is all meaningful. She is ready to give her life for love. She has known this since she was a child. So when the man came into her life, who seemed to personify this love in all its nobility, she gave her yes hugely."

Yes! Yes! and she wrote it large on the big sheet of letter paper, full size turning the sheet, so the Yes was filling the page.

It was filling me. *I was the Yes*. I shouted it into the winds for it to be blown across the miles to my love. I shouted it into the river for it to be carried to my love. I shouted my Yes to the stars . . .

Shine it, shine it, shine my Yes to him, my love.

I did not heed my Mother's far seeing words: "This Yes will bring you immeasurable sorrow and suffering."

Yes was my heart. Yes was all of me. And I realised that I had given myself into this love at the first fateful encounter with this man four years earlier. It was so brief and so fateful, "Hello, you are Clara, I have heard so much about you."

I was lying, thin and haggard, recovering from blood poisoning, that had taken me to the brink of life. " You are . . ?"

"Adam", he quickly answered.

And in my heart, I finished my greeting, 'my love come at last.'

This one meeting had not just struck a note in me, but had made me into a jubilating song. The opportunity was not given to get to know this man, not even the most ordinary things, how old he was, where he came from. So I built him. I built him in awe and wonder into the most noble of love, into the most aware and awake of beings. A shining presence, who was pure and whole in his human being.

I built Apollo.

And in the building of him, I shone. Other men came into my life, but each one of these could only be a spark of the sublime one that I was building.

*   *   *   *

The voice of the Shaman telling the tale - Clara's voice, deep within her, telling the tale.

. . . Yes, in my bright aspiring to love, to wisdom and to light, I saw my created Adam as this Holy Trinity personified, so that, when we were finally together, I handed my life over to him in deepest trust. And my life became meaningful only because of his. We were one.

Thus, we shone and radiated our togetherness. Thus we had children. The shadow was not let in, the flaws were not permitted or acknowledged, neither in the togetherness, nor in each one or each other. - This marriage was made in Heaven, and it was like a spell I lived by. - But spells are magic, and magic does not last.

One day, in my fortieth year, I woke to the spell broken.

I stood in the road waving Adam good-bye. I stood on the steep slope of the road in front of our home alone, lost and disconnected. And I formed a funnel round my mouth with my now forlorn hands and I shouted, "Clara, where are you? Clara, where are you?" . . . Where are you, where are you . . . the echoes came back from the Horse-Thief-Valley below.

At that moment, with that cry, a world started to crumble, that shining hands had built. A spell had been broken, that this life had been nourished by and lived by.

- Lest the seed falleth into the dark, into the dark deep of the earth. Behold! It falling.

Words, that Adam had spoken but the night before and that had made a sharp pain in her, Clara repeated to herself, still standing in the road, "But I have never been in you, as you see yourself in me. I have never identified with you. A man loves differently."

Sharp pain and a piercing revelation of a truth Clara had known, but had not wanted to know. And oh, such a far cry from Adam's words written so many years ago, 'I cannot anymore live without you, life has no meaning, it is wrong for us to live apart.' And other words crowded in spoken of love, of being one, of being for ever. They crowded in on Clara standing there forsaken on the steep slope in front of her home in Texas.

She had been subtly informed for sometime, from within and from without, that change was needed, that she was with this man and not because of him. That she must re-member her life, which

64

was separate from his and was unique and precious and needed to be lived.

"But *I am* living my life. My life is this love for husband and children." Thus, Clara would answer to herself, yet somewhere knowing the other and knowing, that an unknown wanted to become and a leap into the dark had to be made yet again. And oh, being so afraid to leap. But now the push was given with a vehemence.

And on that very day, Clara began both wittingly and unwittingly, to dismember what she had for many years lived by.

- Oh, do not reject fate when it offers you a dance. Dance, dance with love, that has become a phantom in your arms.

Clara was still in love. She was in love with whom . . ?

On that memorable day, she told a young student, who like so many had found Clara out as a helper and listener in their troubles, that Adam would be the one to truly help her.

Do not just take a bite out of the apple, eat the whole apple, core and all, then look with wonder on the stem, that you are holding between thumb and pointing finger. Look with wonder on it for this little thing held that apple on the branch of the tree . . . What holds, what let's fall? Is it the same force?

Thus subtly and promptly, happening followed upon happening, that brought down the house of light, that Clara had built with bright hands and shining heart.

Adam became at once infatuated in the girl, was fascinated by her, they became lovers and he got lost to the family.

Clara still waved to her love in the morning, still stood under the door to welcome her love in the evening and wept in the house without windows, without doors, without hearth.

The heart grows up into the throat. Water drips from the tap. Tears are filling the gutters of the house.

- Leaping. Falling. Letting fall. -

One night, Clara asked Adam, 'What if this girl gets pregnant?"

"O, we'll cope with the situation should it occur." - Casually said, lightly and carelessly by the same man who had said to Clara a while back, 'You must not get pregnant again, two children are quite enough.' And so Clara had kept her new pregnancy to herself. And Adam had added, "Anyway, this relationship with Anita is a very special gift to me and it has nothing whatsoever to do with our marriage. Our marriage *is!*"

'Let not my hands grow barren with lovelessness,' Clara had prayed this one morning, and turning in the road to go back into the house, she saw a man, obviously badly injured, coming tumbling drunkenly up the steep slope. She ran to him and half carried, half dragged him home. She threw snow white sheets on the bed and laid the bleeding young man into these. In all his agony, he apologised for soiling these white sheets. But for Clara it was, that her marital bed, dry and hard for so long, was being sanctified at last with the blood of love.

From his hospital bed, this unknown young man, a student, sent her an armful of red roses.

"The emotional stress and strain, the disloyalty and above all the infidelity became too much and a miscarriage was inevitable." The Shaman's voice speaking, while the little room is filling with a foul stench, as he seems to take handfuls of decayed matter from Clara's body, which he is throwing behind him with gestures and sounds of disgust.

"In her loss and grief, this person did not trust herself to anyone, did not seek medical advice or help either and the growth started almost immediately. All the most endangering matter has now been removed. It is advised, for the operation to take place, but it will be easy and without complications. Leave a small personal object behind, a handkerchief, maybe, let us know the date of the operation and we will stand by you.

"Fear not any more. You are in good hands. You are being watched over."

I am lying on the couch. Still. Quiet. I do not move. I breathe regularly. Every now and then I take a deep breath. Warmth flows through me. My belly is very warm. A hearth. The Healer's hands are over it and receiving. What these hands receive, the Healer translates into words and tells the story. I am listening to my own story. With every word, that the Shaman speaks, I am feeling lighter. Fear goes and hope goes and peace takes their place.

A still-being.

If Adam listens at all, he is hearing this story for the first time. And Clara, too, is hearing it for the first time this way, as though it was someone else's story. And so a spell is broken. She could now partake, but need not be involved, need not be identified with it. Yet, it *is* the full story of how *her* illness had come about.

Don't leave the last drop in your glass, drink it! Don't leave the last drop in the wine bottle, drink it!

The tiny fruit-fly-man sings a song of love that lasts for 60 seconds and not without this song is the little fruit-fly-woman ready to receive her little man in mating; if the song lasts 40 seconds only, she'll not be turned on . . . Adam steps out of the session with the Healer with the words, "We must get on, it's a long drive back."

'Adam, Adam, who are you? Whom is it that I love?' In Clara's heart these questions, while her hands were filling with light again, for all the fear had gone.

And in the many hours ride home, Clara came to see clearly that 'love thyself is the beginning of all love and that, as her Mother had said so so long ago, it has to be learned and earned and comes by suffering. Accepting that which is given in every moment and so make it into an inspiring, transforming force in wakefulness and awareness of one's Self.

"Make that which is given into the livingness of yourself. Affirm yourself in this and accept yourself in self-forgiveness. A most lively, lightful Holy-Trinity, that must needs to become Self-love. This power of love is in you a radiant point and is present in every lived moment."

Clara was at the beginning of herself again. A shoot again.

Oh that there was someone to be held by, to flow with . . .

Clara remembered on this journey, how, in all that upheaval those years ago, she had pondered again and again this thing called love. How she had imagined her love so huge, that it was all embracing and that a relationship such as Adam had with Anita could be seen or experienced as an enrichment of their marriage. Need not be a hurt and cause the heart to be desolate and broken.

But her heart broke. Her loving was being betrayed. And one night, when she knew the two were making love, a jealousy took hold of her, in which she envisioned this young woman clearly into her presence and symbolically strangled her. And how frightfully powerful this gesture was! Anita telephoned the next morning and said, "The strangest thing happened last night, Clara, there was your presence as real, and I felt your hands round my neck and felt I was being suffocated by this apparition."

- What power of symbolic act indeed!

Clara had made the gesture at that moment, that she felt she had to suffocate from this grip of jealousy. She felt relieved and free afterwards and sat there in the candle-lit room looking at herself: How dark the underside of the heart, how abysmal the underground of loving. And she knew that she was in a deep crises and that it is well to remember that it means turning point, a challenge!

"Fear not and turn with it, love is as life is." Was it her Angel speaking . . .

The undermining, the disturbance, she herself had called for it. In her depth she knew that it was necessary for her to let go of being identified with another and of being alive only because of

68

and through the other. She knew, that her life must be freed for herself to rise and to become. She knew also, that she could not have been in this marriage in any other way but to give herself wholly into it and to be ready to sacrifice her life for it and the family. In the deepest depth of her however it was known, that this huge love so passionately expressed in a togetherness that brought ecstasy, joy, so much happiness, so much sorrow, was but one adventure of this life in its quest for Selfhood. And that the quest had moved and meandered on within her like an underground stream, its force of radiation finally and suddenly flowing into her awareness like a shocking awakening.

So, Clara, here you are at the beginning of yourself again. - How frightening. How exhilarating.

In a diary of that time, Clara found a dream, that had been given in the early hours after that self-revealing event of that memorable night.

The dream: 'A gloriously shining, beautifully spirited stallion is galloping by me, the movement of his tail is like a banner in the wind, the mane rippling like water. I am urged to race after him, to get hold of him and to leap on his back. He seems to have come right out of the middle of myself. He stops and turns, comes close to me and looks at me out of enormously large most alive eyes: a being of oneness and grace, his physical strength and beauty become through-spirited life as movement and a spontaneous lightful, inspiring energy, like a new force of life, flows into me. - I wake into a great gladness.'

Some notes follow the jotting down of the dream:

'I remember the dream suddenly while cleaning the house and a stillness long not so profoundly experienced comes to me. There is a peace in my heart. And in this stillness, I can see everything in its place, everyone in his role. I am *with* myself. I *hear* the wind in the trees. I *see* the trees. I clean the windows of my home to outwardly express the momentary clarity of my own look out. There is nothing in the way now, not at this moment.

'I see, how necessary it is for my own life and inevitable for the livingness of this togetherness, that I recognise myself "Als Einzelne," an individual, that has his own unique being and way to fulfil. On her own alone, yet within a relationship with another.

'To be thus prepared like the freshly ploughed earth for the seed . . .

'Wait in peace, then, for the new to manifest, that has already happened in the deep of you.

'Listen. Your name is being called.

'Respond.

'Be wakeful.'

The Healer's hands had wrought a transformation. Clara was rejuvenated. She had become a flow of lightful energy. And one day, she took Adam by the hand and led him to a small nest of grass encircled by flowering gorse - a place long sacred to her and kept a secret till this day - and they made love.

The Earth for a sweet moment stopped its turning and a jubilation spread over Her, the Sun spun faster and the Stars fell into the day and a Fragrance rose and was carried by the winds . . . To make love so. The shine of it falling into generations yet to come.

Thus, Clara was light and easy when she entered hospital, and she was filled with a vision of herself being in a new life with a new meaning. A new dream was born from her. In this strength she was able to visit all the other women in the ward she was in, so many of them, who were either waiting for operations or had just undergone severe surgery. With her renewed faith in life, Clara was able to lighten and strengthen each woman a little.

In the early morning of the June-day of her own operation, the Surgeon came to her bed. He sat on the bed and took both her hands in his, "I have come to make sure that you are fully aware of the gravity and severity of the operation that we are going to do shortly, and I want you to tell me, what this operation is all about."

"You are going to cut out the womb and the ovaries because of the growth that is there. I have no fear now. We are in good hands." - Saying this, Clara looked clearly into the Surgeon's eyes.

When she was quite aware of herself again after the operation, the Surgeon appeared again. Again, he sat on the bed and took her hands in his: "I have come because I must tell you, that never in my long practice have I had an easier operation. Because of the state you were in, when we first saw you, we were prepared for every kind of complication, blood transfusion etc. None of these were needed and there was no sign, as far as we can tell at this moment, of the cancer that was about to destroy your life. It was as though my hands were being guided. I have not ever used the word miracle, not in my private life nor in my work, but I am saying it now, a miracle has occurred."

It was then, that Clara took the Surgeon's hands in hers and thanked him and wished him well and said again as in the early morning, "We are in good hands."

By these good hands, Clara was being held. And to her own surprise and that of everyone else, she recovered well and fast. She became of a vitality and a vivacity that was astonishing and that she had not experienced for many years. Even so, she urged her doctor that she should receive the hormone that the body was so abruptly deprived of - for a voice kept coming into her ears 'beware the miracle, this operation always has traumatic consequences.' - But the doctor laughed, "Look at you, the way you are recovering, and we believe, that anyway, you are passed your menopause." Clara insisted, that she was not and knew and should know that she was not. And Adam's pleading for her was not heeded either. - And by and by, the warning voice was overwhelmed by the joy of well being that grew in Clara and by which she was swept along and affected others. She travelled and visited friends far and wide, and she wrote long letters to Adam, sharing impressions and experiences. She felt close to him. She was still in love. And she was in love with life so newly and overwhelmingly having been given to her again.

Everything she did became a love-making; the sexual force was like a wonderful feeling all over her. She did not need the sexual act to express herself in or confirm herself by, or get lost in or be transported by. *She was in a transport* and she was transformed. There was a force, a flow, a dynamic that vitalised itself in herself and turned her on and whoever stepped into her realm. A woman-force, whole, huge and glorious, where every gesture made was Yes, Yes, Yes life, Yes! And joy was brought forth. And every day was new and a celebration.

The sexual act for its own exciting sake never had any meaning without the loving, on the contrary, it was for Clara a painful and deeply hurtful experience. And now, that it was, at least temporarily, made physically impossible because of the operation, Clara felt, that at last a loving will be built the way she had always dreamed it. Where the sexual-force as life-force is in every gesture and a togetherness is created that is pure movement.

Each a dancer. And together a dance. That is the way Clara moved. That is the way she saw herself fulfilled finally in a meaningful togetherness. Turned on to full force in her own womanself and as a togetherness be a force, a power of love.

I look up, and an energy is let loose in him; he looks up, and a force is unleashed in me, a mighty power of love.

I am a dance. He is a dance. Together we are a dance. Our togetherness is a dance.

What flow.

What might.

What force.

How many deserts shall be greening, how many hungry children be fed, how much love made . . .

But Adam was not there, where Clara was. He felt left behind and rejected. And Clara knew in her heart of hearts that he had abandoned her. But she did not want to see it and held fast to her dream and imagining and pretending.

Is such marriage, such togetherness, that is held fast by inner laws, yet moves, evolves, becomes, dies, and is renewed, is it only a reality as an inner happening in oneself . . .

"Clara, build your life. Build it. Build it hugely."

Dear Heart, hold my hand, hold my right hand and do not let it go. Not evermore.

*   *   *   *

72

Abruptly, Clara was thrown into darkness. By the same good hands that had helped her through the operation and held her in radiant health for six months after?

"Yes, it would take about six months," said the doctor of Homeopathy, whom Clara met at a dinner. By then, she had been in and out of Mental Hospital for several years. "Imagine, that all the glands in a woman's body form a pyramid and that the ovaries are the foundation of this pyramid. This foundation is pulled away suddenly; however, the rest of the pyramid would crumble only slowly, imperceptibly and yes, after some six months from one day to another, without forewarning, all the glands would be in disarray, the vital rhythmic communication be disturbed entirely and your mind collapse."

The conventional doctors and psychiatrists had refused to see this most obvious connection. And that the collapse of the mind and the collapse of the natural rhythmic functioning and communing of all the glands together were intimately related and caused by the removal of the most vital and major female gland.

The fact was that Clara's mind was sick. She was insane. Adam, too, finally supported this and actually told the doctors that insanity was in her family. And accordingly, Clara was put in Mental Hospital and treated with drugs.

Her first falling was fast. It was as though she had been thrust into a quag. Plucked from her bright being at that moment when all the threads seemed to have been gathered in again and tied into the life-knot. And a new life was surging in and a love for life and herself growing and her heart was light and flowering, like the heart of spring.

Plucked at this high moment of bliss and shine and dropped into some primal slime.

And suddenly. And without forewarning. And no one could hear her cry for help. It stayed deep within her. And her mouth seemed full of muck.

What did her eyes say? Were they not screaming the fear? Were they vacant . . ? Was her soul eclipsed?

And she sank fast and deeper every day. And she could not get out of the quag she was in. There was no hold on. And she did not recognise her own hands. And there was no hand reaching for her

73

d

hand. She was dismembered.

She was in so many pieces.

Yet, she stood there, a whole body.

Where was I, my Self, where was I? What can I call I but It. the Me-bit: the Me-my Self-bit. The God in me.

'It'. So be it.

The essential being shrunk to the minutest. The most minute. The unfathomably small. 'It', a dot, so small not visible to the eye. But there, in an innermost, not cowering, oh no, but in bright shining awareness of now, this mo-ment. This Augenblick. And seeing and hearing. *Seeing and Hearing* in now and into ahead and long past in time happened and into space happenings not yet here, not yet, but happened there already.

'It', like a huge Third Eye, like an enormous Third Ear, like another Mouth gaping in wonder wide open, like another Pair of Hands with the hearth of nerves in their palms abuzz, like two Extra Feet, the map of this life, mine, deep engraved, deep, oh, I tell you, my love, like Unhealed Wounds passed and yet to be inflicted.

The 'It', there, far in, in the deepest innermost. A dot so minute, not visible to the sharpest eye. Far in and radiant in its knowing and seeing and hearing and glorious by the suffering suffered passed and born ahead of time measurable.

Behold! The smallest is the Biggest in its radiation.
Behold it!

This vital force, then, concentrated in a smallest, a seed again, maybe, in an unfathomably deep innermost. There waiting, there preserving, taking in and registering. But not experiencing, for the experiencer is not there.

Where is she? Where?

Fore-sighting is given of all that passes and foresight of what is yet to pass. Where is she, that sees and hears and foresees and foreknows? Who is the one in the quag, in that morass of horror and fear? Who is the one left mindless, abandoned of all sense of belonging and relating?

This one, who is being utterly helplessly in the grip of forces which are being-less, shape-less, form-less . . . Who is she? - A mass of . . . a mass of . . . What name has it . . ?

Who is she? Where is she? What world is she in?

She had not fallen off this tangible world into another one existing in another sphere. No, the fall was vertical and fast and happened within herself and falling, she had gone to pieces.

Humpty, Dumpty had a great fall . . .

Glutinum mundi! O, where is the pot of this Godly Glue? Or will the spit of a loved one be able to stick the pieces together again? But where can the pieces be found and where the love?

Help! screams the mouth full of muck and no one hears and the hand has no grasp on the slimy ledge and no hand is reaching down to rescue . . .

All the lights had gone out but that one tiny speck of light. Yet, there was some sort of life and there was a body somewhat alive and there was a person.

This person was in terror of day and of night, of dawn and of twilight. By day, she desperately tried to hide within some small dark space, which would shield her from the persecutions of monstrous things that seemed to be all around her. But they were within her, and she could not escape. There *was* no escape. By night, she could not allow herself to go to sleep and might sit up on the small stair to her bedroom facing the long dark passage, staring wide-eyed into it, awaiting in stiff fear the abominable things emerging . . .

From that tiny light in the depth of her, Clara saw herself thus, this shrunken, terrified dismembered creature, this thing-person. That could not recognise what the needle was for or the thread or any once most familiar thing, that saw everyone approaching the house as threatening, that ate and drank, but did not taste, did not relate or respond.

Clara could not hear bird song or feel the wind.

How utterly, utterly abandoned one is, when one's contact with one's soul is lost, the communion with one's Self is gone - you wander in chaos. You are chaos. You fall into a morass of horror. You are sucked ever deeper into a quag:

Help! Help, someone . . . help!

One day, Adam enticed Clara out of the dark space she was hiding in by saying that someone was downstairs who was offering to help her. She was sat beside this kindly, well dressed man on the sofa, who greeted her as though he knew her. He asked her lots of questions the answers of which were formulated somewhere inside her, but could not be uttered, for the her that sat there close beside this man, had no way of answering. It finally hit home, that he was the Head-Psychiatrist of the County Hospital for the mentally ill and that the only real help could come to her by entering this hospital, which was fully equipped to give such help.

Immediately, words, names sprang up in her: Lobotomy, Insulin, Electric Shock Treatment, Drugs. And a host of faces appeared of peoples she had encountered in a far past, who had by such treatment lost their essential being never ever to regain it again. And Clara let out a piercing yell - "Noooooo . . ."

Which hangs in that cottage behind the cliffs like a fore-warning of disaster, so that no one can ever settle there peaceably since.

However, sometime later, a woman psychiatrist was able to make Clara say yes. It was done in such a way, that Clara did not realise that she had said yes or that she may even have given a signature, until she was in the car driven by Adam and discovered by signs along the road, that they were on the way to the Mental Hospital.

76

*   *   *   *

To this day, Clara cannot travel that stretch of country without seeing herself beside Adam at the moment, when she, in a striking lightning flash, *saw* herself being taken to be incarcerated by her own true love and *knew* in an instant of piercing pain an abandonment that was final and glimpsed an endless time ahead of years of a loneliness that was unspeakable.

Clara tried to open the car door and jump out on several occasions, but Adam discovered it each time just in time, stopped and was ever more fierce and hard with her. "You are making my life impossible in the state you are in; these people know what they are doing, they will help you." "If you try to jump out once more, I shall turn back and get the ambulance to take you; you will then lose the chance to go in on your own free will and you will have to stay there as long as they see fit to keep you. It's up to you, entirely."

Adam did not drive into a lay-by and stop, and put his arms around her and just say 'Clara'. That's all. 'Clara' - And somehow to Clara it was that a death sentence was added to all these life sentences, that had been heaped on her: for the crime of unfulfilled desires, angers and griefs stowed away, joys not lived, potentials buried, life unlived, love not loved, tears not shed; laughter not laughed . . . mind collapsed because an operation caused a severe upheaval in her entire interior communications system . . ?

Silent Night - All the Love not loved - All the Hands not touched - All the Eyes not smiled - All the Feet not danced - All the Hearts broken - Holy Night.

- Rose-petals of last years roses lying in the streets and lanes like blood stains yet to come.
- Rose-petals, like drops of blood in all the lanes and streets.

77

- All the broken hearts like rose petals of last year's roses lying invisibly in all the lanes and streets.
- Silent Night. Holy Night.

Clara was delivered into the hands of the ward sister, Sister Margaret - St. Margaret, the helper of women in childbirth - who over the many years that Clara spent in-and-out of Mental Hospital, grew into a rock of strength and support.

A young nurse introduced Clara to the ward: the games room, the quiet lounge, the TV room, the dining-room, the dormitories, all looking out with large windows on an open landscape. A modern one-storey building full of light and plants, a pleasant looking place, not at all like what springs up in front of one, when one says: Mental Hospital.

Clara did not see all this that day, she was encapsulated in the dark fear of being left behind, of being abandoned and forgotten. And when Adam said that he was leaving now, she threw herself at him and clung to him and had to be torn off. And she was being held tight by a nurse as she saw him go down the long hallway, turn by the huge glass entrance and gone.

Deep, deep within, there was one that wept - Clara, a stone, stood there, held tightly by the nurse.

Deep, deep within, there was one that shouted, "Love, love, do not abandon me. Not at this moment when I need you so."

Clara, a stone stood there looking down the wide hallway - held tightly by the nurse.

Deep, deep inside, there was one sobbing, "Love me, love me, love me, *do*."

She was taken to the single bedroom, that was to be her room for a while.

To the dread of being forsaken, of being handed over callously by the one she loved into strange, unknown hands, of being left behind in a vast impersonal clinical place amidst a crowd of men

78

and women, all strangers, was added the unbearable weight of total isolation.

And there was no one and nothing within her that she could call, that she could summon to be held by, to be warmed by, to be protected by, to be loved by.

NO ONE - NOTHING
ICE - OLATION
DREAD.

All the while, deep, deep within was the one, this life? like a radiant speck: noting, registering, marking and utterly helpless. Isolated within the isolated one.

You cannot call my God my dear love my heart my friend my brother my sister my mother my father.

Not even in the deep of within yourself.

That, too, has become icy isolation.

This is Hell, not the fire, but the ice.

If there is a quintessence of horror and fear, Clara was it. Her body stood spread-eagled against a small, dark stretch of corridor, as though she had been blasted on to it. Her body stood thus for hours at a time, until meal-time came around and a nurse appeared to take her to the dining-room. After each meal, she was given drugs, and keeping close to the wall, slouched like a beast burdened back to the same dark space in the otherwise light hall. - A figure of horror and fear enclosed tightly in her own world of horror and fear.

She lost her speech. For some weeks, she could not utter one word. Adam came to visit, but if he had any warmth to give her, she was not able to receive it.

No one could contact her, even if anyone tried to find her inside her hermetically sealed dwelling of her insularity.

- *Be with me, my love, be with me as strength, I need you so.*

Can you for a moment stop and be still and imagine the longing within this being to partake in the living world, to break out of the encapsulation? - Does it not hang out of her eyes . . .Can no one see it, feel it, guess it . . . . - Carl Gustave Jung has long since died.

*   *   *   *

Pressed against the wall, hidden in the only dark little space in the huge hallway, deserted by everything that is meaningful, forsaken by love, and fear looking in and fear looking out, and riddled with fear inside her, Cecil suddenly stands before her.

Clara is in her mid-twenties and on a visit to a private school for boys, who are highly intelligent and deeply emotionally disturbed. During lunch, she had observed four boys. They had sprung to her heart and one, Cecil, in particular. After the meal, the four stood together, and the Head and owner of the school pointed them out saying, "Those four have failed everywhere before and they are failing here. There is really no chance of adjustment for them; if you look at their heads, you will notice that the maladjustment is inborn in each one. They'll be spending their lives in Mental Hospital or in prison."

Clara could not believe her ears: this judgement from a man to whom some 24 children had been trusted. And she said, "You need staff, I shall come and work here and those four boys shall be in my special care."

Not much was known about Cecil's background. That he had lost his speech suddenly when he was about four years old and no one knew why, and that his parents were unknown, and that he had been handed from institution to foster parents and back to institutions. He was now twelve and in the past 8 years no one had ever heard him speak.

Clara intuitively grasped from this, that at four Cecil had undergone a severe emotional shock, a trauma, which instantly cut a vital current, eclipsed his Self, so to speak, which now was banished in an immense depth within, but nevertheless was there, shining bright and very alive.

A rescue-operation!

Cecil was tall and well built, but an absolutely forbidding looking boy with his hunted-animal eyes, deep set and on guard, never trusting. He did not wash and could not be made to change his clothes. And although he did not speak, he had great and fearful power over all the other boys and they were afraid of him.

Unflinchingly and in deepest trust in the speck of light Clara saw was there, Clara built trust. Daily. Slowly. She discovered that Cecil had an amazing relationship with animals and knew their language. A certain call and rabbits would come hopping along out of their warrens, another sound and an owl, no one had seen but him, would fly down out of a tree onto his shoulder, squirrels appeared by some chattering noises he made, a horse grazing in a field some way away, could be made to gallop up to him, jumping hedges on the way. None of these creatures were afraid in his presence, he was obviously in some magical rapport with them.

As he could truly relate to them and a light for a short while came to his eyes, Clara allowed Cecil to bring an owl back to the school one time, another time a couple of squirrels. The other boys in his dormitory were let into the secret, which had to be kept a deadly secret, as they were not allowed pets.

To find that Clara kept the secret and was able to get everyone else to keep it, was a first breakthrough in trust, and she was therefore able to make Cecil aware that these creatures must go back to the wild.

He started to have a bath once a week and change into clean clothes. And he joined a small group of boys with whom Clara was making musical instruments out of any kind of scrap material from which, in one way or another, one could get sound. Cecil, with most diligent, sensitive fingers, twisted long strands of raffia into strings which were strung on a wooden board and plucked.

The first real, almost tangible light appeared on this boy, when he plucked his primitive instrument. And inspired by this obvious gift in his hands, Clara left on a table in her room - to which Cecil had entry - a block of wood and her sharp bladed Swiss pocket-knife.

While she sat there, writing some report for the visiting psychiatrist, Cecil carved. He was completely absorbed in what he was doing. And after he left, Clara found on the table a carved male figure in a position of deep and troubled thought, the head, with clearly carved features, held in both hands. Most expressive and skilfully done. Reminiscent of Rodin's 'Thinker'. Later, lumps of clay were worked by him into figure after figure burdened and tormented ones, again and again. Then slowly, a different movement came into them; a rhythm of light and a lightness, and it reflected on the boy: the way he moved, the way he was with others, the way the other boys' fears of him changed into a kind of 'follow the inspired leader', the way his eyes

81

changed.

Discovering that Cecil had lots of music in him from the way he created those sculptures and the manner in which he plucked his home-made instrument, Clara got him a fiddle. Immediately, he set to tuning it and to playing tunefully simple melodies, which came out of himself as of one truly gifted with music.

The first real signs of the emergence of that utterly sensitive and highly gifted human being, that Clara had 'seen' at the very first meeting some three months earlier, began to show.

Then one morning, after playing his fiddle quite seraphically, Cecil spoke.

There was urgency in his telling, but he spoke clearly.

"There is something I know, that nobody else knows, and I need to tell you about it. You can keep a secret. No one else must ever know about it. You must come to the attic-room on Saturday at noon and you must lock all the doors behind you. No one must be told about our meeting and you must come alone."

Clara gave Cecil her word. She was aware of the risk.

On the day, she did as promised. Cecil's first move was to check, that all the doors leading up to the attic had been locked and that no one was hidden anywhere. When he returned, he showed Clara a large poker and told her that had she failed in any way, he would have used that poker on her.

She had had a good inkling of Cecil not really being able to believe that he could trust anyone, so deep was his injury.

"When I was four, I was evacuated from London to a farm in the West Country. Every day I played with a little girl of the same age who belonged to the farm. We often played by a stream near the farm. One day, the stream was swollen with water from heavy rainfalls and was flowing rapidly and the little girl was suddenly not by my side any more. She had fallen in and the stream had taken her away. Everyone on the farm and in the village accused me that I had pushed the girl in. I was called 'the little murderer.'

"No one wanted to know me anymore and my parents rejected me also. 'This monster', they called me. I lost my speech then and there instantly. I spent the past eight years mostly in institutions. I don't know anyone. You are the first person who trusted me. Frankly, when you left that sharp pocket-knife for me on the table, I thought 'this woman is crazy, I could kill her with this knife'." - Clara had been aware of the possibility at the time. - At

82

this very moment, that Cecil speaks of this trust given him for the first time since that traumatic event so many years earlier, a transfiguration happens: The Cecil now standing in front of Clara is new.

For a moment be still. Be still. And then in this stillness see, *see* this child emerge in its radiance, that had been banished for the past eight years in the darkest recesses of itself. That deepest wound, wide open and unbearably painful, inflicted to a small, vulnerable little boy of four some eight years earlier, is healed in a moment of *a word*.

Trust, it would seem, is a radiant vibrant creative force, that kindles a fire, where there was only a spark.
Trust is a transformer.
Trust is a healer.

There was a joy in that attic-room and Clara took Cecil in her arms and thanked him for his trust.

Cecil then said that now he was fully ready to learn to read and to write and to catch up with all the learning that he had missed.

"Therefore," Clara explained, "it is vital, that you extend your trust to others, especially the Head of the school, who will be able to help you into the world that is now wide open to you. I will be there for you should you need me and always as a friend. But the work that we had to do *together* is now done.

"Let's go, and have lunch."

As Cecil and Clara entered the dining-room, where everyone had been waiting for them, all eyes went wide with astonishment at the shining entrance of Cecil's, so striking was the change that had been wrought in him, and the Head offered him the place on his right.

Inside Clara, her small body pressed tightly against the wall of the hallway, Cecil's story is being played and watched and heard by the highly awake Self, that is but a tiny dot in a deep innermost. Is there not the slightest bit of light shining through her eyes from there, that might be discovered by someone . . ?

In a strange and inexplicable way, this dot, her awareness, is known to Clara and at the same time not known. She is, it would seem, so many pieces that do not hold together. She cannot connect the one with the other.

She is a shattered song.

To everyone, Clara was deranged. No one could or would see that the madness she was accused of was but a blind, albeit opaque, and that behind it was a woman longing to mingle and mix with time and life of every day. Longing desperately and screaming desperately 'let me out! let me out! I have a story to tell, believe me. My story. Hear me, hear me, do!'

My hell is, that time is no more, nothing is any more. I am a shattered song. But I know what there was, what there is, what there will be. 'It' knows, the radiant spinning speck that is my Self.

Let me out! O, let me out . . .

But no words came out. They were caught and suffocated inside. And maybe nothing of the dark fear she was in was visible to anyone. And not to anyone was visible the agony of the banishment to a hell, where her life, her spirit did not move anymore, but stood stock still, was frozen into an isolation.

At least, if anyone saw anything, it was not this.

They saw a case.

A case. And no one seemed to care other than take her from her dark place on the wall in the hall and sit her down in the dining-room at meal time, at night call her to bed, in the morning, call her to get up. And she was given drugs. All done with great kindness.

After a while, Clara was sometimes allowed to join a group of other patients on walks round the grounds of the hospital. The drugs made her shuffle and made all her senses dull. She was listless. But deep inside was 'It', taking in, registering, remembering, seeing, hearing and unspeakably lonely and abandoned.

No one asks, Clara, how are you? Clara, where are you? Clara, are you here?

Look, look, and see that I am here, right here. Lift the mask that you call disease of the mind. Roll up the blind of insanity and see me, *see me, my Self.* I need you, help me. I want to tell you my story. I want to sing you my song.

Listen! Ask! Ask me something, anything. Touch my hand. Show me, that you know that I am here. *That I am* and that I am real and substantial.

Real and substantial.

Of which you have no grasp, if you don't take off your coded glasses and let flow yourself and let yourself mingle with myself. For although I do not fit any code of normality, *I am a life.* I am a meaningful and unique life.

Take your spectacles off and rub your eyes and see, I am a human being with a meaningful story. *My story.*

In one moment, in a sudden moment, this story was cut, the vital current switched off, the flow ceased, the spirit shrunk and life banned to a dark innermost.

With the spectacles of your learned normality, you see me as insane, my mind as diseased. But judge not, drug not, for there is meaning in the state that I am in of which you have no grasp. There is meaning as there is meaning in dream and vision.

You judge. You give my disease a name and drugs and other treatment according to this name. You see the surface only, if that, the symptom only. You do not see my reality. You are doing me wrong. You are doing me harm. You are acting from ignorance and yet you make out you know. Ignorance becomes arrogance, when you *think* that there is no sense in my condition and you think, that you have to make sense and you treat me according to this self-appointed authority over me. And you take possession of me and my life is not mine anymore.

*   *   *   *

Woe, woe, my story.
Woe, woe, the song that I am.

But you are acting from a great distance of me and my reality. You are putting yourself on a height and are acting from above down to me. From the assumption: here is a shattered personality, a deranged mind.

Come, oh, come down to my smallness, open yourselves and receive me in. Look at me and see me. *See* me. Listen to me. Listen to my silence. I am a human being with a story. *I am a life.* I am a song. Do not judge me, but respect me.

From somewhere within me I can see you and I know that I am done wrong, that the drugs do not bring healing but slowly and gradually take that away, which is uniquely me and destroy my body. And your very presence, instead of being and bringing healing, frightens me.

Is there someone somewhere, who understands that drugs and those other accepted conventional treatments cannot bring back the song, cannot give the rhythm to make me a well being again, the whole-being that I truly am. That they cannot recover the melody of my song, gather in the torn threads that make my story.

Is there someone somewhere, who understands: I am music. I am a symphony. I am perpetual movement, flow, a force in rhythmic harmony with the force of life itself.

I am a dance. And I am a dancer.

A new fear gets hold of Clara, that her Self is being taken away from her and that she is being made into someone, that others want her to be, with no will of her own. And she retreats deeper into herself and so appears more disturbed.

New drugs are being given and she senses a more severe judgement having been hung over her.

*   *   *   *

86

One night, her speech returns at the moment when nurse Phyllis tries to force her to take the sleeping pill from which she had begged to be exempt. Clara screamed suddenly and shouted, "Don't do it, don't do it." And the nurse sat herself heavily on Clara's forcibly lain down body and forced the pill down into her. She then threatened Clara with a transference to a grim ward in the old part of the hospital with barred windows and strict rules:

"The proper place for a devil-woman like you!"

So yet another fear was added to the many piled up. The nurse would be listened to and Clara would not be able to defend herself. But with her new found speech she went to see Ward Sister Margaret the next day and had it confirmed, that it is written on her sheet, that she must not be forced to take sleeping pills.

But this made it worse for Clara and each night when nurse Phyllis was on duty, Clara was exposed to one tortuous way or another to force the sleeping pill into her. And as day nurse, she as often as she could exposed Clara to ridicule and made her a scapegoat or accused her wrongly of one thing or another.

One time, Clara asked to see a TV-programme, one of a series called Evolution. She had talked to some patients who watched TV regularly and found that they were interested. She then got permission from the Ward Sister to arrange it with night nurse Phyllis, who was to be present and make sure the right channel was turned on.

It was Clara's very first appearance in the TV room. She sat quietly at the end of a row, waiting for the show to start, but the TV was tuned to the wrong channel and she remarked on it. At the very same moment as she spoke, her glasses-case tumbled from her lap onto the floor with a clatter. Nurse Phyllis shot up, grabbed hold of Clara and bent her down with force to pick up the case threatening her with an injection, as such violent behaviour could and would not be tolerated. A report of the incident would have to go to the Ward Sister. In addition, Clara was forbidden ever to enter the TV room again. She was shattered, and there was no word possible of self-defence.

*   *   *   *

87

Some years later, when Clara was in an all women's ward, she heard that nurse Phyllis had become Ward Sister of that mixed ward of her very first hospitalisation. She went to visit Sister Phyllis to ask her why she had had such a negative attitude towards her. She received Clara kindly and said, "I am glad you came. I am deeply sorry for having treated you in this way. I was terribly unhappy at the time both in my work and in my private life. And although you were very ill, through your mental sickness was shining a very together and wonderful person, and I was envious, and I was envious of that strength and envious too, that you seemed to be a favourite of the then Ward Sister Margaret, who is indeed very fond of you and has high regards for you.

"I used you to show that I had power, because you were the most vulnerable of all the patients. Please forgive me. I shall never forget you."

And with that, Sister Phyllis took Clara in her arms.

To ask to see the film had been an enormous step for Clara. To come out of her isolation and to begin a communication with others. To sit with others in the same room. To share in something with others, maybe to talk to one or the other, to have a conversation.

But nurse Phyllis' action pushed her back and farther in to the soundless, lightless space.

Stiff, her head pulled into her shoulders, arms pressed icily to her body, vision sunk in fear, coldly separate from herself, from everyone and everything, she shuffled the hallway day in, day out, or pressed her body against the wall of her chosen dark corner.

Somewhere within, *she was.* She was real and substantial. And somewhere within, she feared and despaired, that she might be condemned to being imprisoned in a state that is insanity, if she, herself, cannot communicate with her Self or find just one note of the song that she is.

But the rhythm of the song is disturbed and the melody of the song is gone into a lightless forgetfulness.

*   *   *   *

I am not understood as life at all. I am frightened. Whom do I turn to? Even in this state of insanity, I know that this treatment with drugs is fundamentally wrong. A kind of levelling-out process is being achieved. A kind of normality is brought about, where the will is deadened, the senses are lulled and the mind is dulled, the soul made bland and the body is gradually destroyed. - Such damned lifeless normality that death has more life in it. Indeed, death has more life in it. Look! there is movement in death, a dynamic force! *See, how Spring is born from Winter-death!*

I am life. But I am not understood as life. Deathly death is handed out here.

And today, they are preparing the beds for those, that are treated with Electric Shock. Fear is thickening the air in the place. A very young, most beautiful girl is brought in from outside the clinic to receive this most destructive treatment.

Help me, someone! I can see this girl levelled out, the fire of her young life extinguished. O, I can see her lightless. Help me, someone, help! If I scream, I shall get an injection. But I can see this girl, her life dispirited. Will Adam ever remember James and Charles and Moira, will he? And never give his consenting signature for me to be given this horror-treatment?

Hear me, someone! I have been put in this institution to be helped and look, daily, I am more afraid and helpless.

And now this girl. This beautiful, young girl. I call her Lucia because her beauty is like light. *Light!* to be extinguished, snuffed out for ever.

Clara is over filled with this anxiety and she is afraid, that she will have to scream. She presses her face to the wall, so that if she did scream, the wall would dampen the sound. She waits and waits. She will need to see Lucia come out of that forsaken place.

When Lucia emerges, held by nurses, her eyes glass and her face distorted with blotches, Clara screams "Noooo . . . Murderers . . ." Sister Margaret takes Clara to her office.

"What is it, Clara?"

"The beautiful young girl, you are killing her."

"She is very ill and the treatment she is receiving will help her. You may sit in my office for a while."

Tears, live tears are running down Clara's cheeks. She hadn't cried, not for joy, not for sadness for months. She lets them run down and gathers them, a little salted pool in the cup of her hand. - How deep the little pond of tears, how deep the tears in the little pool.

Who is weeping . . .

In front of Clara's inner eye is moving by a procession of slouching people's led by James and Charles and Moira whose life-impulse was destroyed by electric shock and drugs and injections. Clara's mouth is filling with scream again. She bites her fist and pushes the scream back down inside her. For even Sister Margaret might lose her patience. It was her, after all, who prepared those beds. She is warm, motherly and understanding. But she too is part of this institution. And she too is trained in a science of medicine that is untrue to its name. For is not the root-word 'medeor': to heal, to make whole?

When it is true to its name, it is inspired by and based in life. It creates and enhances life, is life-giving, active, strong and of the spirit. It is then pure movement, makes energy, motion and generates power. It is then the art of restoring and preserving and enhancing health and funding life and cannot but address itself in all its realm of service other than as life to life.

Yet, I am not understood as life. Life, a symphony. *I am a symphony.* All life is music. Is rhythm.

Is dance. Is dancer.

A force.

A dynamic.

My life is. Your life is. The grass blade is. The daisy is. The mouse is and the mole.

Is there someone somewhere, who understands this: that drugs, injections, electric shock deaden the very life that they should heal, because they come from a science of medicine which is based in deathly death. *That death*, which has no movement and therefore brings no resurrection. It gives its drugs names like: antibiotic and pain killer. And these names are true in what they are doing, not healing but violating life. And they carry within

90

them the pain, die Angst, and the horror of the animals and peoples on whom they were experimented on.

I hear the Devil laugh like hell and I see Satan split his sides in his hilarity and I see Lucifer gleeful in his satisfaction of a hugely successful campaign of revenge for his expulsion from the heavenly realm. Indeed, his laughter fills the universe: look at the foetus-market, the kidney-market, the weapons-market, the market in children and whole peoples . . .
Lucifer's blinding light of scientifically proved knowledge is blinding indeed.

The glass-eyes and the red-blotched face of Lucia are inside Clara. And the name Devil-Woman, that nurse Phyllis had thrown at her, is going round and round inside her like a perpetual gramophone disk and filling her out with its sharp, condemning sound.

"Devil-Woman!" Clara is twelve years of age. It is her first week at Secondary School. For the class of Religious Instruction, she chooses to sit in a desk at the back of the first row. The Vicar enters. The class stands up to greet. The register of pupils names is being read, and each one, as the name is being called, makes himself known. That done, the Vicar, a tall strongly built man all in black, stands there and lets his eyes wander from one to the other of pupils. His eyes hit Clara's. His right hand shoots up. The long index-finger points at Clara and his voice as final as the finger pointing thunders, "Beware, the She-Devil is among us!" And his face grows into a smile that hangs like an unhealed wound in it.
Clara loses her breath. All becomes black around her. And momentarily there is the fear, that she is going to faint. Inside her, she calls, 'Mother, help me!'
And soon she feels strong and a resolve is made within her 'You see me as the She-Devil, I shall show you that I am.'
All heads of all the other pupils are turned towards Clara. All the eyes are upon her and a stunned silence has fallen into the room.

"Let us begin the lesson, which is dedicated to the study of The Book of Books. *This*, The Holy Bible, the Only and True Word of God." And saying this, the Vicar is holding the Bible up high for everyone to see.

And that mouth, like an unhealed wound, is smiling, making a gargoyle.

Clara is seeing this smile clearly, now, hanging in front of her like a grotesque mask, as she is standing, back pressed to the wall, in the corridor of the hospital ward.

To have been judged at all and at once and with such finality made it impossible from the very beginning to have a dialogue with the Vicar. She had been so looking forward to such real encounter, where an exchange of thought might be possible, after the stern, forbidding and fixed Sunday School teaching.

She was bursting with questions.

She did not doubt the existence of God, for He had made Himself known before her conscious life and was in her life with a clarity and a might that was real. But she doubted a God that was all light and all love, for within her He showed Himself as of many colours and was manifest in many shades of darkness, at least as thought.

If I am made in the image of God and I am light and darkness, good and evil, then He is this two-fold being too, this awe-full contradiction. And in the wrestling with this paradox, that she had discovered in the humans all around her too, she had come to understand it as the very fundamental living force of life.

A necessary situation of continual Yes-No, Light-Dark, Good-Bad, as impulse. The Negative - the Positive, both, to create the current to make life *Life*, that which flows and grows and dies and resurrects.

At Sunday School, they had killed God with candy-sweet voices. He was fixed and framed. Deadly secure and mighty on His thrown. He was the Judge. He had His huge single Eye on you day and night. He was Love. But unless you fear Him . . .

He sacrificed His only begotten Son to save us humans. Yet, we are born in sin and as sinners. What sense my life in the hands of such God . . . The Dark One, the Devil seemed to have all life on HIS side.

In her father, Clara knew, there was an open and continuous conflict of forces, which made for a depth of enquiry and questioning in which God was constantly unbuilt, built and rebuilt. God was a very alive and dynamic force rather than a mighty Judge. In Mother, God lived and worked as love. She was flowing with the flow that God surely is. She was in harmony with life and inspired others by her very being.

Clara had no such gift; but rather like her father, she had conflict within her and needed to question. Early, she knew her life as a quest, and also, that she is a wanderer. Yes, a wanderer: he who receives every day anew and the answers to his questions not out of someone's mouth or from books, but from being in touch with life and allowing to be touched by life.

A Wanderer: passionately in touch with life. Celebrating life with every step she makes, drinking life with every breath she breathes in, singing life with every breath she breathes out. And never taking life for granted, but being surprised by it every new day.

My God is alive. I am alive. When I call my God, I open my arms; I stand with arms wide open and receive Him so. Not as a sin-loaded sinner, but as one who is built like Him, gloriously alive. Life flows into life, and we become one.

- The dark womb is where the seed falls into and becomes a shoot, a new being.
- *I say, the dark womb, too, is God.*

Vicar! you can keep your bloodless God, your judgemental God, your suffocating God. You can keep your God in whose name people kill, maim, indoctrinate, missionise, hate, judge, create apartheid, make money, support poverty and ignorance.

Keep your prepacked, deep frozen God!

My God is alive. And I am alive. And I am not to be enslaved in your fixed idea of God and I am not to be ensnared in the worship of an idolised, unliving God!

I need to celebrate! I need to love! And my celebration is for a God alive. And my love is for a God alive. And my celebration is for a life alive. And my love is for a life alive. I need to be as vast as I am meant to be and that has no limits.

I have wings, Vicar. And you shall not clip them. I have a will to be as alive as alive and neither you, Vicar, nor anyone else, shall bend that will.

Clara turned to the poets and she sang with them and danced with them and laughed with them and wept with them. And they shared with her deeply her solitary becoming.

> *'Denn sie, die uns das himmlische Feuer leihn,*
> *Die Goetter, schenken heiliges Leid uns auch.*
> *Drum bleibe dies. Ein Sohn der Erde*
> *Schein ich: zu lieben gemacht, zu leiden.'*
> Hoelderlin: Die Heimat.

> *'In unermesslich tiefen Stunden*
> *Hast du, in ahnungsvollem Schmerz,*
> *Den Geist des Weltalls nie empfunden,*
> *Der niederflammte in dein Herz?'*
> Friedrich Hebbel: Erleuchtung.

> *'Ich fuerchte mich so vor der Menschen Wort.*
> *Sie sprechen alles so deutlich aus:*
> *und dieses heisst Hund und jenes heisst Haus,*
> *und hier ist Beginn und das Ende ist dort.'*
> Rilke.

'Wie ist das klein, womit wir ringen,
was mit uns ringt, wie ist das gross;
liessen wir, aehnlicher den Dingen,
Uns so vom grossen Sturm bezwingen,
Wir wuerden weit und namenlos."
                    Rilke. Der Schauende.

"Dennoch, Himmel, immer mir nur
Dieses Eine mir: fuer das Lied
Jedes freien Vogels im Blau
Eine Seele, die mit ihm zieht,
Nur fuer jeden kaerglichen Strahl
Meinen farbig schillernden Saum,
Jeder warmen Hand meinen Druck,
Und fuer jedes Glueck meinen Traum.
            Annette von Droste - Huelshoff: Im Grase.

Ich steh auf hohem Balkone am Turm,
Umstrichen vom schreienden Stare, .
Und lass gleich einer Maenade den Sturm
Mir wuehlen im flatternden Haare;
O wilder Geselle, O toller Fant,
Ich moechte dich kraeftig umschlingen
Und Sehne an Sehne zwei Schritte vom Rand,
Auf Tod und Leben dann ringen."
            Annette von Droste - Huelshoff: Am Turme.*

The measure is not: good or evil, dark or light, but how alive
Life, how alive God and how alive my Self.
And 0, I like a God that is alive and grows with me.

Clara, her back pushed flat and stiff against the wall of the
corridor of the hospital is watching Clara of twelve, thirteen,
fourteen, who does not allow herself to be crushed by the Vicar's
verdict, on the contrary, makes it into a banner. And carrying it

*English translations of poems on pages 244/245

95

high, she is not silent when she feels that there is need to speak. And she challenges the Vicar's words and behaviour in respect to The Word. Soon, she is being called 'De Revolutz' by her schoolmates.

But in her own inner-world, in the lit-up silence, there she swings in the Himmelhoch-Jauchzend and in the Zu-Tode-Betruebt, that belongs to the time of her emerging from childhood. And she grows deep in laughter and tears.

She knows a terrible loneliness, but also again and again, she knows that she is being held.

This Child-Clara, being deeply and happy-sadly in a world of her own - in her own world - is there now vivid in front of Clara. A Clara whose world is lost and who seems lost to the world, who has no hold on and is held by no one, who knows nothing and who is in an unspeakably lonely lostness, that has no tears.

Yet, someone is weeping inside her. But no tears are running down her cheeks. Someone is longing, longing inside her. And the longing for time and life of ordinary everyday becomes so huge, that she is terrified with the fear of being in this hermetically sealed capsule of isolation for ever.

She wants to howl her guts out, but hears just in time Nurse Phyllis' voice 'injection' 'ward with barred windows', and she shoves her fist into her mouth and presses her left hand into her belly to soothe the fierce pain that the suppressed howls give her.

There is no one. She reaches out for that Child-Clara. But that Child-Clara has blown like a seed in the wind. She is growing in another soil, in an other land, in an other time, in an other life.

Adam! Who is Adam? Your husband.
Husband?
        Only Moira is real.
        Only Charles is real.
        Only James is real.
And they are in pieces.

*   *   *   *

Howl!
          Scream!
                              Shout!
Murderers!   Murderers!   Murderers!
          Killers!
                    Killers!
                    Killers!
All you Killers!
Howl!
          Scream!
                              Shout!
Shout!
                    Howl!
                              Scream!

Also
the
Face
of
God
&
Mine

Also
the
Voice
of
God
&
Mine

          *   *   *   *

97

e

Moira, tall, gold-blonde hair cascading down her back. Large green eyes, they are translucent and you can see wonder-wonderland at the bottom of them. She is wild. She dances. She paints. She sings. She makes poems. She is young. She is a mother and soon she is going to be a mother again. Things go wrong at the birth. She receives injections and does not witness the birthing. She rejects the baby as not hers when it is brought to her after she comes to. She does not recover herself. She falls deeper and deeper into depression. She is taken away. She is declared schizophrenic. Her loving husband, impressed by the psychiatrists, that electric shock is the only real help in such cases, signs the fatal piece of paper.

Moira. Head stands stiff on a long slim stiff neck. Eyes are large, muddy-green, sea before a storm. Eyes have no light. Arms are spread out from body and are stiff, fingers of hands spread and stiff, swollen, like hands drawn by a child. Eyes have no light and they are enormous. Hair hangs like wind-beaten washing.

Sing. Dance. Paint. Motherhood. Moira. Poems. Names of foreign countries. Never been. Never seen. Never heard of.

Is there anyone at home? Knock, knock. Is there anyone at home? Knock. Knock. Is there anyone at home? Knock. Knock.

One morning, looking in the mirror, she saw Moira, the young woman with a waterfall of gold-blonde hair down her back and joy of life shining on her forehead. She was struck and alight with the light of realising: it was him, my own husband, who signed my death-warrant. And she snatched the sharpest carving knife from the magnet-knife board and charged into the early morning-sun-lit bedroom, where this thief, this murderer, this man, this husband was lying fast asleep and smiling seraphically in a sweet dreaming.

Moira drew the coverlet down and held the knife poised above his heart. The bangles clanging on her wrist woke the man.

Moira. Motherhood. Sing. Dance. Paint. Make poems. Names of foreign countries. Never been. Never seen. Never heard of.

*　　*　　*　　*

Moira: somewhere deep, deep within a spark of human dignity and splendour.

Your heart breaks.

Hold me, someone! Hold me, someone! Someone hold me . . .

The nurses come running down the corridor. Sister Margaret appears, "Bring Clara to my office." Sister Margaret is too busy to ask questions, but says kindly, "Sit here, Clara, until you feel better."

But Moira comes down the road towards Clara, immensely tall, her arms and hands spread from her body like a chick, that has just discovered that it has wings, her large eyes lightless but staring horror, her mouth wide open, frozen at the moment of her last scream.
Moira had just stepped out of a painting by Munch.
Moira walks by. She does not see Clara.
Moira flies with chicks wings into the endless distance.
The winds gather her frozen screams and scatter them.
Hail as large as dove's eggs is falling all over the land.

"You have got to have heart, miles and miles of heart." Someone is singing somewhere. But there is only the sound, every now and then, of Sister Margaret taking a paper out of a file and putting another one in and the sound of the pen moving on the paper.

'Sister. Adam does not love me.' 'What makes you think that? He writes to you and comes to see you as often as he can.' But Clara does not say this out loud. The conversation is inside her.

*   *   *   *

"Adam!"

"Just a moment."

"Adam!"

"Just a moment."

"A-D-A-M!"

"Justamomentjustamomentjustamomentjustamomentjustamo-
mentjustamomentjustamomentjustamomentjustamomentjusta-
momentjustamomentjusta . . .

"You have got to have heart, miles and miles of heart." -
Someone is singing somewhere.

Clara is sitting through a million of Adam's 'justamoments' in
Sister Margaret's office. And then it is lunch-time. Clara is
terrified at lunch-times. They fill her platter with so much food
and she has to stuff it all down. It's all being written down.
Everything is. And the black pill is replaced by the red one and a
green one added to the three other ones, casually, "Here, Clara,
for you. Want some water to wash them down with? Here."
Sweetly, done. Sweetly, by the nurses.

Coming out of the dining-room stuffed out of her eyes with
double helpings, Clara sees the wide hallway paved with hearts in
all the rainbow colours. She lifts the hem of her long wide skirt
so that it makes a big pocket and one by one picks up the hearts
and puts them in. 'Adam!' she calls. 'Adam! the wheel barrow,
there are too many hearts for my pocket.' 'Justamoment,' from a
far distance and in the same moment, the already cracked hand-
basin breaks in two and the jagged porcelain edge slashes her
right leg and the impact of the weight makes her fall on the steep
slippery slope under the ancient crooked plum tree, and she is
lying there, blood gushing. When some strength comes back, she
calls, "Adam, Adam!"

"What is it for God's sake?"

"Adam!"

Perhaps he heard in Clara's voice some anguish. He sticks his
head out of his study window and sees her lying there. He comes

100

rushing out. "Why did you have to carry this basin, it was cracked!" He then rushes back into the house to get a towel to stem the blood and then rushes her to the nearest doctor. - For more than a year, every now and then, Clara had asked for the basin to be removed - 'Justamoment'. 'Justamoment'. 'Justamoment'.

Where does love go in justamoment? Where does love go when it's gone?
Borne away on the wings of the wind to No-man's-land.
Down the Black Hole into the fire.
Into the fire in No-man's-land.
What is it, that comes out of the White Hole?

"When you are much older, the scar will remind you of this nasty cut; the severed nerves will never heal."
The country doctor's eyes said, 'a broken heart never heals'.

Clara went to Sister Margaret's office. "Could I go out to find the gardener. I need a wheel barrow."
"What ever for, Clara?"
"To put the hearts in, see my skirt is over flowing."
"Sit here, Clara, for a while, until you feel better."

"You have grown fat, Clara."
"It's the hearts, Adam."
"You must lose weight, Clara."
"It's the hearts, Adam. See, the heart is full to overflowing."
- 'In sickness and in all kinds of weather, I shall love you for ever'

For the rest of the day, Clara stands in her dark corner in the corridor, back pressed against the wall, holding up her skirt full of hearts calling, "Have a heart, love." "Have a heart, love." She carries them into supper. She must not let go of the skirt.

"Put that skirt down, fancy walking like that into the dining-room."

"The hearts, nurse, they'll break."

'Oh we ain't got a barrel of money
Maybe we look ragged and funny
But we are travelling along
Singing a song
Side by side
Through all kinds of weather, who cares if the sun doesn't shine - as long as we are together . . .'

Young Clara is riding at Adam's side in a borrowed car through the length of the island down to Dorset to their first home. A semi-detached two-bedroomed farm hand's cottage on top of a hill. They are singing together all the way. They are happy. They are in love.

The nurse repeats, "Put that skirt down, you hussy, you are in the dining-room!"

"The hearts they'll break."

The nurse opens Clara's clenched hands that hold the skirt up tightly.

They paint their bedroom a tender shade of rose and bath in the one-shilling-tin-tub and bake their own bread and make love in the 2/6 French Bed.

Clara throws herself down over the scattered broken hearts. The nurse is getting angry.

- Miles and miles of hearts away, Clara is weeping.

Not a tear is falling on the dining-room floor.

Clara is allowed to go for a drive with Adam. Out of the gates of the hospital! Out into the world! With Adam alone! But he looks sternly on the road. Doesn't reach across every now and then or give her a glance. "Travelling along, singing a song, side by side . . ." it's singing in her ears, a snatch of a song, a memory from years and years ago.

"Adam, don't stop." "Adam, drive on forever." "Adam, let's get lost, so we cannot find our way back." "Adam, why do you keep me in this hospital? I am not any better."

"You are, you know."

And inside her, 'Adam, you don't love me any more. Adam, you don't even care for me any more. Adam, I am a burden to you.'

"Adam!" she screams and the car swerves and brakes screech.

Adam is angry. "It's no good. I thought it'd be a nice change for you to go for a drive. But it's obviously too much for you all of a sudden. We'd better turn back."

> 'O willow weep for me,
> weep in sympathy.
> O willow, weep for me . . .'

From the back of the car comes this sad song. No body is singing.

Back in the hospital, they sit side by side in the quiet lounge. Clara sees an endless distance between them. Will they never meet again . . .

> 'O willow, weep for me'
> weep in sympathy . . .'

This deep Negro-voice singing inside her.

Clara a willow, weeping inside her . . .

No tears falling into her lonely lap.

Adam looking at his watch.

From an endless distance in the chair beside her, "Bye Darling, see you in a week's time." Clara sits motionless. Inside her she hears the words falling. The words said, and unsaid. Each one falls like a stone dropped into a narrow shaft.

Clara is listless. But she listens. She hears each word, how it falls like a stone on a pile of stones. Deep down in an innermost. Which *is* real. Which *is* her being.

Words, gestures, faces, things said and not said, longings, yearnings that happen somewhere inside her, sadness, loneliness, they pile up at the bottom of the shaft. An ever growing pile of stones.

Everything is being intensely received in the deep within, but the receiver has no gestures to express, no words to express, no words to tell. She cannot translate and transform anything, for the light of experiencing, that light which through-lightens all experience, is not shining.

Listen!
No sound - the stone is falling.
Listen!
The sound of the stone falling on stones.
Listen!
The sound of stones shifting.
Listen!
No sound.
Listen!
Dead silence.

Clara is motionless. She is listless. But she listens: The sound of a daffodil-bud bursting, emerging sun-golden - the sound of it opening, wider and wider into its own golden radiance.

To open one's Self like a Daffodil.
To be one's own golden radiance.

In the very far distance inside herself, Clara sees the tight palest green Daffodil bud in its silken sheath. She sees the moment when the bud is ready to unfold through-warmed by the sun and the sheath bursts. The sheath, two crumpled leaves now like old parchment, makes a cup out of which thrusts the gold-golden flower. A tight bud at first. Now, open, a chalice of pure gold.

In the far distance within herself, Clara sees herself thus. And an unspeakable longing is there, in that far away place within her. And a terrible fear also, that the warmth of love needed for her unfolding will not be given, that the sun of her life has grown white and cold like the winter sun.

And the fear grows monstrous: she sees the bizarre face of frozen isolation. And the terror is like a nightmare in which you scream, but there is no sound from you.

And she sees the gargoyle face of un-loved-ness grinning toothless and hairless into her face, coming closer to kiss her with its outward turned bulging slimy lips like fat slugs. And she sees herself become this face utterly abandoned by love. And she sees herself amidst the gargoyle-people, where no one relates to anyone or anything.

The dumb mouldy hell of the forsaken.

She opens her mouth to scream at the unbearably foreboding vision, but the terror snatches her voice away and the quiet lounge resounds with scornful laughter. While hoards of gargoyle-people surround her, claw at her and pointing at her are sticking out their thick lecherous tongues.

Stiff and in motionless terror, Clara sits in this hell. She might suffocate. There seems to be no breath in her, no breath outside her.

To be forsaken so. To die so, in the hell of unlovedness.

On a far far horizon within herself, Clara sees a procession of people: her mother, her father, her brothers, her sisters, her children, lovers and loved ones, they all look her way, they are very close, but they do not recognise her. She waves as one drowning, but they do not see her. They do not recognise her.

This is hell, to see yourself so, yet to be in a voiceless, gesture-less helplessness, and seeing everyone clearly and recognising them, but not being seen and not being recognised.

Thrown into this motionless space, abandoned by her own voice and gestures, slowly suffocated by the stinking breath of the gargoyle-people, Clara dwells for days, for weeks maybe.

*　　*　　*　　*

Time has abandoned time. Endlessly, day and night, the procession of the loved ones. All these beloved faces from all her past looking at her and not one of them waving, not one of them recognising her.

This is Hell.

The finality of Hell.

In the far distance, yet as near as her inner Self, there is someone, a minute someone, seeing, hearing, registering, receiving. But the one who transforms, shapes, creates, makes light, makes life, is banished to a terror of helplessness.

To be for just one moment
The radiance of one daffodil . . .

One morning, a young and jolly student nurse invites Clara to the canteen. The single large room is full of people. They sit round tables or stand around forlornly. There are shouts. The room is full of smoke. The nurse is at the counter ordering coffee. Clara stands and looks and *sees*, as though straight out of her nightmare vision, a hairless, toothless woman coming through the crowd like an arrow towards her. She is pointing at Clara and mumbles. Clara wants to flee, but is glued where she stands. And this awful thing with bristles and bulging red-shot eyes and monstrous slug-lips is upon her pressing and wriggling her shapeless body into Clara's and pushing her slimy lips and thick tongue into Clara's mouth. Her breath is foul with nicotine. When she finally lets go, she stands back and grins and mumbles thickly, "Make love to you, you beautiful."

And over her face, that seemed to be so grotesquely ugly, a smile spreads and lights it gently, and Clara sees, for the moment of a glance, a beautiful child with palest grey eyes.

"Bella," pointing at herself, "me beautiful too." And Bella parades like a fashion model in front of Clara holding up her hanging breasts and lifting her brightly flowered short dress to show her shapely legs, giggling, when her frilly knickers appear and smacking her lips pointing at what is there in between . . .

And stroking her make believe hair she says, "Touch ringlets, they lovely and soft."

Bella sits down at table with Clara, sunk into herself at first, then she lifts her face, this ugly mask of unlovedness and grins, "You my lover," licking and smacking her outrageous lips. On leaving, she blows kisses, loud and smacking kisses.

Clara sees herself as Bella. One day, very soon, that is what *she* will be like. And she goes to the canteen at every opportunity to find Bella and let her believe that she is her lover.

One day, soon, when I am hairless and toothless and my eyes bulge and my lips are like fat slugs and my tongue is thick and my speech is mumbles and my breasts hang like old money bags, when everyone has forsaken me and no one remembers me and no one recognises me, will there be one that will be my lover?

A postcard arrives with greetings. Clara cannot recognise the name of the sender, but who ever it is says that the sunflower shown on it always reminded her of Clara. - Receiving these words and with them the joyous radiance of the sunflower, suddenly makes an opening into Clara's morbid darkness. And a ray of light enters and touches and lightens somewhere deeply forgotten happenings and wakens sleeping beauty.

And Clara remembers. She remembers her seventh birthday and the huge tall sunflower in the garden, that had grown from one of the seeds she had thrown out into the snow for the winter birds and that had opened its shining face on that very day for her. She knew it was a gift for her and she stood under it looking up into its sun brightness and thanked it, and they had a communion.

And for a moment, Clara feels the power of that moment now: A sunflower radiance of so many years ago shining a ray into her darkness now.

And Clara remembers. She remembers emerging from the passion of loving that had transported her into the bliss of conception and how her own radiance merged with the radiance of the sunflower-face, that had shone down on the lovers on the balcony with the stars in all its magnificence. A shining sun-wheel in the depth of the deep summer-blue night. - Her daughter Maya was conceived in that memorable night and from the beginning she was known as Sunshine.

Will the opening widen, and ray after ray reach and waken the slumbering Self . . .

Is the one that is dismembered and dwells in terror and darkness, is she the disguise, underneath which in the deep is sprouting from the Self as seed in sacred silence and in its own sacred time and space a one that is new, a one that is to become its own wholeness . . .

O, blessed be the cloak of madness, then.

Blessed be the mask of insanity, if it is to shield the sacred inner space. The inner of the temple, that is the mystery, where the spirit quickens into life and the true Self is being born.

This postcard said that there is a woman called Caroline, who has Clara in her loving thoughts and more, to whom Clara is the presence of the radiance of a sunflower.

Clara is real and present in someone's life, whom she cannot remember.

Many times a day, Clara goes to the wardrobe by her bed to take this card from a little ledge and to re-read it and to gaze at the picture of the sunflower. And so, for very brief moments everyday, she is in a little light of a communion with another human being, that is reaching her and touching her in her dark dwelling.

And the few words and the picture of a sunflower bring to light events of Clara's life that are of joy. She is able to have glimpses, as through a sudden and momentary lifting of a thick mist, of herself alive and well.

But they are rare gifts and she cannot make them appear. And when she is quickly thrown back into the suffocating space of the dark fear, they are being held in front of her teasingly and scorn-fully as life that was and was never to return.

*   *   *   *

However, Clara slowly grew receptive and open and started to communicate with one or the other of the fellow patients in the ward. One of them had a hymn book, and she got him to teach her some of the songs, the words of which were uplifting.

Painstakingly, Clara copied these songs holding the pen with her stiffened fingers, writing without rhythm and sharp and pointed. But by this doing, a movement happened within her, and when George taught her the beautiful song:

'Abide with me . . .' she found herself sobbing.

At the same time, in the outside world, a conspiracy of loving and caring happened. Daily, Clara received words from people remembered and not remembered, that confirmed lovingly her real presence in their lives.

These words of love and the singing of the hymns, even though the once beautiful voice was more croaking than singing, helped like healing faith and healing prayer to through-lighten the darkness more and more and to pierce through the wall of terror and fear and break down the fence of isolation.

Encouraged, Clara found herself brave enough to ask to spend a weekend at home.

The closer they came to home, the more of the fearful enclosure in which Clara had been so tightly shut in seemed to vanish. And when they were at the top of the steep country lane that ran down to the house, she needed to get out of the car and walk. She flung her arms open and shouted, "Paradise! This is Paradise!"

On either side of the lane were processions of majestic fox-gloves and all the gold of the gorse in bloom. Clara walked slowly and waved her hand in greeting and she was greeted back by all this beauty, that surely was there for her welcome. In the house she felt that the little things recognised her and there was a gladness coming to her, that she had not been in for so long.

Stepping out onto the terrace, she was greeted by countless sunflowers, half-grown only, but scattered all the length and width of the stone-hedged meadow and like a ring-a-ring-dance round the huge boulder in the middle. It was onto this magical

109

rock, that Clara had strewn the seeds, so many months ago, for the winter birds. What splendour of gold it will be, when they are all in bloom. Oh, she will have to be truly home long before then.

Was not every breath she breathed in, already in the few moments of being home, like a healing . . . Why was she not here, anyway . . . Why not . . . Here, she belonged. On this bit of land, that could not and would not be tamed by humans. Here, where the weather was made, near by the sea and the wild moors above.

Only here can she truly recover.

But she must not spoil her short stay with thoughts of the hospital. She must take it all in, arms and arms full of this beauty.

Was it possible, that she could feel again as huge a feeling as gladness . . . Something was happening to her. She was feeling touched and in touch and was able to touch.

But where was Adam in all this? Might she intrude on a privacy he had created for himself in her long absence . . . Had the distance of time made the inner distance wider still . . .

Even He-She, the seagull, came tap-tapping on the windows and with some urgency, and apparently it had not been seen or heard since the day after Clara left. And the two dogs were crazy with excitement at seeing her and followed her closely wherever she went and were outside her bedroom next morning, where they obviously had spent the night, and they licked her toes and leaped up in an exuberant welcome.

Was it not gladness and joy for Adam, that Clara was here, that she was well enough to see things and recognise them, and partake somewhat? That there were glimpses of her Self recovering? Could he really not see, that she did not need drugs and hospital to get well, but simply his love?

That dread in the darkness of her night, that she was already not really there any more in his life was that true? And that the collapse of her mind had as much to do with the fear of this loss as with the consequence of the operation, was that true . . ?

- 'Build your own life, Clara,
      Build it.'

Who Is saying this . . .

      'Build the respect for yourself, Clara.'
      'Build the love for yourself and so build your own life. Yours.'

110

Somewhere inside her, this voice.
To *hear* this voice . . .

Her life is coming back to her. But will she be able to hear it without the love from Adam? *She needs to be loved and she needs to love.* That is all she needs.

What happened to the one she was before she trusted her whole life into Adam's hands? What had she expected that Adam be or do for her that she is meant to be or do for herself?

Her love is more and stronger now having been tried in so many trials of this togetherness. But who is her love for? Who is this man, Adam? Cool, aloof, distant, when he should be crazy with gladness at Clara's being here . . . He should . . . why should he? - Because I love him?

I am expecting something of Adam, which he is not expecting of himself. I can only be expectant in myself of my Self. I have made my loving a bondage. I must let go. Let go. I must trust myself. I must recover the one that went under when my life was handed over to Adam.

One cannot and must not hand over one's life. Nor must we allow ourselves to be taken over by another life. My life is mine. And I alone am responsible for it. And my responsibility is to live it. Live it in its given fullness and hugeness. And love it.

Is this the lesson that I must learn in the darkness of my own Self: To build the respect for my Self and grow it into the love of my Self . . .

And ever grow and flow and respond to all life with love as life . . . A process of ever becoming . . . Where, being in awareness, in a great wakefulness, there is no more fear. Where every step is lightful and every gesture makes gladness . . .

This then is my task: to make myself whole, which is merely to rediscover, what I truly am. To gladden every step. To lighten every gesture. To be a power-station of love.

- O, Beloved, give me a sign to confirm my in-seeing.

*   *   *   *

111

Thus, Clara muses, while she is walking some distance behind Adam down to Wicca Pool, the magical sea-and-rock pool, where only some months before she had had an urge to make it into her oblivion.

Clara hears a sound, clear and fluty, a bird-call she never ever had heard before: 'Who-are-you-oo . . . Who-are-you-oo . . .' And look, there is a flash of pure shining gold in a bush right close to her and becoming a large golden bird flying by her.

Out of the middle of herself it might have flown and just as real if it had, as seeing it now sitting a bit farther away on top of a bush.

The Vogel Gryf, the Golden Bird that appears once only in a hundred years, that only one in a crowd is destined to see and to receive the one golden feather that it drops or to find the three golden eggs that it is the sacred guardian of. This one is the fool. He, who goes the path of the heart. The youngest son, who has done all the tasks given him on the way in the innocence of his heart. Simplicius, who answered truthfully all the questions put to him and who, child-like, asked the right questions at the right moment.

Oriolus, oriolus - the Golden Oriole - not native to this blessed land and like Clara become a native by choice, or, per chance, by being chosen . . . the sign?

Oriolus oriolus the sign, the symbol for Clara's becoming?

Wherever you are, Clara, in what ever space you are in, remember Oriolus oriolus, the Golden Bird, that sings like a reed-flute:

Who-are-you-oo, who-are-you-oo. Do never, never, never forget this.

Clara makes a chalice with her inner hands and puts this secret of the Oriolus oriolus within to make it sacred. There it will grow like a dream grows into a vision.

Oriolus oriolus: the sign, the symbol.

It's been given in an instant of looking up, a flash of gold to a questing heart: "Follow your heart, this innocent, this fool. The Golden Feather and The Three Golden Eggs are in your within."

Pray, to never ever forget, not in the pitch of any darkness of my Self this flash of gold given, this treasure of in-sight in a lightful moment of listening-in.

Like in childhood, when her pockets were always bulging with treasures: bits of moss, pebbles, shells, leaves, thus Clara returned to the hospital, the pockets in her inner filled with these many treasures gathered in her short weekend-stay at home.

With this sustenance and the daily singing of hymns with George, she would soon be ready for a ten day sojourn at home, that always lead, as she had observed with other patients, to a final discharge from the hospital.

To help herself further, Clara felt she needed to paint and she got permission to join in the occupational therapy, where she painted with large brushes on large sheets of white paper endlessly the same theme: The Shoot. Imagining a seed, imagining it becoming the shoot, imagining its growing happening within a field of radiation of the seven colours of the rainbow. In doing so, she became the seed that became the shoot that was within this rainbow-field of light. And she felt bereaved each time, when the clock-time ended the doing. But the shine of it wove itself into the endless hours left, that otherwise would have been barren and wasted, walking up and down the long hallway.

Clara became rich, innerly, very rich. And where was the fear? Did she need to ask this?

The light got lighter with every day. There was tangible life. There was life: shoot after shoot after shoot. The abundance of a great spring-time.

The drugs? Clara swallowed them, they could not affect her anymore, not harm her anymore, surely?

*　　*　　*　　*

At her return to the hospital from her short stay at home, Clara was received by every one of the patients with a warm welcome. They had missed her, she was being told, and since then she had contact with each one of them, even if it was just a greeting.

Martha, a very bright woman in a wheel-chair, who at her first entry to the ward had frightened Clara with her alert and alive being, became very close to Clara and told her why she was in this hospital.

In a motorcycle accident, she had broken her back and she came out of the operation paralysed from her waist down. The doctors did not accept that something might have gone wrong in the operation, but insisted on saying that the paralysis was in her imagination. And she had been brought here to eventually undergo hypnosis, if all other Psychotherapy failed.

Clara said, "Give me your left hand," and she held Martha's left hand in her right hand and she received the message, "Martha, you have a trapped nerve. A vital nerve was trapped during the operation and you have to undergo another operation to free this nerve." Clara spoke these words into Martha's hand, most astonished at them herself, as they came to her tongue.

Martha grew pale and started to shake and sobbing she said that her most faithful and dearest friend, a faith-healer, had received the same message. "But I have not wanted to believe it, because I am scared stiff to put myself under the knife once more."

Hence, she had allowed herself to be persuaded that the paralysis was all in her mind and that the only thing that could possibly help her was Psychiatry. However, so far, Martha said, the psychotherapy had only helped to undermine her being and her self-confidence and to make her lose her trust in her Self more and more. "The Psychotherapist is reading all these things into my life. It doesn't make any sense at all and every session makes me more uneasy."

On the day that Martha was told that she now had no alternative than to give herself over to hypnosis, as all the psychiatrists and psychotherapists insisted that it was the only thing now that could cure her, she was in total panic. Clara, who had an absolute mistrust of this practice, which she had encountered during her

114

work with emotionally disturbed children, could only put her arms round Martha and tell her that she would be with her in thought and prayer.

When Martha finally reappeared in the ward, about a week later, Clara could not recognise her. Martha could not recognise herself. Still afflicted with the severe paralysis she was completely crushed and could not stop sobbing. The shining spirit, that had made her such a vital, inspiring being in spite of her total confinement to the wheel-chair, was banished or extinguished. And where laughter had lit up her large vivid eyes, there was terror now. With the little of will that she had left, she summoned a relative to take her away from the hospital.

Clara was haunted by Martha. Will she have been protected enough to find the light of her soul again . . . to restore her life again, even the one that had to be in a wheel-chair?

Martha had had such command: she had danced with the wheel-chair. She had zummed around the dining-room laying the tables and clearing them, all in a jiffy. She had organised games, told stories, created fun and laughter. Martha had been so alive. And now this wreck!

To Clara it was inconceivable, that anyone seeing Martha, this glorious woman, could even begin to believe that she was making herself paralysed by imagining it. Why should she want to be paralysed? She was, even now, crazy about motorcycles and would, 'as soon as she was freed from the paralysis, ride her steel-horse all over the world'.

She is so obviously a Knight Errand of the Holy Order of the Steel-Horse! She carries that shining spirit that comes from a great quest.

And it was exactly that, which had intimidated and frightened Clara at first meeting, for then Clara was in a space in which she could not see herself to be ever again of a great and inspiring spirit-force like Martha's.

The most frightening thing that Martha had said to Clara

before she left hospital abruptly was, "I am so bewildered, I don't know if I am or not."

Is not the experiment with another human being or any other creature an evil, springing directly from a total ignorance of life, its source and its being?

Clara was haunted and always will be by this image of these terribly clever psychologists and psychiatrists sucking out Martha's soul and making it into so many pieces, a fair share for each one to enhance and feed their own egos with. She would add this dreadful image to so many actual happenings, which she had encountered and witnessed in her working contact with the 'Knowers of the Human Soul', where a verdict fell on a child that could only be likened to a sentence for life.

What barren, spiritless power is at work here, that allows such destructive interference with a human life: *A woman's life that was huge?*

Abandoned by the passion of the spirit, the mind has become parched. And an intellect is at work that is so frighteningly stagnant, that it shrinks even consciousness down to that which can be 'understood' and named and is instantly grasped.

God help the mankind of the Western World, where there is such material affluence, and all life is based on it, and such unspeakable impoverishment of the spirit.

And the heart lies in the gutter.

Who is sick? Is it I or those that are put above me to cure me? Cure me of what? Cure me of my spirited, bright, vital being? Where spirit as passion dwells, a great passion for life and to live, just as it does in Martha? Cure me of the fire that burns in me, that fire, that is ready to light a whole new life, that has its roots in the unfathomable time of God's first word? Cure me of my life, mine, that one which belongs to me and me alone? Cure me out of my wits, so that I am as limp as a washing-up rag and as malleable, with no will of my own, no impulse to live? Cure me into Zombi-hood, a nice obedient citizen, not able to be responsible in his own right, who never even says as much as 'pap'?

I, Clara rage, rage against these All-Knowers, who travel under the banner of science, whatever science, and with their arid intellect lay waste to life.

I, Clara, rage, rage against these pompous All-Knowers, who think that think is all there is to thinking and think for thinking's sake alone and with this lop-sided view from a self-enthroned enthronement speak down their compartmentalised and blinkered expertise findings and judgements like Gods.

There has, I believe, never been such poverty of the spirit, such impoverished heart, such total loss of the vital connection, and communion of life with life. And never has Man been so distant from his God, his source of inspiration.

Inspiration! It cannot be measured, nor weighed or packaged by any science. There is no yard-stick long enough, nor any container big enough . . .

I am judged insane! By whom? By representatives of a medical science that is based in the very same fuddled spirit, which was able to mistake the power of the atom as the greatest possible force of destruction and use it as such!

I, Clara, rage, rage that such blatant insanity runs the world and dictates the peoples of the world what to do, and not to do and thinks itself right and infallible.

I, Clara, rage, rage against my own womankind! For we should know better than allow such violation of life and with it the violation of our own Kind. Which has led to the outrageous indoctrinations, that so easily undermine by fear all that makes womankind. Allow a woman to accept that pregnancy is a sickness and birthing a mechanical act and breast-feeding something ugly and deforming.

Fear has taken hold of womankind. Fear in every realm that is hers by birth.

And life has become sick. And womankind has become bewildered and diseased.

As a woman, I am in touch with the majestic silence. In it, I wait and listen. From it, I am being nourished.

The intuition, which is my greatest womanly gift, has its source in the Pool of Life itself.

I am still. I wait. I listen. I am receptive. I am given all that I need for my nourishment and all that I need to nurture those that are given into my trust.

As a woman, I am from the source.

As a woman, I am not alien to the Earth nor to Heaven, for I am of both.

As a woman, I trust then in that which I am endowed with: the gifts both of Earth and of Heaven.

As a woman, I am endowed with life hugely. And my task is to give life and to preserve it. To give it from my body and from my being in vast gestures. To preserve it with might and with courage.

As a woman, the gift of love is mine from the beginning. From that moment in measureless time, when the first gesture was made, the gift of love has been mine.

As a woman, I am love. I give it. I receive it. I need it. With it, I nurture, I heal, I harbour, I shelter and I shield and I feed and I create and I harvest.

*　　*　　*　　*

As a woman, I rage against myself for allowing my womanhood to be man-handled and violated and by that, assisting the perversion and the abuse of the human spirit.

As a woman, I am the keeper of the sacred and I keep sacred life and all things created and thus my gestures are made in celebration and in thanksgiving.

As a woman, *I am celebration*. Through me and by me, life is being celebrated. With every breath I breathe in, I renew my sacred being, with every breath I breathe out, I celebrate my life. With every step I make, I create hallelujah, with every gesture I make, I sow love.

Clara is not screaming this woe to woman, this ode to woman off her heart into the sixteen winds or onto the four walls, but she is writing it down. She is writing it down in a beautifully bound red-and-gold note-book, that was yet another gift from someone, whose name did not recall a face, but who says that she is thinking of Clara and that she has her in her prayers and that she remembers all the enriching conversations they had had together, word for word.

And the more Clara uses the pen, that came with this beautiful gift, the more rhythmic her writing becomes and the more urgently the words are being received to express herself by.

Like the singing of the hymns and the painting, the act of writing and the finding of words to tell of herself, are creating flow and this flow returns into her as healing force.

One morning, Clara wakes so lightfully, that she is able to write '*WomanKind is a celebration*. Sing it. Dance it. Celebrate, then the celebration that womankind is.'

'One day, I must write the Ode to WomanKind. It is given me to transform all woman's woe and make it joy. Joy and Gladness. A power of love.'

'So I see myself fulfilling my life in truth as the work which

119

was given me to do this time round on my Earth-round.'
'Write the Ode, Clara, and live it! Sing it living!'

Suddenly this breakthrough. This gift to Clara. This Yes.

So it became that the space that Clara was in was more open and lightful. And she found that she affected the other patients by it and made them come up to her and trust their stories to her. And by listening, Clara was healing also.

One of the first to trust herself to Clara was Sylvia.
"Are you here because of your great secret?"
Apart from lifting her left hand in greeting every morning, Sylvia had never spoken to Clara before.
"Yes, I am."
"You never told anyone?"
"No, not anyone."
"I told it to Him-Her" (pointing to Heaven) "who has no name, but Him-Her did not hear not ever. Then I turned the gas on. That's another sin. I am dark with sin. That's why I am here. Have you tried to kill yourself?"
"Yes, I walked into the sea, someone fished me out."
"When I was sixteen, I gave birth to a son. I was wild. I had a beautiful voice and I sang in clubs. I fell in love with this man so much older than me. I was crazy about him. He made out that he was mad about me, too. I had gorgeous auburn hair falling down over shoulders and back, down to my knees. I had a soft sweet body. I was full of fun. I made eyes at all the good-looking men, but I was in love with this one. He told me I was his first and only sweetheart. It flattered me to death. He was my first. We made love in the back seat of his car. When I got pregnant, he confessed, that he had mislead me, that he was a married man and father of three children. I broke down and stuck my head into the gas oven. My mother found me. She called me a whore and I was sent to a home for unmarried mothers. My baby-boy was beautiful and very cheerful. He suckled my overflowing breasts. When he was three months old, I carried him in my own arms

to . . . in my own arms to . . . in my own arms to . . ."

Sylvia broke down and wailed. Wails, that have not been heard since Mary uttered them at the foot of the cross. And Sylvia sank into a flood of tears.

Clara pressed her to her and wept with her. "Tears, tears, I haven't wept since that day, when he was three months old and I carried him in my own arms to . . . to . . . to . . . I haven't seen him since. I don't know if he is dead or alive. The only being I ever loved. My little boy. When I gave him away, I gave my life away and my love. I never sang another song. My voice died. I heaped sin upon sin. I never loved the man I married or the children we had together. All my love went with my little boy. All this has been my secret until today. And now you know it. I don't know why I am telling you all this. I haven't seen my mother or my father again since the day my mother forbad me to ever come home again. And my children don't want to know me since I have been in and out of Mental Institutions. I don't want morning to come. I don't want to wake up. Why do they keep me alive? I don't want to live. I am full of black sin. I murdered my own heart. I gave my baby-boy away. I carried him in these arms and with these hands I handed him over like a parcel. No, No, No! I don't want to live. Where will I go when I die? Woe, woe, woe, there is no forgiveness for murdering your own love. I could have been a great singer. I had a beautiful voice. Deep and beautiful. And my auburn hair fell down over my shoulders to my knees. Why am I telling you all this? Now I haven't got my deepest secret any more. Now I am hollowed out. Now I am just an empty shell. What's my life worth? What's the use of someone like me? My life is tough. Look, how tough my body has become from the weight of carrying that secret for forty years and never able to shed a tear. Look, how tough my skin is, just like sole-leather, all the tears that have become knots. I am all knots, inside and out. I am too tough to die. I am a fossil. I want to hold my little baby-boy in my arms. But I am terrified. Will he want to know his mother, this heap of sin and misery, who handed him over like a parcel. I want to die."

And Sylvia's wailing is as heart rending as the wailing of the Mother Elephant whose baby is shot in front of her eyes.

* * * *

121

f

All of us in here, in this institution for mentally ill, are given names like: schizoid, schizophrenic, like psychopath, like severe endogenous involutional/depression, like manic-depressive psychoses, like hypomanic etc. etc. etc. . . .

And we are all being given drugs, injections, electric-shock treatment and so forth, to cure our ills.

Our ills.

No one listens to the story each one of us has to tell. If anyone did, more than not, our names would be: broken-heart, unshed tears, want-to-die, unloved-unloved, cannot-love, etc. etc. etc.

We all need ears that listen, hearts that beat, arms that hold, eyes that weep for us, hands that reach out, words that are like healing balm.

The only thing we all need is Love.

"Tears, tears, tears, I haven't wept since I was sixteen. I was made for love. I thwarted all my power of love. I never sang again. Tearless, my heart has been crying for forty years. I ruined my marriage and my children's lives. I died that day, when I carried my baby-boy in my arms to hand him over like a parcel into unknown hands. The burden of guilt is too heavy. My hands are dirty. Why didn't my mother push me farther into the gas oven instead of rescuing me? She pushed me out of the house for good afterwards anyway."

- Did the father of her son ever ponder for one moment only, only for one moment, and gaze at his hands and ponder; for one moment only: What has become of Sylvia, my 'first' love . . .

Sylvia's story is too much for Clara. It brings up too many shattering unlived experiences from her own life, and she wept quietly for days.

We give so much. We give so much and we expect so much. And our loving is used and abused. Woe to be born a woman, whose meaning to live is to love. Woe, woe, woman, when your life means to respond with your whole being to life and so to be fully responsible for life and deeply respectful of it. How open and vulnerable you are in the sacredness of your so-being.

Thus, in trust, you hand this wonderful womanly inheritance over into a relationship and soon it is taken for granted and becomes a possession of the other. Used to bear from hundreds of generations of bearing and submitting, you bear and submit. And you lose your life. Daily a little bit more. And the demand on you to give, spoken and unspoken, grows daily. Guilty, because you expect to be rewarded for your loving with love and afraid, because the relationship into which you have given yourself by deep inner commitment, that you have understood to be reciprocal, turns out to be an illusion, your bewilderment grows. Suddenly, you stand naked and alone and helpless in a life you have given your word to but have not been in the least prepared for.

You suffer and you bear, quietly, you keep a brave face, you accept, because you learnt it from your mother and because the word you gave is sacred like your life.

Instead of living hugely the hugeness of our woman selves, we are afraid of it. A fear conditioned by generations of women submitting to and accepting a sole male dominance, that has distorted and defaced every aspect of living and life and caused a grave imbalance of forces.

By allowing the feminine - the force of life itself - to be exploited, undermined, abused and suppressed, we have degraded all of life.

Nothing is sacred anymore. And we do not anymore know as to who we are and what the meaning is of our lives. There is a severance from life itself. And there is a deep bewilderment. Bewilderment makes muddle. Muddle muddles, muddles, muddles.

Woman is called upon, *urgently* called upon, to remember her Self. She must at once undertake a journey of self-discovery. She must at once step out, fearlessly, into the unknown and bravely become a warrior. A warrior, whose only weapon is her ever growing love for her Self as she recovers, step by step and thrust by thrust, the treasures of her womanhood so long forgotten, so long seemingly lost.

Woman is called upon urgently, for life is given into her hands. She has to recover it and restore to it its meaning.

For woman is the measure. She is the balancer, the treasure and the treasurer. She gives the tone.

She is born of her own Kind and thus, from the beginning, she responds deeply and hugely to life and stands full square within it.

Unless woman becomes fully respectful of and responsive to her Self and sees and grasps her innate power of womanhood - this power of life and love - and that it stands quite alone and easy and glad without any support, strong and beautiful all of its own and out of itself, a relationship of balance and harmony with man and the world is not possible.

Woman! Submit not to false values. Know: you are value unto yourself. You possess the greatest gifts and the greatest responsibility. Live the hugeness that you are!

Naturally are.

Let your love flow!

Let your life flow!

Let's create a flood! Open the sluice gates and create a flood of love and life.

And let there be greening. Let the barren mankind be greening by the flood of love and life.

Woman! You are called upon to be aware of your gifts: Life is in your hands and Love is in your hands.

In sacred trust, they are given you from the beginning from the silence of the great womb, even and long before The Word!

From the awareness of the sacred-being of these gifts, you must respond in the whole of your being and in the whole of your doing with clarity and lightful strength.

Life nor love know any half-measures. *You are full measure, measure accordingly.*

*　　*　　*　　*

This light thus created, shine it into the face of fear. Shine it brightly into the face of fear that rules and dominates all mankind and de-humanises in such a way, that mankind cannot even remember anymore to become Humankind. And creates values, that are contrary to life, thus opening life and nature to total exploitation and the loss of their sacred being.

The fear has taken on monstrous proportions, so that whole peoples are able to be made to believe, that peace can only be kept by a huge arsenal of horrifically destructive weapons.

Fear is ground and foundation of all mankind now. And what humankind could be built there on . . .

Fear has created a madness, that has befallen all mankind.

Woman waken!
Waken, woman!
It is highest time.
Woman, awake!
Waken! And speak and act!
It is highest time to break your long and deep silence of centuries.
Speak! You are ready *now.*
And say the word:
Let there be day after the long black night of the human heart.
Let there be light after the long eclipse of the human soul.
Let there be joy.
Let there be gladness.
Let there be love.
Let there be life.

Roar it.   Roar it.   Roar it.

Thus, the red-and-gold notebook of Clara's is filling its pages with words. They are written from her being, wrenched from her innermost being, and she feels at once the pain and the healing.

The Sunflowers, the Golden Oriole, He-She, the seagull that

had not been to tap the window since the day Clara left for hospital and then was there to tap its greeting at her short visit, Cuckoo singing all through the night, both Dogs sleeping in front of her bedroom door and licking her toes on stepping out in the morning . . .

Adam. Adam.

The Garden of Eden is the Earth.

The Kingdom of Heaven is within me.

So many of her fellow-patients had trusted their story to Clara and slowly, what seemed once an alien lot of people became a sisterhood and a brotherhood. In each story, Clara found bits of her own story. Each of these lives was her life also.

And when she left for her ten-day leave, the preliminary to her final dismissal, it was like leaving a trusting family and Adam and home, that which once she had put her trust in entirely, became the alien, the estranged.

It was, then, with great trepidations, that she made herself comfortable beside Adam, as he drove with her out of the main gates of the hospital.

And suddenly there was fear again. Clara opened the window wide to get air fast and strong into her face.

Adam had not been in joy at their meeting. She had been like a child. So expectant. But his haste and nervousness took all her openness away and she turned round to the circle of friends who saw her off as if to say to them: 'Help me, I don't want to go. I am going to a foreign land.'

They waved, wished her well and blew kisses.

In spite of the blast of air, the atmosphere in the car was thick and uneasy. Wasn't there so much to tell, so much to share, now that they were together and had ten days of togetherness in front of them . . ?

When they left the main road and turned into a side-road that was an entirely different direction from home, Clara said, "O, are we having a pleasure ride through the countryside before going home?"

"Well, yes and no. You are going to spend a week with our friends Elsa and Basil. You have been to their home before, we sat in their beautiful garden and we have shared meals. They like

126

you. You see, what with one thing and another, I have fallen behind with my work and this week will be vital for me to be able to be ready before the deadline."

"Oh." That's all Clara was able to say. And she fell deep into herself and could not hear Adam's voice. All the light, that had started to become in her and with it a confidence and even a trust in herself, went instantly and she felt within and without in a thick impenetrable fog.

Air! more air!

Adam took a suitcase out of the car. He had thought of everything.

They were in time for lunch, which was a colourful spread on a round table in Elsa's sunlit garden. Immediately after the meal, Adam was off and Clara had not another moment alone with him.

"See you in a week's time if all goes as planned. Bye, my darling."

- Dearling - darling - dearling - darling:
Ten thousand such dearling-darlings over the many years . . .

Clara was intimidated by the efficiency in which the children, husband, garden, household and business from home were run. Efficiency! And the way the 'Daily' wiped daily every grain of dust.

They were kind to Clara. Very kind. She was treated as though she was an invalid. And she was being watched. Obviously, they felt very responsible. And Adam had given instructions. She was to have a soothing bath every day, and he left oils. She must be accompanied on walks. She should be introduced to preparing meals and may help with some garden work as she had forgotten all these things.

How well Adam knew the things, that Clara had forgotten . . .

*   *   *   *

127

But she was completely intimidated by the way the day was laid out and programmed. Every moment was prescribed. And this paralysed Clara so that she found it difficult even to chop parsley or to wash vegetables, all those little things and doings, that she had hoped she would easily remember again once back in her familiar surroundings. - O, to prepare a meal again with imagination and joy! But fear thickened her. These two people were so big in their capacity to run their lives. There was no fault. Everything and everywhere perfection.

No room to improvise.

No space to dance.

No time to play.

Good people. Very good people. And kind. Very kind!

Clara found herself a spot in the garden, a little hide-out, a small space in a thicket of undergrowth. She went there with the red-and-gold notebook and a pen. And she saw herself write, over and over again, write 'There is a way of killing another, and it is never called murder.'

Her writing was spindly, spiky and spidery. She turned the pages. She read and wondered: who wrote that and whose hand is that . . . and who is this one sitting here writing this?

In the kitchen, Clara found a cook-book. And as she suddenly was possessed with the idea that she should never ever be able to be inspired to cook as she used to do without recipes and from her fingertips, creating each meal like a work of art, she copied into her note book recipe after recipe frantically, almost like a thief that might be caught at any moment at his misdeed.

She was undermined. There wasn't a shred of confidence. And in her are churning the words, 'What will become of me? Where is the me, that I am, surely am?'

O, to love and to be loved.

And she thickened with fear.

Air! more air!

Air! more air!

*   *   *   *

After a few days, Clara asked to go for a walk on her own. On one of the walks with Elsa, she had spotted a rock by the stream, and she had felt that she would want to sit there, take her shoes off and let the water flow over her feet and listen.

Clara left her sandals on the grass ledge, hitched her skirt and waded into the stream. She pushed her feet into fine pebbly sand and a delicious sensation ran up into her body.

For a moment, she was Clara the child, and she bent and pushed both her hands into the sand, and bringing up hands full of it, she let it stream back through her fingers into the water. A sensuous sweetness spreads through her body. A delight fills every cell. She could forget herself. She could be here forever and simply not remember that she is the now-Clara, the one whose mind is supposed to be astray.

She waded to the rock. Her skirt was wet. There was a seat in the rock. Just made for her and just high enough for her feet to dangle in the water.

To forget herself . . . to forget herself . . .

Lifting her head, her eyes are dazzled by a flashing bright blue light . . . a Kingfisher! Like a bright dream from her own Self. Under his wings glitters pure gold. Next, she sees him clinging to a bush opposite, directly in her sight, shining brightly his amazing colours at her: the blue, the green, the white, the chestnut-red.

Clara remembers. And she is being filled with the warmth of a promise, for the Kingfisher, so rarely seen, is an omen of portending good tidings.

Good tidings. A gift.

And in a few delicious moments, Clara loses herself in a time of long ago and mingles with a Clara so carefree, so spirited, so wild. And all of a sudden it seems, that *that one is the real one, the true one:* colourful, bright-shining like the Kingfisher. A flash of ungraspable life. A life alive. And the one of recent times is like a cloak over that one, a guise, temporarily, even if it was for so many years, still temporarily, to protect like a shield, to cover like an armour the one which in stillness *needed to become.*

The King-Fisher.

The King-Fisher.

The King-Fisher.

The Fisher-King . . .

Long happened. Long happened. Deep inside. Fathoms deep inside. That which is real and true: *I have to be the Kingfisher, the Fisher-King.*

And a dream shoots into Clara's memory, that was given her in slightly different versions at different times soon after she had joined with Adam. This is the first time in so long, that Clara recalls it:

Clara is sitting by a pond, the water of which is wonderfully clear. She knows it as the 'bottomless pond' as it is endlessly deep. She knows, too, that what she is looking for is in this pond, and that whatever it is can only be found by herself diving in. 'Make the leap, Clara, dive.' Out of her own Self this voice and an instant readiness to leap. In the same instant appears a Kingfisher and he says, 'You called me. I am the Fisher King's diver. I am your servant. Command!'

And Clara speaks with certainty: 'There are three keys at the bottom of this pond, a silver one, a golden one and a crystal one. These are to be mine. They lie at different depths, the crystal one lies deepest. You have to dive three times.'

As the Kingfisher returns from his first dive and drops the Silver-Key in her lap, the voice says, 'To open the door to your unconscious.' With the dropping of the Golden Key, the voice says, 'To open the door to the forces of creation indwelling you,' and with the Crystal Key in her lap, the voice says, 'To open the door to your own immortal life.'

With that, the Kingfisher becomes the Fisher-King, which is her Self.

On waking, Clara reaches for the Keys, the dream having been so real. And for the brief moment of this gesture, Clara knows that the three keys *are* in her lap and that only she her-self will find the Keyholes to fit these Keys to open those doors with. And that it cannot happen by union with another, but only by the union of herself with her Self.

*   *   *   *

130

The Kingfisher like a vision and the Fisher-King dream as a gift of remembrance.

I am so rich, so rich. Even in moments when I feel completely abandoned, I am being seen.

Maybe what seemed to be an irresponsible off-loading of me by Adam into the hands of people only superficially known, is turning into a blessing . . .

Back in Elsa's garden, Clara wrote in a hand more in rhythm again of the encounter with the Kingfisher and the Fisher-King dream as she had recalled it. And she felt thankful to Elsa and Basil for having taken her on. For how could they know what they did take on, when just the mention of mental illness makes such strangely coloured pictures in people's minds and causes such immediate apprehension.

And was there forgiveness for Adam? Again an act seemingly done against her, turns out to be one for her . . ?

The last two whole days of her ten day sojourn are spent at home with Adam. Clara is delighted at remembering how to make toast on the AGA-cooker and how to make a good cup of tea and coffee. And she makes simple salads and finds how much pleasure it gives her. Fancy, to ever have forgotten those simple gestures and to have been so terrified, lest she should never again remember how to make them.

But one day, they all had fallen out of her over night and she had stood there with empty hands.

And now, were her hands being filled again . . ?

When they were sitting at the last supper on the eve of her return to the hospital, Adam suddenly said, "Why are you still wearing the engagement ring, the diamond fell out years ago, what does it mean to you? You can't let go, can you. How you hang on to yesterday."

What did this little stoneless platinum-ring call up in Adam?

Clara had only slipped it on that morning in jest, so to speak. She had not worn it again since that devastating morning some years before, when she pulled her hands out of the old-fashioned washing-trough, where the last rinsing water was just vanishing down the drains with funny noises and looking at her wrinkled hands, she found with shock the diamond missing. Two local men searched the drains. They were so sweetly concerned, but the brilliant treasure, that had over the years so minutely and accurately registered all her moods by the way it glittered or lacked shine, was gone.

Clara had been stunned for days, and she had known instantly, that some vital part of her relationship had come to an end and *that she must face it.*

The stoneless ring was dropped into the back of the bottom drawer of her jewellery chest well out of sight, but the ring-finger and the heart could never forget.

That morning, Clara had been playing with her jewellery and had had such fun and pleasure, putting on finger-rings and earrings and necklaces and filling her arms with all manner of bracelets and looking at herself in the mirror and remembering the occasions most associated with each of these lovely things. Then she found the hollow ring. It did not fit on her ring-finger anymore, so she pushed it on her little finger and then quite forgot to take it off.

But in putting it on, Clara had relived vividly the moment of her first encounter with the ring: They had been walking in St James Park, when Adam took her by the hand and running said, "Let's go and buy you an engagement ring." Like children they had run and laughed while they were running. Then they stood in front of this small jewellery shop. It looked rich. Terribly rich. Clara felt exhilarated. To enter this shop. Was she dressed well enough . . . To buy a ring . . . oh . . . "How much money have you got with you?" She heard Adam say. - A strange thing to ask - They entered. She was wearing an ankle-long golden-honey coloured wide-ribbed corduroy skirt which had pockets going down to the bottom seam and a purple knitted cotton top with a

132

simple circular neck-line and three-quarter slightly bat-winged sleeves, dainty, flat-soled suede shoes of the same purple. Her skin was tanned nut brown by much sun and a pure-gold-circle broach, a gift from her Mother, adorned her. She knew her eyes were shining. Was the gracious and well spoken gentleman in a frock coat or did she in her excitement and her astonishment at finding herself in Aladdin's Cave make him wear one . . . Finally, he brought out this one fingering on a crimson velvet cushion. For a moment, Clara was a Princess.

"This is a most beautiful diamond, it is vastly reduced in price" - had he guessed our pockets - "as we have not in so many years been able to find a finger slender enough to fit it. It has obviously been waiting for you, madam."

And it slipped on her ring-finger so gladly, so sweetly, so simply. There it was. Belonging. Clara turned all red and hot. It was *her ring*. It had been waiting for her finger all these years. Had it been on another hand ever before and if so who could it have been . . . It cost exactly the seventeen pounds sterling that Clara possessed in all the world . . . she had slipped it to Adam before they had entered the magical shop. The money, as she remembered, was carried away on a black velvet cushion, or did she make this up . . .

That shop had appeared on the edge of St James Park just for that most magical moment. Then it sank back into a time long past and gone.

In their very secret meeting place in St James Park, Adam slipped the ring on her slim ring-finger and then he took her in his arms and she sank and she sank and she sank. And he kissed her, he kissed her, oh, he kissed her - the land of Bliss forever and this sparkling jewel its radiant symbol.

Clara had forgotten those moments and this morning in play, they had returned.

"You and your yesterdays . . ."

Adam's voice.

Clara with a smile, "Can you make a step today without the one you made yesterday . . ?"

But pain is in her throat and pain is in her heart.

*   *   *   *

When the diamond fell out, Clara did not heed its message. She tried to continue the relationship as it had been or maybe, as she wanted it to be. She had been asked to look herself in the face without fear and to look into Adam's face without fear and at their relationship with open clear eyes.

She pretended not to know, not to see, not to hear.

It was strongly in her, to make believe.

When the relationship as it had been had died, they did not together acknowledge this and find in the dying the tiny seed of something new and other that might have wanted to grow. Like the Giant Rhubarb every spring grows from this heap of 'ugh', this mess of soggy brown pulp, unshapely, formless, lying there in a wintering death. Then one day there is movement and a first emerging and imperceptibly, it begins to grow. And soon and suddenly, there is this dome textured with minute spikes and covered in finest shining silver hairs. And this tomorrow is seen to unfold and a leaf shape becomes and as the days go by, a stem pushes up and the leaf unfolds opening ever wider and growing larger and larger. Meanwhile, other domes have grown of a different structure, but from the same 'ugh'. They are intricately built and sculptured by a hand of genius, and the largest one ends in a tri-pointed crown. Today, this form is revealing lots of fingers held tightly together - maybe, these will become flowers.

When we have become the wintering mess of decay and death in our relationship or in ourselves, oh, let's remember the 'ugh' from which the magnificent Giant Rhubarb is born every Spring.

'Hold my hand and trust.' It is your Self speaking. 'I have been built by generations of builders.'

Listen! The voice . . .

'Fear not, there is a life in you that belongs to you. That is yours and yours alone. You are becoming this life. It does not depend on another.'

'Fear not and trust.'

'The Earth is speaking to you and the Heavens. They are both speaking to you.'

Tune in, Clara.

Listen!

The Voice!

How much we stow away into the far corners of ourselves, until one time, when we are forced to shine these hiding places and are asked to bring all forward and lay all in front of our eyes, spread it all in front of ourselves and look at all and each one.

The voice that asks is strong and unrelenting and clear.

It ceases not, until we hear it and are heedful of it.

It is at our own peril, that we do not take heed of it.

Clara is being returned to the hospital in time for tea. In the ten days so much had happened within her and it struck her fiercely, almost like a blow between her eyes, that she had not shared anything with Adam at all.

Each had been a guarded, encapsulated world. Clara realised with a pain in her, that she was alone.

Oh, not the glad aloneness, that is a gift of being all one and one with all. Nay, not that, but that shocking and painful separateness.

"Shocking and necessary. Necessary!" She repeated it aloud, looking up and into a new face belonging to a young woman sitting opposite her.

"You are Clara," she says, gently, looking at Clara with her pure emerald-green eyes, that are without shine, and one looking in and the other looking out from under a huge chaotic mass of burnt-copper-red curls. Her face, white and translucent, of a beauty born of a Northland night of the Aurora Borealis or of an Irish night of flying mists, the pale moon riding in it like a phantom Unicorn, or the fast white-rider-wave of a Spring-tide stormy sea.

On the white silken skin in the drop shape of the neckline

hangs a sun-golden tear pendant on a simple golden chain that is finely linked. No earrings. A thin circle of gold, woven in a celtic pattern, adorns the little finger of her left hand, which rests on the table. Her dress, the green of her eyes, is of silk.

Her long slim white hand moves across the table and Clara meets her half-way in a hand-greeting. "My name is Deirdre." And in a gesture towards the other tables, Deirdre says, "They talked about you, they say you listen."

"O, did they?"

Out of this unearthly looking creature comes a voice that has no tone. "I am asked to come to the dining-room, but I have no appetite. I don't feel like eating and I don't want to eat and the food doesn't want to go down. It's called Anorexia. I have no desire to live, you see. It's all the same."

And Deirdre sits there, her long white slender hands lying on either side of her filled plate and her egg-shell face looking down on the food in front of her. A nurse comes up to encourage her to eat. But the coaxing is of no avail.

Deirdre is apathetic. She is removed and isolated. Clara is in sympathy. She feels herself into this other world, where Deirdre seems to be. Had she not been there herself, but a short while ago? And Clara is struck by the other-worldly beauty of Deirdre. It conjures up images in her: an inner woman, like a dream-image of herself, that seems an aspect of her Self almost like a mirror-face under water. And in Clara is wakened a magic of pure sound dance-music, experienced as a small child in a cave hung with icicles, the falling drops of the slowly melting ice being the musicians and the music. - Why this particular image drawn up from the deep well of memory at this moment by the presence of Deirdre with the green green eyes . . . Ah! Clara had not recalled that magical spell of the icicle-music in all her life until now . . .

She must tell Deirdre, maybe that it bring a light to her eyes.

And her name rings the verses of J.M. Synge's drama 'Deirdre of the Sorrows', that many years ago had moved Clara so.

Deirdre is destined to be the bride of a King, but she falls in love with another, with whom she spends idyllic times on the shores of a lake. Cruelly, her sweetheart and his two brothers are slain by the King and Deirdre's song of love becomes her lament.

The mother knew this song that gave Deirdre her name, perhaps it was her own name and she handed it on like some sorrow. - It happens. We do it. As though we were making an endowment, and we do not realise that it is already there as an inheritance in the bone and in the marrow.

They walked out of the dining-room hand in hand. Seeing herself so small beside the tall thin figure of Deirdre, as in Cecil Collins's painting 'The Pilgrim Fool' appears, and Clara sees herself the little girl in it holding hands with the tall, white-faced paper crowned fool.

In the quiet-lounge, they sit on one of the wide window sills. And still holding hands, whispering now, Deirdre begins her story:

"I am misbegotten. I should never have been born. And so was my mother and so was her mother before her. In a fit of unbearable remorse, my mother confessed to me on my twelfth birthday, that she had tried everything to get rid of the pregnancy of me, as I had been conceived, as she herself, in violence. Fear, hatred and distrust of men had been handed down by the women of her family and she had not ever wanted any children. Breaking down and sobbing, my mother poured out the story of the violent night in which I was conceived. How she had once more refused her father her bed, but blind-drunk and in blind-rage, he had forced his way to what he considered his right.

"I had been brought up in a household of women. There was nothing unusual in this; there were many such homes, as so many men had died in the wars. That is what I had been made to believe up to the moment of the horrible truth of how I got into this world. And it was then that the shining image I had created of my father was smashed and a monster took its place.

"And I found, that the three women, great grand-mother, grand-mother and mother, had brought me up in an unreal world filled with make-believe. They meant well. They wanted to shield me 'from a world, more full of weeping than you can understand'.

"Do you know W B Yeat's poem 'The Stolen Child'?"

Clara was thrown. Did she know this poem? Indeed she did! When her daughter Maya was but eight years old, this poem was being read one evening and so captivated was this small child by it and so haunted, especially by the refrain:

'Come away, O human Child!
To the waters and the wild
With a Faery hand in hand
For the world's more full of weeping
Than you can understand.'

that she learnt the whole poem by heart at once and would have no evening reading, without this poem being included.

And Clara remembered the pain she had felt for her daughter, for somewhere in the small deeply feeling child, there was a knowing of that weeping and of that sorrow. And to Clara it was that Maya, who was so much a small child and yet so old, had a foreknowing of the weeping and sorrowing that was awaiting her in the world.

And here on this window-sill in this Mental Hospital Ward, so many years later, Clara is holding hands with a young woman only a few years older than her own daughter, who is asking her, does she know this poem . . ! And then tells her, that as a small child it was read to her and she was overtaken by it so over-whelmingly, that she learnt it by heart and recited it to herself before sleeping for weeks, maybe for months every night and wept herself to sleep with it.

Somewhere inside her she knew, said Deirdre, that this world more full of weeping was waiting for her and was the real world, and that the world the three women in her life were keeping her in was but a dream.

Then on her twelfth birthday, Deirdre's idyllic life was rent like a beautiful colourful and precious garment. And she was naked and injured in her deepest depth, as she was cruelly torn from her dream-world by the same mother, who had kept her so well hidden in it for those many years.

"The load of being misbegotten, of being conceived in violence and of being born unwanted, that has been carried from generation to generation by the mothers in my family, is thrust on me when I am twelve years old and culminates in me becoming the murderess of my own unwanted baby-daughter by suffocating her with a pillow. I did not want her to live to carry on the inherited curse. It would have been better to have stuffed a pillow over my own face too. My life ended before it began. I stood trial. I confessed to the crime. I was declared insane."

Deirdre's voice is voiceless. There is no voice in her. Clara felt, if only Deirdre could yell, shout, bellow, howl, roar her story and her burnt copper-red hair could go up in flames of redemption . . . Clara pressed Deirdre's hand. It must have pained her, so hard did Clara press that white hand and she dissolved in tears.

And Deirdre's green green eyes were there, one looking in, one looking out, but motionless, lightless and tearless. As if arrested in a moment of horror in a time past and held fast and fixed in that moment for ever, never to move again, never to be moved again.

Are the unshed tears becoming crystals in her or cancer or blind stones . . .

Deirdre, Deirdre of the unending sorrow.

Since her return, Clara was allowed to go for walks on her own within a prescribed area of the hospital grounds. She found some places which seemed to speak to her, and one of them was a small walled rose-garden. An enchantment of fragrant climbing roses and rambling roses, delightful small rose-trees and bushes of roses and rock-roses growing between the paving stones. The ancient Albertine, Clara's most beloved rose beside the wild rose of the hedges, cascaded its masses of sweetly scented blossoms and deep-rose buds over an old crooked apple tree and in its arbour Clara loved to sit and to dream.

Dream! She was able to dream again! And to remember times of idyll under the flowering trees of her childhood and young girlhood. The bliss of being in a sudden shower of blossom-petals, and how she could become any kind of magical being under the spell of the flowering trees fragrance and unearthly beauty.

Clara could never quite believe that the rose-garden was real but that the tipsy green wooden gate hanging drunkenly on loose hinges just simply appeared in that high wall every time she happened to pass. And never being able to resist any such doors or gates, she pushed it a little and gazed in astonishment into the little paradise. The rose-garden became her secret and her love and her daily walk a pilgrimage to the shrine of roses, where, in a blissful lightfulness, she could lose herself.

Lose herself! And be drunk of roses, roses, roses . . .

A poem by Christian Morgenstern is being remembered:

> *'Oh wer um alle Rosen wuesste,*
> *die rings in stillen Gaerten stehn -*
> *Oh, wer um alle wuesste, muesste*
> *wie im Rausch durch's Leben gehn.'*

And Clara remembers how, so long ago, she had recited the whole poem up and down a country-lane in which she was floating in the scent of masses of wild roses in its hedge-rows. A first overwhelming welcoming experience of an untamed English countryside, soon after her entry into her now adopted, beloved land.

On the day before leaving the Mental Hospital finally - she could not see herself ever to return there - Clara took Thomas, the farmer, to her secret garden. He too was allowed to go for walks on his own, and they had on a few occasions shared their walking. But Clara would then go different paths and make sure not to come near her dream place.

Clara had made the rose garden deeply hers and in it she had not only dreamed and reminisced, but also dwelt on the stories which had been trusted to her by her fellow patients.

And Thomas' story had preoccupied her a lot. Again and again, it came to the fore, and it was as though he was standing beside her listening to the potent silence of the little paradise of roses.

140

Clara felt suddenly that not only must she share her secret garden this once with Thomas, but that she had to put it into his hands in trust, as it were. For she felt hidden in him a heart-breaking sensibility, injured and broken almost, but the fire of his life had not died out. There were small glowing embers to be rekindled and a passion for life to be let loose that was shut into a huge yearning heart, and a soul delighted that was languishing. There was a tear in the fabric of his being, where life still flowed in and out.

In speaking to her, Thomas could change suddenly, and for a split-moment the hard shell, dark and lightless, show a minute crack and a light appear in his black eyes, that were otherwise hung as with heavy curtains, and a shine flicker on his otherwise heavily loaded brow.

In the rose-garden, Thomas might find not only solace but rediscovery of himself and healing and by that the courage and will he so much needed.

It was a few days after Deirdre had told Clara her story, that Thomas stopped her as she passed by his table and asked to talk to her after the meal. They had had chats, mostly about farming, as when Clara discovered him to be a farmer, she told him that she had grown up on a farm on the continent. And as he was immediately interested, she had been glad to share some memories with him.

Clara suggested, that they walk together and by chance, they came to the ancient gnarled weeping ash-tree under which Clara had sat but once and had had a kind of visitation or apparition.

On that day, this ash tree had called to her, and she sat under it with her back to the trunk. It was shortly after she had been allowed to take walks unaccompanied. It seemed that she dozed off and in this spell of semi-sleep, she saw a young woman all in white, her fine light-gold hair falling over her shoulders. In her right hand, she held a round hand-mirror that was in a golden frame of the entwined snakes, and in her left hand was a wooden comb, the rectangular piece above the handle was carved in a relief of eight-petalled roses. A procession of lepers appeared. Each one's hair was being combed and by that simple gesture, they received healing. It was as though the pure light which this wonderful creature seemed to be in, became purifying flame in the comb. Indeed, Clara saw the comb become flame, as it passed through each sick person's hair. Not a word was spoken. But in the mirror held in front of each one, they saw their healing confirmed.

A pure white light was left under the tree, as the newly healed danced round the ash in thankful celebration.

Clara had on several of her walks tried to find this weeping ash-tree again, but had failed and had finally accepted, that she might come upon it by chance again, as she had done on that day, when she had received the gift of vision of the Healing Woman.

And now, here they were right upon it, having literally walked straight up to it. So this is the place then, where Thomas will tell her his story . . .

"I like to come here, it seems that I can forget myself under this age-old ash-tree. I come here most days and just sit with my back against its trunk. Sometimes I doze off and have curious dreams. In the ward, I never dream. In fact, I sleep rather badly, there are so many in the dormitory and those fierce little piercing lights are very disturbing. I don't know what it is about those lights, but they make me uneasy."

Clara does not say it, but she too suffers terribly from those night-lights, and she, too, has not been able to dream and her sleep was very disturbed.

"Most times I sit and just watch the branches move. They always seem to move. And I imagine myself by a stream that runs through the farm, very old basket-willows grow along it. In my childhood, all the baskets were made on the farm."

"It was the same on our farm, crude ones for the potatoes and finer ones for the fruit," Clara said this with memories flooding her. But it was Thomas' story and she could see that it was difficult for him to truly begin.

"Each time, when I step out from under this beloved and bewitching weeping-ash, I am resolute and clear that I must summon my wife and reveal to her the dreadful guilt that has been undermining my mind for so many years. But as soon as I am back in the ward again, I cannot do it.

"This huge fear of losing her love grabs hold of me each time, and I sink back into my gloomy hopeless guilt riddled world.

"You see, Clara, I am a broken-up man. I am sure it hangs all over me for you and everyone to see. But there is something about you that makes me feel, that you will not judge me."

Thomas's voice is warm and deep, a heart-voice. Clara is moved by him.

"I am the oldest of five sons. We grew up on the ancient farm that I am now the head of. We seemed to have had a lot of time to play and make music. One of our favourite games was the stick-throwing game, which was a lot of fun.

"Instead of playing the game with sharpened sticks, which are to hit a marked spot in the ground, I suggested one day, that it would be more fun to throw knives and try to hit a marked spot in a tree. My youngest brother, Benjamin, won this game each time. I had suggested to use knives, because I had practised my knife on the tree in secret and had hit the marked spot each time accurately. Now playing together, I lost the game each time. A rage built up in me and a jealousy, Benjamin also always won everyone's heart. He was outgoing and had a great charm. I was inclined to be solitary and separate. A brooder. To be the loser each time made me the laughing stock. The rage already huge in me took hold of me one time entirely and blind with it, I flung my knife and it flew straight into my brother Benjamin's head.

"I tucked the incident deep down into forgetfulness and Benjamin never showed any resentment."

When Benjamin died on the day of his 30th birthday in an operation to remove a malignant brain-tumour, the incident of the knife was suddenly pointing at Thomas like a gigantic accusing finger: 'You killed Benjamin!' 'You killed Benjamin.' A perpetual mill in his head of these three words. Whatever anyone said to him, Thomas could never hear anything else anymore than this terrible accusation. He could not eat nor sleep any more and failed totally in seeing any sense or meaning any more in anything.

He would ride out to a field on his tractor and just sit there sunk in himself and helplessly utter, "I killed Benjamin, my beloved brother." And making music with his family and brothers broke him up so badly, that he had to give it up.

"It is now five years since Benjamin's death. It seems a world ago and yet at the same time, as though it happened only yesterday. So far away and unreal and so close and so real."

"My family put me into this Mental Hospital, as the farm is going to ruin. I have no more purpose to live, no more pride in my farm. There is no more motivation to do anything, only to sit and to brood. And the guilt becomes more and more of a dull weight inside me, too heavy to bear.

"This is my third time here. Each time I receive electric shock treatment and drugs. And each time I come out of here I am less of a human being. And the treatment has never yet been able to help me find the courage and muster the will to talk to any of my family of my guilt. Yet somewhere I know, if I could but tell them and ask them for help, my will and my courage might not finally be completely broken.

"Good God, Clara, you are weeping!"

And Thomas reaches out for Clara in a warm gesture.

"I have never grieved for my brother, never yet shed one tear. It is monstrous. This unfounded guilt made an iron man out of me.

"Telling you the story makes me suddenly see that I had not thrown the knife with the intention to harm my brother Benjamin or anyone else, but my rage and jealousy needed an outlet, and in that fatal moment, they overwhelmed me and I acted in a blind fury.

"The very fact, that no one accused me or even reprimanded me, and that without a word about it, the game was never ever played again, should have been enough to make me aware of this dark passion in me, that made it possible for me to be so deadly envious of the very one I loved so much.

"Clara, did you hear me saying this? Deadly envious? Deadly envious! After all these many years, I am saying this. Could it be that I was not setting out to harm but that in the very depth of this dark power was hidden the intent to hurt, hence the knife flying straight to the target? Could it be, too, that in the same dark depth was a wish to punish myself? - I have heard it said, that the power of the unconscious is real power.

"Clara, what am I saying? I hear myself saying all these things

144

and I don't know where they are coming from. But I suddenly *see* that I am a passionate man full of huge feelings that never ever really have been expressed. What have I done to myself, Clara!"

And this tall strong man is shaken by sobs. Like huge shivers they run through his body.

"When I was a little boy of ten or eleven, paddling in the basket-willow stream, I was suddenly overwhelmed with this clear vision of myself, that I would become a man of love like Jesus. And today, right now, I remember this, and I *see* the happy careless boy Thomas clearly and how he did not once question what this meant, to be a man of love, but just continued messing about in the stream and never ever to remember it until this moment."

With this, Thomas grips Clara's arm. "Clara, it's as though I had just woken from a long sleep full of nightmares. To hang up with guilt as I have done is a way out of facing the truth of my life and is making Benjamin's death uneasy. I am sure of it.

"Clara, I am like the Blind man who suddenly is given the sight of his eyes. I can see everything clearly. I refused to suffer and missed my life. It's strange, but it just occurred to me, likely I am afraid of life rather than of death . . .

"I shall live yet, Clara! And its all in my hands, Clara. *It's all in my hands!*

"With the help of God, I shall yet be the man that I am meant to be in this life and little boy Thomas knew of when he waded in the basket-willow stream!

"How can I thank you, Clara . . . I shall always remember you."

Thomas's eyes are shining brightly. There is a veritable fire in them. And Clara is shaken, for it is as though she was looking into the eyes of her father: eyes of a mysterious power like the black tourmaline.

And Thomas's story brought so much up in her. So much! That she had not looked into for a long time.

She, too, had a fatal moment in her childhood where in a rage,

g

brought about by what she heard as a callous remark by the youngest of her brothers, her most beloved one, she flung her small garden tool in the air and it landed, tooth-bit first, in her dearest-heart-brother's head. There it stuck, blood gushing and him pale and paler and fainting. Clara fainting.

Later, being heart-broken at finding her sweet brother and best friend with his head in white bandages as white as maiden-snow and looking from under them with his large deep-blue eyes, that were now larger and full of wonder, Clara was sobbing. Kurt was looking angelical and in the presence of so much inexplicable hugeness, Clara sobbing, her little body shivering and shaking, said over and over, "I didn't mean to hurt you, I didn't mean to hurt you," and inside her 'dearest love!' But she couldn't get those and these other words out 'will you forgive me?'

And her brother never seemed ever to have a grudge on her or revenge himself. On the contrary, he treated her with ever more love and courtesy.

And how strange, that he too, like Benjamin, was the victim of a rage and possibly jealousy in the very same stick-game, that also had become the knife throwing game.

Clara was present at the incident, which happened in the back garden of the family home. All three of her brothers played and an older boy from the village. There was suddenly an argument: fair-unfair etc, and it became quite hot. Clara's brother Martin was, like herself, prone to have fast flaring tempers and he lost his temper suddenly and just threw the knife and walked away. The knife went straight into Kurt's head.

And Kurt, too, died in an operation, the second one, to remove a malignant tumour on his brain. It happened on his 40th birthday. Everyone's arms full of flowers meant to shower him with after the operation, became the sweet lining of his coffin . . . Three years before - knowing already that he was seriously ill - he carried a gift of a cloak to Clara all the way from Columbia to wherever Clara was at the time. He had had it woven for her by a native Indian woman in finest handspun wool in the chequered pattern of the three natural colours of sheep's wool: black and white and brown. 'The Life-pattern', the Indians called it, so her brother told Clara. "After telling this wonderful wise Indian woman of you, it is this pattern that was seen by her as the one meant for you."

*   *   *   *

How much of the light and the dark and all the shades in between that make the fabric of our lives is woven for us by others . . .

Oh, could we but be aware that we are all weavers, weaving at the big loom together, weaving the cloth of life together.

In the first night at home, Clara has a dream: She is walking up some narrow steps alongside which a brook is dancing merrily. The trees are all in new-born leaf and the many greens are made translucent by the evening light. The Angelicas stand lush and tall beside the stream in the copse, and a Blackbird sings a jubilation to the sun just vanishing, but pouring everything with abundant golden light. An Albertine-rose tumbles its masses of rosebuds from a little meadow over a rickety fence into the narrow brook and beside it, an Elderberry is just come into blooming. Clara picks a blossom and crushes it in her hand. She will have to make Elderberry-blossom champagne again. Ha! how it quickens and runs like young love through the body! At the top of the lane, Clara encounters The Queen of May, a might and magnificence of a May-tree in full bloom. A magical bride . . . newly fallen snow . . . Clara follows her feet.

Brushing against the huge leaves of a Giant Rhubarb, she hears it whisper, 'Be watchful of every sign. Signs are signals. Go where your feet go.' She crosses a path, goes up a few steps and is in a large meadow. She reaches a high stone-stile. Standing on the topmost stone, her view is a vast circle, and land and sea and sky are in a transport of an unearthly light.

She walks across one meadow after another, stone-stiles connect them all. At the foot of the one, that leads her into a farmyard, she picks camomile; it makes a little pond there, and she carries it with her like a posy. She crosses a main road and finds another stone-stile and leaps from it into a field freshly rolled. But a-one-foot-before-another-path runs diagonally through it to a stile just visible in a hedge ahead. It is a little chilly. The sun has gone down entirely, and there is a hush of magic of a haze of pale blue over everything.

As Clara stands on the large flat stone of a very high stile, she hears the beautiful deep voice of a man singing the German Wander Vogel song 'Das Wandern ist des Muellers Lust, das Wandern. Das muss ein schlechter Mueller sein, dem niemals fiel das Wandern ein, das Wandern.' She cannot see anyone. But in the middle of the large square meadow of lush deep green grass stands a Standing Stone brightly lit by sunlight. There is no sunlight anywhere else. But the Stone stands in a Glory of Light.

It beckons! Clara runs to it. It's a Standing Stone! It's a Woman! It's a Goddess! . . . In awe, Clara stands in front of it and she lifts both arms and palms of hands towards it; she greets it as she greets the rising sun every morning.

Thomas, the farmer, is suddenly beside her. He takes her left hand and presses it on one place of the Stone. It is radiantly warm and Clara feels a throbbing as of a heart beating. "The Heart of the Stone, Clara, it is pulsating."

Thomas takes the right hand, too, and presses both her hands to the Stone "The Heart of the Stone, Clara, it is alive."

As he had appeared, so Thomas disappeared. Clara presses her whole body against the Stone holding it like a life in her embrace and feeling herself being irradiated through and through with light and warmth.

She stands back. The Stone is lightless now. But some gentle light is touching the highest tips of a spinney of mountain-pines in a distance towards the now rose-tinted evening sky to the east. Across the sea, one window-pane has caught the last of the sun.

Clara feels so one with all that is around her, as if she was fused with it. Lit up and luminous as the Stone had been, she is lifted by this force as if by wings, and she flies floats all the way home . . . But home is not the home she knows, but the Heart of a village she vaguely remembers.

It is The Heart, it is Home. - Is it a pre-vision of a life ahead?

This dream is written in Clara's red and gold notebook. And immediately after its entry it says, 'This then is what I must do, to hand myself over to the Unknowable Hugeness, *to Naught*.

'In deepest trust, empty-handed and without hold on to this or that, I must *leap* into the invisibility of the sea of mist, the

148

Unknown. Make myself void in readiness for the Void. - Amen.'
That is followed by, 'I pray for the strength and readiness to receive my Self and to be clear and open at the moment of conception of my Self by myself.

My will to merge with The Will.
My light to be absorbed in The Light.
My death to be born as Life.
My life to become Love.
Roots in Earth, firmly, deeply.
Roots in Heaven, firmly, deeply.
Roots in Heart, firmly, deeply.
Love become life become Love life live love Life:
Live and Love.
Live! and Love!
Amen.
So be it.
Praise be. Praise be. Praise be.
Death and Renewal!
The theme of my life. My life's music, if you will.
The tune, that makes my feet dance . . .'

Hallow Shadow! Welcome Shadow!

Enter, and be welcome. Make yourself at home!

Am I discovering, that it is you, that I must put my trust in? You, the Under-Miner? Dance with *you*? Dance *with* you? *Dance with* you?

Hold you close like a lover? You?

Ha! My shadow, my Beloved! Listen to this, all ye peoples! Listen! After a life of making out you don't exist - not in my life - to hail you as the source of my inspiration?

O, come then, come, let me hold you tight!

Enter! Penetrate! And let's make love as never love was made . . . And let there be born from our fusion a force!

A force, that will imperceptibly but with might enter each and everyone everywhere and make each and everyone everywhere wake up one morning and turn the palms of their hands to their eyes and ask, 'What am I doing with the gift of my life?'

JA! *What am I doing with the gift of my life?*

This question to be there early every morning at sunrise,

disturbing the self satisfaction, the sweet equilibrium of make-believe, the lovely 'that's the way it is', the nice and easy 'can't be helped I am only human'; of millions of people . . .

Hail to you Shadow! Dark one, come and be my bed-fellow! Come and be my Lover! Come and be my love!

On the third day after Clara had returned home, in the morning quite early, she had a welcome greeting by telephone from Zarah, "Welcome home, we are all overjoyed at having you back home again." But her cheer changed abruptly into a story of woe: how she was at the end of her tether, as her husband Marc was growing daily more unbearably jealous of her relationship with her two teenage daughters from a previous marriage. And how he indoctrinated their small son often against her, making her bad in his eyes. She ended up shrieking, "If you hear on the Local Radio tomorrow morning the news 'a woman stabbed her husband to death with a carving knife', that is me. I am at my wits end!"

Next morning, Zarah gave an account of what had happened. She did indeed stand over Marc, her husband, poised with the carving knife, freshly sharpened and ready to cut his throat. - "I sharpened it as sharp as a butcher's." - But it was her who started to scream, when she found Marc sitting there "like a bloody Christ, just like a bloody lamb ready for slaughter without a word, just sitting there dumb, quite still, not a budge, his eyes closed, allowing me to do with him whatever I wanted to do. It was unbearable, and I screamed so loud, that a neighbour from across the road could hear me and he came rushing in and quietly took the knife out of my hand. I broke down and wept. Then all three of us had a glass of wine, and we talked till the early hours, and it was decided that Marc and I must, for the best of all, live separately. So Marc will move out into his studio for the time being and then find a place of his own. The children were all three with a friend for the night. They must never ever hear the truth of what I was about to do to Marc!"

Another marriage in pieces that seemed to have been made in heaven. This couple had seemed to be so well together, so inspiring in one another's life and each seemed to be free to do what they love doing, Marc his sculptures, Zarah her work with small children. And there seemed to be that rare respect for one another's individual expression and being, so fundamental to an alive and beautiful relationship.

Surely, it could not all have been show . . . What did happen to break something that seemed so strong and so real?

Clara is shaken and suddenly afraid. The story of her friend brings her own marriage right into her eyes. Right in. But her marriage doesn't need to break, surely, *her* marriage was truly made in heaven.

It must die, Yes, as it is. It must die and newborn become a relationship, created by two people who, too, have died and been made new. The getting used to one another, the taking of one another for granted, both of which do not allow growth - this phenomena of movement and change - these are the killers.

To greet my Self as being new every morning like the day is new, and to greet as new the one I am in close relationship with on this new morning, too, we make new our relating on this new day.

Movement - Change - Growth - Beauty. Togetherness as dance. A new dance with every new day, for *all* is new on this new day. And Easter-morning is every morning in a life that is alive and in a relationship that lives.

Sitting in the small rock-strewn ancient meadow on a rock that stands high and allows her eyes to be wanderers, Clara ponders: What am I afraid of? Losing what? Afraid of life? Not afraid of life, surely? Afraid of what, then?

The sea has suddenly changed from slate to all the peacock colours. She hears He-She, the seagull, knocking the window . . . lifting her head, she sees her first swallow. And she spontaneously makes a cup with her hands and relives moments of a night, how long ago:

151

Clara had stepped out at midnight, as she was want to do in those days, to walk under the stars, to gather herself in and to harvest the silence from the immense silence of the night. On returning and entering her bedroom, she lights the candle as always. The sash-window had been wide open all day. Letting her eyes wander round the room delighting in the play of the shadows that the candle light makes, Clara discovers a ball, shining like a jewel in blue-gold in the light of the candle, lying on top of a pile of unironed washing brought in earlier that evening.

Going close, she discovers it to be a swallow, its head tucked under. She cups her hands around it like a shield. Her nearness wakens the bird and the head appears, and Clara receives a wink from a bright ebony eye, the light from the candle nearby making tiny golden stars in it. Clara whispers, "Swallow, Swallow, heavenly messenger of gladness. Thank you for coming to my room this night and for not being afraid."

Every now and then, the eyelid closes over the dark jewel, then opens once more and Clara and the Swallow look into one another. And then the head is tucked in for the night.

Peace. Deep Peace in the bedroom. Potent Peace.

Clara lies awake a long time. Her hands are lying on her heart. She flies with the Swallow the long hazardous flight across the sea and over the mountains to bring the sun to here from the Land of the Sun. Tonight, the Messenger of the Sun is in her bedroom. One night long, the heart of the Swallow is beating near by her beating heart. The two hearts are beating together through this summer's night.

The gladness of this fills her.

At dawn, the swallow wakens.

A last looking-in, one in the other, the Swallow and Clara, one in the other - and out the window she flies, clear out and high. Soaring high.

Clara is soaring high into the dawn . . . What a morning, with the Swallow's eye in mine and me become flight of the Swallow . . .

Ever and ever, the Swallow-Morning will be in my heart as gladness.

*   *   *   *

There is a tickling sensation on her neck, and something slithers inside her monk's cotton blouse into the sleeve, and into the still cupped hands tumbles a small lizard and lifting its dear head, eyes Clara.

Clara is in jubilation! A Lizard! She had not seen one for years. She whistled to it tunes as they came to her tongue, just as she had done in childhood on the Lizard Hill. One magical small hill - quite sacred, as it was known as a most ancient people's place - that was so deliciously rounded, that child Clara was sure the Earthfolk had their dwelling there as well as the Lizards. Thus whistling and humming, she entranced whole Lizard-Clans out of the Hill until she was surrounded by all these delightful little creatures who were spellbound by her tunes.

And here, today, is this one little Lizard sitting in the cup of her hands so very much at home. Delighting in it, Clara is transported back some 15 years.

Pitch, the cat, which her then six-year-old son had pulled out of a water pipe in which the starved little thing had been hidden in fright, when recovered, used to vanish into the surrounding wilderness for days and on returning, always lay a live offering at Michael's feet. One time, this was a lizard. The lizard was too stunned to move and looked quite without life. But lying there, it soon got warmed through by the sun and eyed its surroundings. As it slithered away, Michael's sister, Maya, not yet three, said: "Look, look, the sun alived it."

The Swallow unafraid and the Lizard alived . . .

Adam is suddenly beside Clara. She is startled. She was reading a letter, which had tumbled out of a volume of poetry, that she had pulled out of a bookshelf in her room earlier in the morning. She had put it into the large pocket in her skirt and forgotten about it. After the lizard had slithered off her hands, she remembered it. Two pressed flowers were stuck to the paper by the delicate stamens and in the folding they had imprinted them-selves to the letter. No date on the letter. Just 'Friday'.

'Darling,

I walked barefoot over the fields with the sun upon my face in the lush summer grass and over the hot stones by the riverside and in the cool of the river itself - and O I wanted you to be at my side to share the silence, the space, the burn of the sun.

I have nothing to tell you but this, but it is so much . . . Adam.'

It was like Heimweh, and Clara was quietly weeping.

"You received a letter this morning?"

"Yes, it's taken a long time in reaching me."

"Who is it from?"

"One named Adam."

And Clara reads the letter aloud.

"Things change, Clara, you must learn to accept that."

- It is always I who has to accept. Please do not give me one of your sermons.

And aloud Clara says, "I cannot accept that things change to become less, much less, than what they were to begin with." And she emphasises her words by a vigorous spiral movement of her hands. She reads the last two lines again. 'O I wanted you to be at my side to share the silence, the space, the burn of the sun. I have nothing to tell you but this, but it is so much.'

"Why should not the much be much mucher now after so much daily sharing of these many years of our togetherness? I must *accept* change, *see* the reality of a situation, *become* aware of this and that . . . do you, Adam, ask the same of yourself?

"Words spoken - words lived! - When I was about ten, I said to my father after one of his eloquent word-pourings, 'Father, make your words flesh.' I earned a smite on each cheek by one that had never slapped anyone before. And later in the day, I received the gift of a brand new bicycle with gears, a great novelty at the time.

"I accept change as an inner reality, not as something that happens like an affliction from outside. I accept it as becoming, growing, aliving, so that the silence spoken of in that letter of long ago, is now a silence that penetrates this relationship *now*. Words are become gestures of the heart, glances become words unspoken. A communication so present and real and spontaneous, that the one is in communion with the other at any one moment, willed or unwilled, spoken or unspoken. The very air we breathe in is life and love.

"I must speak this once. *I must.* I feel that in your eyes, I have let you down. The one that you wanted at your side at the moment of which the letter speaks, I have never been able to live up to.

"I must live and fulfil that which I am meant to be in this earth-given life. *I must!* It is ever more urgent in me to do so. *I cannot* exist to be an image that someone has made of me. However beloved the someone maybe. I cannot! It is the love for my Self that I must build and in the building grow to be fulfilled in the meaning that my journey on this earth this time round has. There is no other way for me. I knew this terribly early in my life. I knew it before I knew.

"You once said, in an awful undone moment of our together-ness *'Our love is!'* Well, I say my love is and will always be. But I cannot, *can not* anymore hand my life over, *I have to live it to the full.*

"You stand aloft and aloof, as though the daily life had nothing to do with *your* life, as though you had arrived in a high place not to be reached by an ordinary mortal. I say that the truly spiritual man is the one, who is hugely, deeply, highly, broadly immersed in life and is alive as life itself is alive.

"And this *is*, what my life is meant to be. To be vibrantly alive even in my stillness and to drink the moment like wine. Life and Love belong together. Love is alivest life, that state of being, when the word has become flesh and does not need to be spoken anymore.

"JA! A State of being! It is not I anymore, nor this or that, but Being! - Sein! A German word I have always been deeply fond of.

"You talk down to me about Experiencing, the Now, Centring, all this jargon! I say to you, Adam, step down from your head into your feet! You got very wide feet. They are meant for walking.

"I have nothing more to tell you but this, but it is so much. Signed Clara."

The delicious cup of coffee that Adam had carried out to Clara on the rock had become stone cold. But Clara felt warmed through and wonderfully relieved. - It had been a long time, since she had spoken openly.

*　　*　　*　　*

A flock of birds is flying over from the west. Marvellous uplifting sound the wings of a flock of birds. For the small spell of an eye-lids flicker you become Niels Holgerson flying with them.

Marvellous! So many wings! The wind! The wind!

- Der Wind, der Wind, das himmlische Kind - Farther in the eastern sky, the birds look as though a gigantic hand had scattered large lightful seeds.

Hands full of light into the light . . .

Strange, watching these birds brings to Clara's ears these words 'Dear meandering heart, you must forgive yourself.'

Clara feels Adam's hand on her head and hears him say, "I am sorry."

Less than a month later, Clara found herself back in Mental Hospital.

Never ever did she remember the journey there, but always, that she woke up in a small barren room, which in her mind became the mortuary. She tried to move, but her body was stiff. An abominable fear made everything black, and she screamed. But no sound came out of her. Horrible thoughts of having been mistaken for dead were flashing like lightning all around her.

However, that tiny little speck of awareness, the light of a fire fly, was there and called out 'Breathe!' 'Breathe deeply.' And with the first real out-breath, she knew, momentarily, that she was in a hospital room. Momentarily, there was some relief.

But questions tumbled over her: how did she get here? Who brought her here? Why? What had she done? Was she out of her mind?

And then, the moment of light was snatched by a huge hand coming close and snatching it. And in the sound of devilish-scornful laughter, a wall came down in front of her and the air became thick, thickening her fear. And her breathing was in tiny frightened snatches. The wall came closer, and it was suffocating. All of her body was stiff as a board.

But again, a glow-worm size light brought a speck of clarity to Clara and she heard herself read: 'When Toad found himself immured in a dank and noisome dungeon, and knew that the grim darkness of a medieval fortress lay between him and the outer world of sunshine . . .' 'Sunshine'. Clara shouted it. But no shout was heard. And she read on 'Sudden and magnificent, the sun's broad golden disc showed itself over the horizon . . . Dulce Domum, Dulce Domum . . . Prima Lux . . . Prima Lux . . .

There was a Clara lying there stiff as a board and blotted out with fear and another one inhabiting her, who, although also removed from the reality of the space and time of her Self and the day, nevertheless was in small instant glimpses aware of herself as *I alive*, but as another.

God help, where was she, Clara, the whole one . . . And she heard her own voice say, 'This time she was removed from the border of sanity to an impenetrable dark Hinterland.'

But no one spoke.

Then the wall, as though on a swivel, swivelled to an horizontal position and came slowly, very slowly down on her. And Clara watching it and saying, 'Fear, fear is the basis of everything. Fear instead of Love.'

Clara, as well as feeling that she was being suffocated, experienced the belly-sinking fear that always came over her in a descending lift - was she in a lift out of control? Where was she? In a crashing aeroplane?

There was a very fast movement downwards, and she was being slowly suffocated by something heavy on top of her. And that sinking, sagging feeling - speechless fear - was taking her over.

Whatever she was travelling in crashed and broke.

Her world was split down the middle and between the two bits was a wide deep dizzy abyss. Clara stood on the one side that was barren like a desert, eery in its deathly silence and awful stillness. Across, as though she was looking through binoculars the wrong way round, a long distance away, she saw a version of her Self in golden sunlight in amongst tropical growth. A bright shining Self moving like water, like wind.

Somewhere within her, in a sudden moment, Clara understood that, that which had crashed and had split was herself and that the tangible one, the one within the physical body was in a banishment and that the place of banishment was a cavern within her Self. A dank place in which fierce light lit up a cauldron, where Clara's fears and bits of unlived life were boiling wildly and bubbling, and foaming and threatening to flow over and drown her, unless she stirred the stinking mass ceaselessly with the large leaden-weight wooden spoon. One or the other time, daring to lift her head, she had a glimpse of the other one - like a teasing - recognised as her split off Self - seeing her dancing, joying, moving like water, like wind, shining like the star in the morning before sunrise and radiating her surroundings with the gentle light of the dawn.

But at once with a jerk, Clara was back at her miserable task relentlessly, ceaselessly stirring the foul smelling contents of the cauldron in a fierce and suffocating heat.

Somewhere within her, it was known that there is no choice but to persevere, to submit to the unyielding force, that she was in the grip of.

She! She had no face, no name. She was at once the one that had to stir this stinking decomposing mass, the foulness of which choked her throat and made her gasp for breath and she was the mass and the cauldron, too.

She! There was no She. There was something that was being willed to be disintegrated.

And dis-integrate 'She-It' did. 'She-It' became a no-thing in a no-man's-land. A non-being in a lightless silence.

In whose hands was 'She-It'? Was She? Was It? Were there hands to hold?

'She-It' was contained in a silence, in a stillness, a moveless mass . . ?

*   *   *   *

158

And was there a silent, nameless force at work, which allowed a pinhead-size light in, which came through a pinhead-size hole through which in a split of a moment, in a flash of awareness, could be seen a far, far distance away, a one, she herself, the whole one, lit up and shining and moving?

Alive?

And in this flash of awareness, a yearning filled the absent, the non-being. It filled it so full, to bursting full. A yearning for to *be*. To be in time and place and communion with another. And then at once nothing again. No thing. Blank. A stillness of frozen horror. No movement.

Nothing.

Not having been in it, you cannot grasp my words, not what they are saying, not what they mean and tell and describe.

And again and again, like pain, this fierce awareness of a self alive. Seeing this through a quick and sudden minute opening, a little hole the size of a fly's mark on a newly shined window-pane. Through this a peep of a 'me-alive', like looking in into heaven for a spit's moment, then the pain of having seen, then the fear of never ever to be again. Then nothing.

The No-Thing: not aware of dark, not aware of light. Not aware. No voice. No movement.

Fathom it, if you can. This for weeks maybe, maybe for months. Goaded like one damned in moments of light that came like a devilish teasing to the shapeless nameless mass 'She-It'.

- Ah! but the seed must needs fall in the earth and perish there and in the perishing *is* the new life.

The perishing then is at once the death and the resurrection.

* * * *

159

Do not, then, O All-Knowers, *do* not, do not throw your all-knowing hands in! Let the perishing be! Let it happen! Stand by in awe and in prayer and hold my hands and stroke my head.

It is the mystery: the life is in the perishing. Right in it. And there is the whole new life. Waiting, waiting for the sound of the trumpet!

Allow me this complete and utter removal from the norm, from every day, from everything, from myself.

Allow me to be this, seemingly, unconscious mass, that is before the seed, before the egg. Allow me to be it.

Do not call me incurably insane simply because you are baffled out of your wits at the sight of me.

For listen! It is an early time of gestation. I am in a womb again. I am back in a womb. I am being fired a second time in the hot heat of the kiln of becoming.

A state of being, as it may be, that happens to befall all growing things at one time or another. - So still. So secluded from the outside. So guarded from all that may disturb it in its essential beginning of becoming that, which in essence it is.

The Self is becoming itself, integral and whole.

A Death becoming Life.

Death dancing with Life.

And awareness holds me and guides me of which I am not aware. I am not allowed to be aware of. For what happens in this state of non-being is not to be known. Never.

It is the mystery of life itself.

All growing happens in silence in dark places, in stillness and comes from nameless mass, consciousless mass. Yet, consciousness is at work.

The fire is the mystery.

Who lights it?

Who feeds it?

Who keeps it going?

Please, do not with drugs extinguish it!
Please do not with electric shock destroy its kernel!
Please, honour the nameless, seemingly unconscious mass that I am. For in it, ignorant All-Knowers, I am being fired for a second time to become that which I am meant to be.

I am in the inner most holy space of the temple that I am. I am there on my own perish or live!

Pray, *pray* dear Sirs. do not pry!

Later, Clara found in the recesses of herself, that there was no memory of the actual hospitalisation of that time, of how she ate, slept, spent the days or was in relation to others. But the state of being that she had been in, she could find somewhere within herself and look at it.

It was confirmed to Clara later by one of the Psychiatrists who had become a friend, that during many weeks there was absolutely no response to anything or anyone and that one came to the conclusion of incurable insanity. Adam was therefore urged on three occasions to give his signature, as the electric shock treatment seemed now the only possible chance to bring some life back.

Adam refused to sign. He remembered - so well this once, Heaven be thanked - how Clara had, many years before, told him of this insight she had had in the presence of just such absence of the soul as she had been in, that the fire of life was burning on, albeit no sign was given outwardly. But as in a coma of the body, the coma of the soul was a time of gestation and *must* be honoured.

*   *   *   *

When I am in a coma of the body or the soul, both are eclipsed. So hold my hands in yours and never let go and stroke gently, lovingly my head as you would a beloved child's, kiss the sole of my feet and embrace my ankles, touch with the pointing finger of your right hand, every now and then, the place where my third eye slumbers. Tell me beautiful stories. Recite poems. Sing songs.

You see, somewhere inside me, this loving will be received. This current of your loving will be received and be transformed and be made into life.

When Clara finally emerged, it was like a great morning's awakening from a deep and wholesome sleep. And no memory at all was there, of where she had been. It was as though she had been thrust, as a shoot is thrust, through the crust of the earth into the day.

And at once Clara's eyes were held by a postcard lying on her bedside table on top of a pile of post. A reproduction of a painting by her beloved friend and soul-sister Flora.
'Spring Force is the name of this painting and it is the name I give you, Clara, when I think of you. - Love, always, Flora.'

What a greeting on waking!
Flora had shunned Clara, almost from the moment that her mind had wandered into dark spaces. In lucid and clear moments, Clara felt her soul-sister's distance like a pain of abandonment and yet she could see; that her abrupt and unforeseen mental break up bewildered and filled with fear precisely those of her friends who were innerly close to her. As it did all the dear, oh, so dearest members of her family.
She became Taboo - the name given a person who has been set apart, being either sacred or accursed.

If your mother or wife or best friend has cancer, you speak of it, but if your mother or wife or best friend is in Mental Hospital, you keep it quiet or you whisper it and you look straight in front of you, lest someone might ask you the pertinent question. You dissociate yourself, even if the mad person is your mother or your wife or your deepest friend, for the disturbance it causes *you* is all too disturbing.

O, but could you, all of you out there, you sane and complete ones, you full of vim and vigour ones and you all-knowing ones be aware, for a moment only, that I am still a human being, and not a monstrous aberration. And that, having fallen off the accepted norm, having been split and dismembered, having become mad, I have merely gone out of my mind to enter The Mind, not as I or person, but as son - sound.

Sound rejoins The Sound from hence it originally came to be re-fired, re-fined, re-newed, re-turned and re-composed.

Re-lit! Son est Lumière: Sound is Light.

Do not abandon me. Do not judge me. Do not harden your senses with fear. But rather be with me in thought and in prayer and in touch. For I am in the chaos that is before logos, the word, but which is the impetus for the word that gives form and for this form to be re-formed and to be re-lit. *A process of initiation.* Which cannot but take place in the inner of inners, where in deepest secret and seclusion, the forces of creation are at work.

A lightless place? Or is it a place, where light is so concentrated that it becomes light-less, seemingly so . . ?

Here, in a no-thing, a no-doing, no-experiencing, no-willing, a state of being in the hands of what, of whom? In the hands of a force? The very force of growing and becoming of life itself . . ?

- Behold the Source. It is above and below.
   It receives and It gives.

But Clara, on this morning of her return, was not as wide awake as Olaf Aesterson had been awake after his long sleep, in which he had travelled through under and overworlds and now, fully awake and new, was able to tell all and sundry of what had been given him to see and to hear in his thirteen-day slumber.

During her 'absence', Clara had been as she was now, treated with drugs, three different kinds three times daily. She could hear and see now, but her mind was rather blank. She could not fully take in all that was being said in the pile of post that she now was reading, but somewhere within her, there was a harvester, that gathered these transmissions and from where she received a kind of warmth. And that was like an assurance 'Yes, I exist.' And that was good. And Clara did look around her and partake in the everyday somewhat. That was something.

Adam's visit is announced. Clara brushes her hair. Although her hand is clumsy and unwilling, she brushes her hair a long time. From the small wardrobe, out of the few garments, she chooses a full length frock in the pale blue, that sometimes miraculously appears over sea and land on an evening after sunset in late summer or early autumn. It has, all around the wide hemline, printed in gold, the tree-of-life pattern.

Clara is both apprehensive and expectant. When she is looking in the mirror, the only one in the clinic, she wonders whose face she is looking at. "If I am wondering if this is my face I am seeing in there, will Adam recognise it as mine? Will he want to recognise it?"

It is cool in the corridor where Clara is waiting. Her dress is cool. But sweat pours out of her. She is afraid.

Adam comes. And with him is a glamorous woman. She walks just a little behind him. Clara's feet are lead. She stands struck, like a pillar of salt. The choke in her throat tightens. And in her heart is singing a morbid song 'murder me softly, murder me softly with your love . . .' And standing like a monument in front of her speechlessness is Adam cheerfully introducing Anita,

164

"Who could not possibly return to the States without having seen you."

The words pile up in Clara and she cannot say them: 'The mockery! Why, Adam, are you doing this to me? Why bringing this woman here from a yet undigested past, when it is difficult enough for me to face and meet you alone, deformed in body and soul as I am? Adam, your cruelty has no limits. What are you punishing me for?'

"Come, Clara, are you ready? Is this what you are going to wear? We are going sight-seeing."

There is such animation in Adam's voice, excitement, even. "Anita wants to see some of the places associated with Tristan and Iseult. I have permission to take you out. Surely, you want to come with us?"

There is a place there at Tintagel, remember, a little cove, quite magical, where quietly and unnoticed, you can walk into oblivion.

With this macabre summons repeating itself over and over in her ears, Clara finds herself in the backseat of Adam's car. She does not see anything. The two in the front seat are very absorbed.

On arrival they are so taken over by one another, that they forget about Clara. And she quietly slips away and turns into the path to the cove.

She takes off her shoes and her stockings. And she walks into the water. As she is knee-deep, it is not fear that overtakes her, but a sudden vision of herself as her Self comes to her and the words 'you are building yourself, your own life and you do not depend on another. Let the tide wash away your old Self, not your life. Your true life is yet to be. You haven't lived.'

And as Clara stands on the edge of the tide, only her feet gently lapped by the sea, floating straight to her and lain down right by her toes, is a small beautifully shaped snow white tree. It has no roots, but forms a small, pure round base on which it stands.

"The Tree of Life! The Tree of Life!" Clara shouts it, holding this sea-given symbol like a Godsend in her hands. She is overwhelmed and weeps and laughs and shouts: "Thank you, Angel of the sea for this gift. *I know now, I must live to live.*"

And she kisses the small white sea-born tree in her hands, and

165

she blows kisses to the invisible Sea-Angel.

Then she suddenly feels violently sick, and she vomits and vomits. It is as though she had to vomit the hell out of her.

Something huge is happening to her. The sea's sounds have now become a chant. No words now.

But holding the small white tree in both hands in front of her, Clara walks out of the cove, rich with promise and upright. The soaked dress is heavy round her legs. Up the winding path she walks slowly, as if she was heading a procession.

'You are on the verge of your life now, now, at this moment! Rejoice!'

The sea, the wind, the ragged rock-strewn land around her are a choral singing this. Clara singing it in her heart carrying in her hands tenderly the great gift of the sea, the gentle little white tree.

Who hears your voice on high and
Who down in the deep . . .
Who knows all of you, more than
You will ever know . . .
Who throws the life-line down from
on high, up from down deep . . .
Who hears the cry for help that you
have not even shouted . . .
Whose ears up on high, down in the
deep . . .

Is the Angel of Hell the Angel
of Light also . . .
Is the Angel of Death the Angel
of Life also . . .

It is not long after, that the Psychiatrists decided that Clara was recovered well enough to return home. Just the one drug,

Lithium, was given on her way and lots of good wishes and a letter to her GP, with whom she must make an immediate appointment.

Ah! but I have an appointment with Life! This is the real appointment. How to keep it? The Lithium is hindering the very vitality of my life. It keeps my mind at a drab level. Not harmony, not balance, level! Not rhythm, movement, dance, life!
- Who the hell wants to be level!
There are plenty, who are kept that way and don't mind, *are* not to mind. Besides, my hair is falling out alarmingly and the roots of my teeth are being dissolved and the bones in my whole body are starting to rattle. Lithium, a natural salt harvested in some mountains or other, so my GP tells me, but in the form given me, it is most unnatural to my body. I call it the Grey Squirrel, as it demands supremacy over all the other minerals so vital to my health. And it somehow causes them to be washed out and so the blood fights to find the sustenance it needs in bones and hair and teeth. My mouth is a mess of loose and painful teeth, dreadful sore gums, a split tongue that hurts and cannot taste anything, and the roof of the mouth is inflamed! And my mind is level!
Who calls this living . . . God help me.

I have to live! I need to live! What else is the meaning of my life? Any life, for that matter.

Clara is talking to herself. She is talking to the walls, the air, the grass under her feet. She is in a dilemma.
Every week, the level of lithium is being tested. If she dared to take less than the prescribed amount, it would be noticed at once and all ears would prick! 'Want to go back to Mental Hospital, now that you are doing so nicely?'
'Nicely'. The word causes my very guts to scream. 'Be good', 'be nice', 'be kind'. Not: 'have joy', 'have fun'. Not: 'live, live, live woman, live! Clara live, for God's sake, live!'
And she hears all the experts voices, 'Once on lithium, always

on lithium.'

Clara does not believe this at all. On the contrary, somewhere within her, she knows much better than that. But the GP says it, all the Psychiatrists say it, and even a Naturopathic Healer with the highest qualifications blows the same out-worn trumpet.

She says, "I can help you with the side-effects caused by Lithium with my herbal remedies, but not without the knowledge of your GP and your Psychiatrist." - Hells, bells, it's all one gigantic plot!

Life has to be kept level, it is too dangerous let loose . . .

Clara suddenly leaps up from the hump of grass she was sitting on. Sunlit thistle-down is floating on the wind. Sunlit-silver-light-spheres. The minute brown body - the eye-shaped seed - is hung fragilely, but oh, so godly well from the ethereal parachute made up of radiant hairy rays: a gladness of pure light.

Clara joins in the magical dance of the sailing thistle-down, catching one or the other of these floating wonders. One chooses to somersault off the palm of her hand, up her bare arm and off on to her blouse, where it clings. Clara blows gently on it, and it floats away. She opens her palms to the breeze, so that the thistle-down is caught on them, and there is laughter in her and delight.

She is wondering at so much light in such a small unearthly thing, and how the brown of the seed becomes gold, when the sunlight falls on it. And she is made aware of the palms of her hands, of the radiance of light that is there, how light-filled the lines are and how very different one palm is from the other. Each a radiant miraculous landscape. Her life written there in hiero-glyphs, as the sea writes its life in the sand or the birds in their flight in the air.

One thistle seed is left in the palm of Clara's left hand. A little brown forlorn naked thing. The silver-lit parachute floats away carelessly . . .

She wonders and ponders on the two opposite forces, that are at work in the thistle-down and the seed suspended from it and transported by it: the thistledown light-ness, its levity - the anti-gravity - so to speak and the gravity of the seed . . .

The one *and* the other to fulfil the purpose of the seed.

A dance of light and time.

A ring-a-ring-around of the ethereal and the substantial . . .
An endless play of the light-ness and the dark-ness . . .
Forces concentrated into a point, the seed, earthward bound;
forces radiating outward into the plane, the parachute, heaven-
ward bound . . .
This and that in a forever changing.
And never the same. Not twice the same ever, but based in the
same unaltered simplicity - Einfachheit - that was from the
beginning.

Adam received a phone call to be involved in the making of a
film, which had been in the offing for some time; and within a
few hours he was packed and gone. "For a few months, for a year,
maybe," he said.
"Bye darling. I'll be in touch."

Clara is not thrown about by this. She does not feel anything
this way or that way. The electric current is kept so low by the
drugs, that whatever is being transmitted by the outside world or
even the world of her within, is barely being received. The
receiver is off the hook, so to speak. The watcher, the guardian
and the harvester are there somewhere, however cowed, and once
in a while, one or the other is able to make himself heard as
warning or confirming: 'Get off the levelling-drug, so you can
make your way into your own light,' or: 'take advantage, it is
your own life now.'
But no council is given of how to go about it.

Then, one early morning, Adam had been gone but a short
while, a call came from the Mental Hospital that Clara must at
once reduce by half the amount of lithium tablets taken and that
this is urgent. - No explanation. - Within three days, Clara was
plunged into a state of total worthlessness, emptiness, hollow-
ness. And indeed, she called herself 'The Hollow Woman.'
That *was* her name now.

*   *   *   *

h

What sense there might have been in her life, vanished. What little life there might have been was gone. There was no more meaning within her or in the world without her. She could not receive anything or give anything. And there was no sense in keeping herself by eating and sleeping.

When seeing the psychiatrist by special appointment to urgently help her out of this hollow place, he was at a loss. He could not help. Clara had to see it through, he said. And, "You will be all right in the end."

"But doctor, you pushed me into this hollow."

"It will be all right in the end."

Later, Clara saw a young assistant, a woman psychiatrist. And she asked her directly, why the lithium was reduced and why this had such devastating consequences. "Lithium affects the electro-magnetic field in the cells, the vital part of the cell. It is a most powerful drug and must be carefully monitored. If there is too much in the blood, you might fall into a coma from which you might not wake up. And once the cells have been interfered with in this way, bewilderment is caused in the body's communication system, where everything is interdependent and delicately balanced."

When Clara confronted her main psychiatrist with this news and said that it was frightening to see that none of them really knew what they were doing or undoing with these drugs given, as was clearly shown by what had happened to her, he was obviously disturbed, that Clara should have such inside informa-tion. - She never saw the young woman psychiatrist again, who had indeed been the rare one to have had some interest in Clara as an individual person and who had given time to listen and had been open to questions. And above all, she had brought some understanding into a situation.

Clara was in a hollow. She was this hollow. She was hollow.

And there was no help. None from the outside. None from within herself. Nobody was there. Nothing was there. Everything was without meaning. Herself had no meaning.

She was The Hollow Woman.

One Sunday morning, The Hollow-Woman left her home and walked up the hill and out on to the cliff path. There was no one on the cliff at this hour. Hollow Woman can vanish without a trace.

She made it onto a ledge of a steep rock-face quite high above the sea, where in better times she had often been tempted to fly off from. This urge to fly, simply open her arms and fly, she had had on mountain tops, too.

She started to count aloud to make it quite clear to herself, that by three she would not fly, but leap into death's open arms. One 'two', arms fold around her, gently.

"Clara, how wonderful to see you on this early Sunday morning, it's been quite a few years." A man's voice. Clara turns round.

"I am not Clara. I might have been once, I am The Hollow Woman now, a worthless, empty life to be thrown over the cliff."

A young pregnant woman steps forward: "I am David's wife Elisabeth, he has often spoken of you. No, no, you are not hollow. On the contrary, you are beautiful and there is a light all over you, and I can see that you are full of riches. I have so much wanted to meet you. Come, let's go back to the village, and I shall stay with you."

The Hollow-Woman steps down from the ridge and stands in front of the young couple. "Knock here," she says, pointing to her head. "Knock and you hear hollow, hollow, hollow. - Knock here," pointing to her heart. "Knock, and you hear hollow, hollow, hollow." - "Knock here," pointing to her solar plexus. "Knock and all you hear is hollow, hollow, hollow." And she shouts, "Hear it, hollow, hollow, hollow." And she laughs a gargoyle's laughter, "The Hollow Woman I am and there is no help for me but to end it over the cliff."

"Come, do not talk like this. It is not true. I see you as you truly are, radiant with life. Come."

And Elisabeth and David take The Hollow Woman by the hand and bring her back to her home.

Elisabeth stayed with Clara for many weeks and at the beautifully prepared and served meals, David joins them.

"It reminds me of those years ago, Clara, when as a young, unknown and rather starved painter you opened your doors so generously to me. I have often told Elisabeth, how through you, I have learned to appreciate that the most simple of meals can be a feast and is a celebration. And you said once 'my kitchen sink is my shrine.' Only much later, I understood this to mean that the most humble of tasks like preparing food, like washing dishes, are like an offering. When I said to you, you live so very differently from anyone I know, you said, 'that I live like a lover is a gift from my mother. For her everything was alive and whatever she did was a thanksgiving, and she lived accordingly.' "

Elisabeth massaged the stiff and knotted body of Clara's daily and gave her a bath fragrant with oil of Rosmarin in the morning and a soothing Lavender-oil bath in the evening. She took her for walks and outings in her car. And she made every effort to make Clara see that there is meaning in her and all around her. It was a most patient task. For what Elisabeth might have thought to have brought about by her patience and abiding, like a small crack through which Clara could momentarily see and affirm: 'Yes, someone *is* there and it *is* worthwhile to persevere in rediscovering this someone;' this might by the evening or the next morning have vanished and the fixed and helpless Hollow Woman was all present again.

Clara could hear when David talked about all the wonderful things that he had been made aware of in those far off days, when he had stayed for some months in her home. But she could not take it in, that it had anything to do with her.

For there was no one home.

If her own being had caused this state of being 'The Hollow Woman', the flow of love that came through and from Elisabeth might have been able to bring about a quickening, an aliving. But

172

as Clara had been drugged for so long and indeed this 'fall' had been caused directly through the sudden drastic reduction of lithium intake, the situation was an artificial one, that the psychiatrists more than ever were helpless about. So what could Elisabeth appeal to, when literally 'no one was home'?

And her faith and trust in Clara's recovery must have been shaken badly, when one early morning, Clara came dishevelled to her bed shouting, "I cannot see my face in the mirror, only a hand waving good-bye. Now I haven't got a face anymore, look, I haven't got a face anymore. I am finished."

And Clara ran down the stairs out of the house, down the steep granite steps at the end of the lane and over the jagged rocks at flying speed, intent to finish the already finished.

In her nighty and barefoot, Elisabeth caught up with Clara and sat her on a rock and sat down beside her. And she took Clara's right hand and lifted it up to her face and made the hand move over the face gently, tracing, as it were, every bit of it as a blind person might discover the face of a beloved one. Elisabeth did that with the left hand too, and again with the right hand and the left hand. Until Clara was able to say, "There is a face there, but is it *my* face?"

"It is *your* face, Clara, and it is beautiful and full of promise."

This wonderful gesture of Elisabeth's made a breakthrough. A ray fell in and touched a vital point, so that during breakfast Clara suddenly said, "I think this is Clara eating breakfast."

"Hurrah," Elisabeth shouted and she leaped up and took Clara in her arms. A long warm embrace. And a flow came up through Clara's feet and gradually filled her.

"I am home again," Clara said. "Let's ring the bells." - And the two women went through the house ringing the bells. Tibetan temple bells, goats bells from Greece, bells from the Andes, bells from India. Bells, bells. And the two women were ringing and the whole house was ringing and bells were ringing and all the spaces were filling with winged sound.

And Clara had a connection with her Self again.
Her Name was Clara again.

To help her further in this new affirmation and to confirm her in it, Elisabeth took Clara to a woman-healer, who had as a girl of seven discovered her gift of healing.

Outside her home a dog had been run over and was left for dead, as no heart-beat could be found. But the little girl pulled him into her lap and held him there and prayed, and the dog revived.

She was by now known even in circles of conventional medicine and was called in by doctors to diagnose, in which she was particularly gifted, also to give healing at the bedside to hospitalised patients.

Elisabeth herself had received much help at a time of terrible self-doubt and depression. 'In her healing presence, which truly radiates, it is as though knots were undone, blockages freed and heavy became light.'

Rose, the healer, has the presence of an early Spring day. It is a transforming energy that she is gifted with. The muddy water that you are becomes clear as a spring.

Recalling the encounter with Rose later, Clara said that it felt as though her whole being had been stood under a gentle rain and then was being penetrated by gentle and delicious sun rays that made her feel clear as a crystal. She said, "I was in the presence of love."

And it was, when still in the presence of this truly beautiful woman, that Clara had her first insight, only like a flash, of how misbegotten it was to use radio-active treatment. This artificially

174

produced highly dangerous radiation which never heals and at best cures and causes so much destruction, devastation and pain, when it is love, that is the true radio-active force.

Love, the healer, that orders, where there is disorder.
Love, the healer, that arrays, where there is disarray.
Love, the healer, that restores the vital current, where it has been cut.
Love the healer, that makes harmony, where there has been disharmony.

"All that you are undergoing now," said Rose, "is preparing you for a life that you have yet to live on this earth-round. In so far as we are being healed, we may bring healing to others. You are and have been and yet will be put through many fires to become strong in yourself and clear in your expression.

"As I see you, you have a huge gift to communicate, and it is this wonderful instrument, that is being tuned through these many years of illness and suffering. Understand that all illness is given, and that it is given to allow you to align yourself anew to your Self and the world, as well as to create a new relationship between body, mind and soul.

"Could all illness, be it of body, mind or soul, be seen in this light, as turning-point and a challenge, how different would be our standing in it and how drastically different the attitude of those that are appointed to help."

Rose gave Clara faith in herself and affirmed Clara in this, that she never had had a sick mind or tarnished soul, but that she must see it all as a passage in her journey, a kind of Odyssey of Self-discovery, during which she has been and yet will be tried by many trials. But enriched and matured by the adventures, she will be landing where she had started and be ready and strong for the life that was to be her own.

"You have wonderful guidance and guardianship, which will

see you through and help you to safe anchorage in the harbour of your destiny, which is the harbour you sailed out from at the beginning of your voyage. You will disembark and know your work, as you will find strength and clarity in unison in your self, an inner harmony, and your great gifts of creativity flowing."

By meeting Rose, Clara's will is ignited. This fire-force that is so vital in the process of living and the growing of the awareness. So important to her in particular that she needs to earth herself, that is, to listen to her feet. To listen and to rhyme with the Earth's rhythm.

Ah! to be thus alert and awake!
Imagine! to be threaded thus by the Earth's and Heaven's threads!
Imagine! to be alight thus with Earth's and Heaven's fires!
Imagine! to be gladly and lightly the seed again and again . . .
Imagine! to push through and out into the light, the shoot . . .

Clara was regaining the vision of herself again and in her was growing a dream again.

She suddenly remembers her son Michael as a little boy of five coming from his bed one morning sobbing, "I don't have the dream anymore, it has fallen out of me!" and how this sorrow and heartbreak of her small son had hit her right in the middle of herself: had the dream not fallen out of her too . . ?

By the encounter with the healer Rose, Clara receives a glimpse of how the imbalance within herself is also an imbalance of herself to the Earth and the All, and that to be out of tune with one's Self is also falling out of step and tune with The Tune, The Dance.

*　　*　　*　　*

In a flash, Clara understands, that she 'was sent' on this hazardous journey to truly discover her spiritual nature and find the key to the store of the secrets and riches of her unconscious and to become a master-builder. Who, with truly gifted hands not only builds himself but skills others.

Flash of insight.
Flash of insight.
Flash of insight.

But the wild goose doesn't fly ready and cooked into your mouth.

The red thread that runs through a life and seemed to have been cut or torn is threading her life again. Clara has dreams. On three consecutive nights a dream is given.

First Night: I am standing on top of a steeply sloping narrow path. The sea is raging below in a high incoming tide. My arms are wide to wind and sea. A feeling of exhilaration is over me and there is laughter in me.

Then the sighting of a man struggling for his life, one moment clearly visible, the next moment gone.

An old man, sea-foam white hair and beard. I run down to rescue and half-way down into my arms flies a baby-boy. He reaches for one of my breasts and starts to suckle and laughs and says 'You are too old, it doesn't flow' and he leaps off and runs helter-skelter down the path. I after him. A huge wave swallows both of us.

I am washed ashore, feeling invigorated, young, new.

Second Night: In this dream, that begins the same way, I throw myself into the raging sea to rescue the old man, but instead of allowing me to rescue him, he is pulling me down into the turbulence of the wild sea.

Later, I find myself sitting above the becalmed sea miraculously young and rejuvenated with the radiant baby-boy suckling my overspilling breast.

Third Night: All happens the same at the beginning, but I actually rescue the old man. However, at the very moment that he is out of the raging sea, he changes into the beautiful baby-boy. And putting him to my breast, he flows into me as a powerful force of transformation and I am a rejuvenated, glorious woman.

Each of these dreams reaches into Clara's days. She carries them with her. They seem meaningful.
A process of whole-y-ing . . ?

She feels encouraged into her own life. She throws the lithium away. Down the loo 'here you go, who needs crutches!' She wants to give herself into her own hands and be out of the grip and grasp of drugs and doctors and psychiatrists.

Clara experiences a gradual lightening of herself. Body, mind and soul: lighter. And daily she grows in light. And she comes to understand that she does not own anything, nor her life, but that she is in a kind of mercy, in a grace, that in all her doing, thinking and being she must answer in kind.

With every morning, more light is in her hands and in her feet. And the clumsiness in which they had been bound falls away. Her senses are becoming clearer. In the growing light, they are being shined.

And there is growing delight. Ah, to taste the green of a lettuce leaf . . . to touch an object and to hold it . . . to look at a face and to see this face . . . to listen to music and hear it . . . to feel . . . to feel with another and for another . . . to have a dream again and dream . . .

All through the house, Clara is building shrines with candles and flowers and handcrafted, beautiful objects. Not for worship but for celebration. And the numberless gestures that are a woman's in her ordinary everyday become a thanksgiving.

She has come home after a long homelessness.

With every morning Clara receives the new day more open-armed and with a renewed joy:

To be alive!

And with the daily growing of this good feeling grows the being in touch. A spontaneity of being with whatever and whoever and a widening and deepening and heightening of perception.

She writes a letter to her absent husband.

17.10

The first blossom in the dancing tree in the courtyard, Michael's tree. Rose, like wild-rose rose. Like the rose that was in and over everything last evening at sunset time. The finest hushed-rose spider-web cloth was laid over the immediate world and all things lay in its gentle shine. Stepping into it, was being of it. Were you there . . ? And then this morning the one blossom. Fragrant of bitter almond. And so many buds, some already with the tip burst and a small, so small a fist of petals showing. And so many leaves on the tree still, most not even in autumn fire yet. - At my feet, I found a small passion fruit, smaller than the polished stone egg put into your hand as a parting gift. I brought it in and put it in a small bowl and am wondering and wondering at the metamorphosis of things: from that winter-death, when the vine hangs like rags and tatters as though it could never live again, to the limbs and vortex fingers that spin round any vital thing to hold on, to the building of the leaves, five fingered with a filigranework of cells and passages, to the blossoms, radiant miraculous suns of palest green-eggshell-purple-white-plum-golden-yellow - the five is there, too, and the ten and the three . . . And then the fruit, egg-shaped, deep orange.

Could you dream any part of it? The blossom into fruit? What unfathomable depth of dream would you have to go, to dream that small, still, shining fruit, that now is in a little dish on my kitchen table . . .

From seed to seed, every moment is a mystery; and every metamorphosis is in the seed as plan; and every moment, every form is before the seed a dream.

There is a honeysuckle still. There are roses. Red ones on the little tree, yellow buds on the rambler. And the Mahonia bealei has made a plumed crown of buds right at the very top of itself. There will be blossoms for the Christmas table, bringing lily-of-the-valley fragrance like spring into the room.

Your Camellia has a few buds, too, I see them grown more every time I look at them. All the fuchsias are still in bloom. The one whose pot was broken and had to be in a make-shift bowl and then just a few days ago received a new pot, has two blossoms and some buds.

The Hallelujah of it all . . . the Ah of it . . . the Oh of it . . . And it all makes me weep this morning.

And I don't know why, but I am being transported onto the 'Bruderfeld', many fields fairly high up on a plane embraced by a woodland, leaving quite a large area open.

Mother and I are working there, the two of us alone. Mad Elisa has just gone down the path. We stop and wait. Soon, we hear her singing in the most beautiful voice in the cathedral of the wood. It is the same song always:

Das Laub faellt von den Baeumen,
das zarte Sommerlaub.
Das Leben mit seinen Traeumen,
das faellt zu Ash und Staub.

Mother always weeps, when she hears that song, and I am moved, too. But I burst and say, 'No, no, no, I shall not have my dreams scattered like leaves. I shall always dream golden dreams to the end. Why, life must always be glorious, whatever happens.

Mother takes me in her arms. And when I feel whole in her warmth, she says, as though to everything. "When God's will happens. When God's will happens."

- A story for Adam, who seems far.

- Clara

*   *   *   *

180

Clara listens to music. The human voice singing, instruments playing. She hears the music. It enters her. She hears with all her being. It pours through every pore into her - it pours in like wine and love - and it is transformed and becomes lightful energy.

She dances. She dances emotions and feelings; she dances silence and music. She is the dancer and becomes the dance. Moving thus in dance, she is in unison with movement that is and she is rhyming with the rhythm that is. Being the dancer and the dance, she is the ever moving, ever peaceful centre and the space!

Dancing, Clara creates a light which, flowing from her and back into her, is a force of new life.

And Clara dances in thanksgiving, in prayer and praise. She dances little things, leaves, daises and teacups and roses.

What else, what else is my Life,
than a dance for God -

What else, what else is my Life,
than a dance with God -

Dancing, she receives this understanding that she has the potential to transform energy, transmute the dark, the negative, the weighty and make light. And more, that the gift is within to harness energy from anywhere of the within, the above and the below.

And she laughs, how we strain and stress and labour and waste so much energy, when we could simply take ourselves and everything lightly.

The breath that we breathe in is here, the air is given each time without our doing.

Life is here, always, effortlessly.

*　　*　　*　　*

181

In her red-and-gold note book, there is an entry of that time: 'I find a life in me of such luminosity and so spacious, that I might enlighten and fill the whole world with it and at the same time there is this little-me, this 1-metre-55-centimetre-body-me . . .'

Clara paints. Images upon images. She is spell-bound in the doing and forgets place and time. - Whence do they come . . ? From farther and deeper than the words . . ?

As these colourful images are flowing through her hand through the paint brush onto sheets of paper, pieces of cardboard and wood, Clara experiences a curious and wonderful thing: her head falls off - look there, it's bobbing out at sea - and in its place a stillness grows, a rich silence, and all babble ceases to be. And it becomes a silence in which she is, or rather, which she is, a potent space from which dreams, insight and wisdom flow.

Clara sees a plan and witnesses an order, where laws as forces are at work that bring about the harmony of movement - the sun's spinning, the earth's turning, the waning and waxing of the moon, the ebbing and tiding of the sea, the orbiting of the celestial bodies - and how all our lives, all life is part of this same, is this same!

This in-seeing, this recognition is divine. This harmony, this divine design is in everything. It is possible to see it, to hear it, to dream it. It is the Godly beauty that is even and also in sorrow, in pain, in poverty and grief, in chaos, in calamity and discord.

And this divine harmony is, in spite of the harm that is being done to the earth, space and outer space.

And Clara suddenly hears her father's voice quite clear and close by: "O, my child, the Godly snowflake, in her is visible what is invisibly in all life. The whole universal harmony is in her, nay, She is it. Imagine, Child, the Godly Snowflake! God, a snowflake!"

Clara is a small child, looking in wonder at a snowflake just landed on her red hand-knitted mitten, her most treasured Christmas-gift.

The whole of me is become a highly sensitive receptacle. This solid that I was, this big obstacle in my own life, is vanished and I am within the harmony of movement and part of it. Not as tangible me, but rather as flow with flow. A force.

I am truly in tune and I flow with whatever.

And there is no effort.

It shows. It is as a visible, almost as a tangible light-presence around me. Children and animals and plants and things respond to me spontaneously, for in a way they are of the same measure of light. Some people, too, enter into it joyfully, others are afraid. - You see, they cannot hide themselves behind themselves, Clara finds them . . .

Clara is up and out in her garden by the sea before dawn. She witnesses the curlew's call that wakens the seabirds. Awake, they fly in silent rhythmic flight. Like music is their flying, until the rising of the sun, when the chorus begins and mounts and mounts and becomes a chorale with the sea's song and the pebbles' sounding.

And I am not. I am not and in my place is a stillness, a richness, a song.

Dreams are given: It is Christmas Eve in the morning. The Christmas tree is the potted Bay-tree, as it has been for the past few years. It is decorated with rose-coloured paper rose-buds, which make the tree look as though it was truly in bud, and hand-blown plain glass balls and white candles.

The Three Kings are there in rich robes, each carrying his gift. The room is expectant. A fourth King arrives, A Queen! She looks radiant and young and is most beautifully arrayed. She tells the story of how she has been wandering for nearly 2,000 years as the Star kept vanishing. But how finally in dreams, she was guided this way to this place.

We all sit down to a breakfast of coffee and croisseaux. After breakfast, The Three Kings and The Queen offer their gifts.

Her's is a heart-shaped box of gold, small and beautiful, it holds one seed, an eight star!

"The seed for the Tree of Love," She says. "Let's go and plant it."

While The Queen and I are planting The Seed of the Tree-of-Love in the front garden, The Three Kings are moving in a circle around us, holding hands. At the moment the seed is dropped in the earth, the single curlew calls the seagulls to wake. And while The Queen blesses the Seed, the seagulls dance their roundelay above us in silence.

At the moment of sunrise, the five of us stand arms raised, palms toward it in greeting. And a second light, more majestic than the sun appears.

The Three Kings and I stand in wonder and awe as The Queen announces, "Behold! The Birth of the Feminine. This is what we are here for, to celebrate today. Look! there, feet first! Wide, wide feet, broad soles, look! and see the map of the whole new age written on them!

"Behold Her in Her might and glory and hear Her laughter. Hear how She laughs! Hear! how the pain of endless centuries has become laughter! Big. Huge rolling belly-laughter. Listen. And join in and laugh and laugh and laugh with Her!" And the five of us join in Her laughter.

Adam has no time to visit Clara, so she is visiting him on his birthday. Although their meeting is in the evening in Leicester Square by the Statue of Charlie Chaplin, she travels the earliest morning train. She carries her big boat-shaped basket full of the first daffodils that some children had gathered for her on the cliffs abandoned flower-meadows.

These radiant messengers of Spring are to be given one by one or in small bunches to the sad people on her journey.

The gift for Adam is a painting she has made:
Behold! The fountain.
It is fed from above and below
and it ceases not.
Behold it!

This is written in gold letters over the painting, which is in the seven colours of the rainbow.

As the train is about to leave the early station, a woman comes rushing into the carriage, quite out of breath and dishevelled. The only seat she can immediately find is opposite Clara's. In time, she remarks on the basket full of daffodils. They discover that they are both travelling up to London to celebrate a birthday. She has made a big birthday cake for the occasion. "I am taking this early train, as there is a lot I want to do while in London, I am to meet my birthday-friend in the evening in Leicester Square . . .!" That's enough. Clara finishes the 'co-incidence' all to herself 'Yes, a friend, his name is Adam . . .'

> String the pearls and make a necklace
> and do not throw them to the swines . . .
> Harness your woman power of Love.

Clara didn't remember how the long day was spent, but by the time she got to Leicester Square in the evening, she was filled to the brim with the smiles and greetings that she had received from countless unknown people.

She is waiting, watching, listening. A sudden wind . . . the bearer of unbearable news that has not yet happened . . ? A wind, a wind of Starlings gusting into Leicester Square from Charing Cross Road and chattering while settling in the trees. The silence, dead silence . . . and there in the trees like black potent overripe fruit . . . all the Starlings from London-town.

Clara dances an homage to Charlie Chaplin to the tune of 'Limelight' which she hums, and she scatters the last daffodils around him. She watches a stunningly beautiful young girl who looks heart-breakingly sad and is obviously waiting for someone. She carries an artist's folder. Clara introduces herself and says: "Why, you are so beautiful and so sad . . ."

The young girl tells how she had come from way up north in great enthusiasm with her collection of fashion designs and how no one wanted to know; she had been making her round for a whole week.

Clara points to the top she is wearing, "Look at my top, I call it stained-glass. See, its several garments in pure colours, they have holes in different places and one shines through the other and gives a stained-glass effect. Go you now and create some such thing and make it all your own and be your own master. You are obviously bright and gifted."

A year later, Clara received a note, 'Just to say I am happy and thank you. I shall always remember Leicester Square.'

Clara laughed with the newspaper seller 'Latest news, latest news!' and everyone passing buying the latest news, which was already yesterday's news! They laughed so much, their bellies hurt and Charlie shook on his one leg . . .

Adam finally turned up, rather late - most unusual - flanked by two women, one of them the bearer of the big home-made birthday cake. She looked quite glamoury-fied . . . There was a brisk greeting from Adam and an introduction to his two friends, Amanda (the cake) and Trudi.

Clara outshone them all - ha! - was she not a-light . . .
- How close pain and high joy.

A table was booked in a Greek-family Restaurant quite close. The Three walked slightly in front. Clara read their backs: we are embarrassed, get lost . . . Clara's heart was light and she smiled 'Wait! The evening hasn't begun yet!' - As they entered the restaurant, the waiter was most courteous; to Clara he said, "You are Greek?'

"For you, my love, tonight, I am Greek!"

- Three people in front of her sank into the floor. - Vanished.

Clara toasted everyone round her table, then the other guests and the waiters and the invisible cook. - Three people at her table fell off their chairs under the table, not to be seen . . .

The meal is wonderful, festive. Clara relishes every morsel . . . The waiter comes, gleaming, holding high a bottle of wine, "Presented to the Lady, who will be a Greek just for Love, this bottle of true Greek wine with the complements of Patera!"

"Let's dance, this is wonderful, let's dance! You have some

186

music? Zorba's dance? Get Patera, the cook, everyone."

Clara, the waiters, the cook, Patera and some of the guests, they dance Zorba the Greek's dance. The place is turned on. At one table, Three people have become stony statues . . .

Clara had that dance in her feet, she had danced it often with the fiery Chilean student Taato, in the sixties in Texas. He *had* to dance, how else could he bear the vision he so intensely had of his beloved homeland's imminent treacherous slaughter . . .

Warmed through, light and feeling wonderful, Clara left the Greek Restaurant with Three completely refrigerated figures.

In the taxi, the Three sat in thick silence. Clara couldn't help being over taken, every now and then, by bursts of laughter at the sight of these Three well dressed, well brought up, well educated people stiff as washing in a sudden severe frost from embarrassment in the presence of pure high joy.

> High joy that was high because of
> the depth of sorrow sadness and pain,
> that was like a pillar holding it there.

"It was an embarrassment to Adam and us all," said Amanda the birthday cake as they were standing in front of the wooden gate opening into the garden surrounding Adam's studio-house.

"Well then, *be* embarrassed at life, when it breaks out in joy, you lifeless sticks!" And turning to Adam, "You are embarrassed, when I am out of my mind - you are embarrassed, when I am in my mind - you are embarrassed when I am alive."

She saw him becoming tighter and tighter and turning white holding in a growing rage that would have wanted to get hold of her . . . like that time on the stairs . . ? She hears her mother say 'Beware every man has a black fire in him, if it doesn't burn it smoulders . . .'

This quiet insidious drip of violence from the life-long bottled anger appearing a life long as sweet-kindness.

"Is love embarrassed in the face of love . . ? Man, Man, you do not love me. Call a taxi, I shall return home on the midnight train."

*   *   *   *

In the taxi, Clara weeps. "You are not shedding tears for that man, he is not worth it, one glance and you see the cold fish who can't love. He is as hard as nails. He would not weep for his mother.

"Weep instead for the young mother who was in my taxi before you, she may not have reached the hospital in time to see her only son alive who had this evening been brutally run down by a car in Charing Cross Road. Weep for her, she needs all our tears and all our love."

At Paddington Station, Seamus the taxi and Clara weep together in one another's arms and he carries her overnight bag and her basket and takes her by the hand and finds a seat for her in the one-minute-to-midnight-train . . .

Clara has always loved that train, ever since in mid-May 1954 when it carried her into the morning of her Beloved. It stops at every Station. People come into the carriage. People leave the carriage.

A young Navy man comes in, he carries a guitar. He sits opposite Clara. She asks him the time. "It's just on one." He plays and sings quietly, sad songs. Suddenly, he breaks down and sobs "It's too much. It's all too much. I can't bear it . . . " Clara reaches across to him. He tells her, how he had had special leave to be with his dying mother and this after he had lost his beloved pal overboard - "Blasted overboard and I witnessed it, in that bloody stupid war . . . We were best pals, we made music together, we had fun together. I made a song for him, I sing it to you . . ."

He played and sang his requiem . . .

Quietly, imperceptibly,
The power of the heart . . .

Just as Clara steps into the little seafront lane that leads to her home, a star-fish splatters at her feet, naked and wet out of the early-morning blue sky . . . she carries it over the rocks to the sea.

It's the last day of February. The morning is brisk and clear. The south-easterly is blowing from the Lizard Point. In the seafront garden seven of the blue dwarf-irises, planted for Adam, are open; and there is a small pool of crocuses here and there of the hundreds Clara had planted in late autumn in the memory of beloved ones . . . Worlds have happened in the 28 hours that she had been gone and come.

> How will they know that the
> sunray that hit their window
> across the bay has become
> an eight-star in my eyes.

Clara dances. She dances Adam. She dances Amanda. She dances Trudi. She dances the young mother who was in the taxi before her and she dances her son. She dances Seamus the taxi. She dances herself.

> Dancing - making Love.
> Dancing - making Life.
> Dancing - Healing.
> Dancing - Awakening.
> Dancing - Awarening.

Clara dances.
She dances and enters timeless time, sacred time.
She dances the song of silence, which has its own measured steps.
She hears the song of silence.
She listens.
She listens the messages that are flowing up from her feet . . .
She listens the silence . . .
She listens the sounds of the silence . . .
She dances.

A dream is dreamed: I walk alone in a vast treeless plain. I walk from the morning into the night, but I do not witness the sunset. The night comes suddenly, and the plain shows - in a momentary light - to be a pure circle. The stars are brilliant, each like a huge Mandala. From the biggest and brightest, some bright things are flying towards me - Angels? Three storks land by me, each laying a new born baby at my feet. There are singing voices as from all around me chanting, 'To tend and to nurture the three-foldness of yourself to become the one which is in the three three times. Amen. Amen.' - The night falls dark.

I wake.

Clara lets this dream fall into her - a gift - to do its work there as it will.

Clara dances. She dances whole days Edith Piaf songs.

Piaf sings every bead on my necklace of sorrow and pain and joy:

    5 for sorrow + 5 for pain + 5 for joy +
    5 for sorrow + 5 for pain + 5 for joy +
    5 for sorrow + 5 for pain + 5 for joy +
    5 for sorrow + 5 for pain = 55 beads
    55 beads-of-mother-of-pearl-for-high-joy.

Sing Piaf - Dance Clara. Sing Piaf - Dance Clara.
Dance Clara, dance.

Clara receives, transforms and irradiates. She experiences herself as a point, a radiant point into which flow rays from a vast circumference around it and from which flow rays into a vastness . . . She experiences this so clearly, that she creates it. The point being a child's toy-horse, a magnificent creation a small child could ride on and in the powerful shape that Clara always had imagined that the very first horse created looked like - das Ur-Pferd. From it flow finest silk-threads, handspun and in the many colours imaginable, in radiation round the room - the horse being the centre - and from points outside, which are being

190

received as most lightful, silk threads flow to it.

Thus, a field of force is being created, that relates directly to that in which Clara is, where communication has become communion.

I enter into, I assimilate the essence of whatever, whoever . . . and from me, the centre, flows a force as radiation of love.

Flash upon fast flash, connections are made with near and far in a wide awake wakefulness, where concrete manifest form and time and space, all are light. All is light, and the seeing goes where that has already happened which is not yet manifest in the here and now.

But in this light there is heightened awareness of the here and now and a deep grasping of the sacredness of life and nature and all. I am in a heightened state of being gifted with a sensory perception, that acts as an encompassing intelligence, which is innate and deep innermost and corresponds with the intelligence that penetrates and informs all and everything.

I am in intimate and spontaneous contact with the subtle rhythm of the cosmic magnetic forces, which enables the eel and the elver and the salmon to make their fabulous journey and the bee to trace in her flight a magical language written in the air in intricate figures and thus transmit life-important messages to the hive.

I am in a heightened state of being to be thus in touch as the bee, as the eel and the elver and the salmon, and as all creatures in which it is divinely simply and simply divine nature.

To me as a human being, it is not simply divine nature. I am in a state of grace, when I am in my divine nature. And I do well to dance in praise and thanksgiving for to partake and to be in this illumined consciousness.

All life lived fully is always full.
It gives itself away, yet is always full.
It is every morning at the spring.

Thus, I am not I but life alive fed at source -
at every moment of itself - the fountain of love.

Young women are drawn into Clara's life. All of them are so much, and mostly sadly and even violently, experienced in the world and rather lost and bewildered in themselves, having had to grow up in a time and a society where the human values have all gone wrong and everything belonging into life is separate from it.

Like sex. - The Big Sex - There is so much shock, trauma and disturbance in these young lives. They have lost touch with their innate gifts, the most precious and powerful being their intuition, the deep truth of themselves. However, there is an eager questioning, seeking and searching, for there is a great and bright life in each one of them and a zest for it, too.

Clara gets them to partake in making bread. All kinds of bread: the wheat loaf, the mixed meal loaf, the braided celebration loaf, the loaf of rye leavened with sour dough.

Kneading in a big wooden bowl on the chunky kitchen-table, one young woman suddenly laughs, lifting her hands streaming with dough, high over the table, and pushing them back into the soft mound of dough with a shout of such sensuous delight, "This is miles better than sex, where have I been for God's sake, let's have more of it!" And she kneaded and sighed such fleshy sighs of delicious joy, that everyone in the room was most wonderfully turned on.

They created meals together. Clara making them aware of the choosing of the foods, of the joy in preparing the different things for each dish and how the ingredients themselves tell how, on each particular occasion, they like to be cut or mixed or what herbs or spices they like to be made savoury with. So you, the cook, the whole of you comes into it and the whole thing is fun and never twice can you repeat yourself for your finger-tips are amazingly gifted creators.

Joy in choosing the bits and pieces, joy in preparing, joy in making, tasting, presenting, serving and you have created a feast even with the most simple foods.

*   *   *   *

What most of these young women know as drudgery and boredom becomes joy. Chopping parsley becomes joying parsley and oneself. Thus in doing with all of oneself the smallest and humblest - shining the sink simply to make it shine: does it not daily give us so much service . . . you create joy in yourself and all around. So, joy then the most honourable Mr Sink and thus create and partake in creating.

I create and I partake in creating. I give and I receive, give and receive . . . And in the process, I discover the hugeness of my womanhood in which the smallest gesture is a creative act. I am in a ritual and in it I am creating myself and I become aware that sex is in all of me as a force and that everything I do can be a sensuous experience. Is a love-making.

I begin to love myself, which is the beginning of all beginning.

Clara's young women-friends began to understand that the first freedom is to be freed from the shackles of oneself. And one such is sex as an existence separate and severed and outside of oneself, for inevitably then it becomes an enslavement and finally is degrading one's feminine human dignity.

Let us come to this and make the love of ourselves so huge that whatever we do is in celebration of life.
Imagine, the power-station each of us will be . . .
Imagine, the current it will cause . . .
Imagine, the mutation: Mankind into Humankind . . .
Imagine, the revolution: man will study war no more but meditate on life and make love make love make love . . .
- And there is more to that than The Big-Dingle-Dongle and Sweet Soft fruits . . .

Let our big over-flowing hearts overflow and let them become streams and rivers. Let them become seas.

193

j

Clara is of a wholeness and in a wholeness. She is exploring the outerspace of her inner space. She is diving ever deeper into the sea of her innermost and brings up treasures, long buried, long lost. She is in a process of innering, as the earth in autumn. Her life is rich and enriches. It flows. It is light and it lightens.

There is a fullness to such living and being so alive. I am in an intimacy with everything, yet I am not overwhelmed nor overtaken by anything, for my life has the same huge measure as life itself and flows with the same flow and rhymes with the same rhythm.

I am a gift and a guidance to those that yearn for their lives to be alive fully and hugely, as each life *must be*, must be, to fulfil its meaning.

I am a threat to those many that fear life and hide it away and convince themselves that they are in the very special grace of God. They polish their voices and enthrone themselves in the throne of self-righteousness and judge and condemn in the name of their God by whom they have been appointed to deal with the un-godly and un-believers. By such compassionate hands Clara was captured one night and brought to judgement.

When some years later, the highly polished and sweeter, much sweeter than candy-floss-voice was asked, why she had acted towards Clara the way she did, not even knowing Clara at all, the sweeter-than-ever-voice said: "You see, God appointed me to act that way. You were so unwell, self-destructive, really and frightening to others, you obviously needed urgent help. God instructed me to do what I did. It was for your own salvation. I always follow God's orders, you see. I am a compassionate believer."

Clara said: "Poor God. Poor, poor God." And walking away she mumbled, "Poor soul, poor soul!"

As every night, Clara had walked out that night to gather in the sea, the stars, the wind, the sailing clouds, the silence of the

194

village lanes and the scenes of the peoples behind the lit and curtained windows. She passed an old cottage and saw in the brightly lit room paintings standing about. Her eye fell intensely on the painting of a head of a man. Spellbound, Clara watched as this head came alive and became the head of a man lying dying in a hospital room. Dying at this very moment of a malignant tumour on his brain and being desperately alone and asking for someone to stand by him in his agony.

Clara pulled herself out of this transfixation, entered a dark open passage and found a door. She knocked. A woman opened the door. "Are you the painter of these works?"

"Yes, all except this portrait," pointing to the head.

"Who is this man?"

"He is my only brother."

"Who painted him?"

"My daughter."

"You know that he is at this moment dying of a malignant tumour on his brain?"

"Good God! how do you know, I heard only this afternoon that he would not live to see the morning."

"It is written all over this portrait, how deathly unwell he is. Why are you not with him? He needs you desperately. He is utterly alone in his agony and he has a message for you. Something he urgently wants to tell you. Something like this: 'Sis, dearest Sis, don't hide your life away as we were taught all our life long, give your life away, Sis, and then it will multiply. Live your life, Sis, I beg you in my last breath. Dearest Sis, live your life. Do!' Go to him at once, it is not too late. He needs you to comfort him in his last hours. Go, I beg you, it is very important for your own life, that you go and share these final dearest moments of his life with your brother."

The woman looked at Clara evermore as though she was seeing a phantom and then let out a yell and charged out of the room.

Clara continued her walk through the night lanes, she didn't want to miss her nightly chit-chat with Mrs Hedgehog, whom she usually encountered as the busy body of the night went on her many errands.

*　　*　　*　　*

As Clara came back to her home, she found a candy-floss voiced woman on her doorstep, whom she did not know but had seen before. She shoved a piece of paper in Clara's hand and said, "You are to urgently call this number, as you couldn't be reached, *I* received this message. It is most urgent."

"Lady, I have seen you around but I do not know you, why then should anyone phone you who is trying to contact me. What humbug is this . . ."

"All I can say is, that it is urgent."

"Well, I am going into my house now, whoever it is will ring me, if it is so urgent. A good night to you."

Quite soon the next morning, the sweet voice came to Clara's house again urging her to ring this number. Clara pointed to her phone and said, "Here is my phone, whoever it is can get in touch with me."

The candy-floss voice turned up again and again until Clara lost patience and dialled the number. It was her GP's practice! In a few minutes, one of his assistants was there, the ambulance waiting outside, the Social Worker stepping in and Clara was removed to the Lunatic Asylum.

- It is frightening, the power of the sugar-tongue of the righteous.

This shining, lightful alive woman was taken abruptly away and declared to be on a self-destructive high and was brought down in an instant and her whole being was fossilised by a mighty dose of depressants . . .

A Life was eclipsed.

The feet that had danced so lightly shuffled. The voice that had sung beautifully was stunned into helplessly trying to shape a word. The arms were stiff and bent and arrested in this position.

Clara was there and bright somewhere and she knew and saw and heard, but as from a distance. A far far distance.

And she was helpless.

God! So helpless.

And she couldn't even cry.

*   *   *   *

196

Again and again from early childhood on and all through her life, Clara is a victim of ignorance.

- God forgive them, for they do not know
  what they are doing.
- Clara, forgive them.

Clara finds herself in an all women's ward in a huge building with one long wide corridor, one big dormitory with so many beds and barred windows, however, the grills are beautifully crafted. This long, high-ceilinged space of the corridor serves as dining-room and sitting-room.

Clara cannot quite make out if it is real, that she is really in this institution, plucked from the bright freedom of herself and thrown into this nightmare imprisonment.

But with every morning, the naked reality of the situation is more strikingly apparent.

How, how has anyone the right and the power to pluck a shining life and incarcerate it and extinguish it with one blow.

Is it because I am a woman and have been in Mental Hospital before . . . I was neither dangerous to myself nor to anyone else, only hugely aware of my life and all life and on the contrary, enriching other lives. And in myself I had found a light - a life generating force - that was akin to the fusion in the highest and deepest moment of lovemaking. I had been close to a great discovery.

And now, come here, anyone come and take a close look and see for yourself: Clara has been made a cripple.

It is unspeakable.

But in a small chamber within her, there is a light and awareness and a force of defiance. A huge Yes, Yes, Yes, I am alive and your treatment cannot finally take this Godly Force from me. No one, not anyone can extinguish the Fire of my Life. And innerly Clara sticks out an enormous long tongue!

And Clara, with the light that's left her, is able to see the other women in the ward. There is not one that is insane or mad. Not one. But in each one the essential life and being is buried under so much rubble. Break-down after break-down piled one on top of another and never even once the cry for help from deep under is detected or received by anyone. In so many there is the wish not to live, which hangs like the rank smell of decay in the air.

At each meal Clara sits at a different table and each time the women ask why she was here, as she didn't look the kind that ought to be here.

And Clara hears many stories. The youngest of the women, she is not yet twenty, suffers from Anorexia!

"If you don't know what it means, it's the wipe-yourself-out-disease, only they won't let me get rid of myself. The men I loved didn't want me anymore when I got pregnant, you see. I have had three abortions. At first you think, oh, what's there to it, just have this thing cleaned out. But afterwards, it's like a huge bit of yourself is gone from you for ever. It's like my life is gone from me. My life is dead and gone. I hate myself. I hate myself."

Then she laughs. And Lorna's laughter sounds like the rattling of a loose plastic gutter in the wind . . .

Clara was still light enough to see Lorna, to see her life, this huge passion, this gift to love cowering in the dimmest corner of her innermost, become the guilt of a murderess; who must now murder her own life . . .

Look and see Lorna's black eyes in which the fire of passion has become terror . . .

Out of every woman in this forsaken establishment screams a life. A life shattered, unlived, unloved.

Like a genetic disease, lovelessness is handed down from one generation to another, until there is come the one, who is born to redeem. In whom the longing for love of all those before has, in a radiance of planetary constellation, brought about a miraculous gene mutation: a great light in the heavens appears and in nine full moon months the bearer of good tidings is born.

The bringer of love.

Clara listens to all the stories, each woman is over-heavy with, like the cows with their gigantic overfilled udders that have their cow-being denied to them, that heavenly contentment, that is their true presence, now that they have become nameless, milk producing machines fed with the most abhorrent feeds.

All life has become the victim of this total ignorance that travels in the guise of All Knowing and inside the smooth garments of Godliness.

How is Clara to keep that light shining in her, when it is being stolen from her, diminished day by day by the drugs that she is being forced to swallow . . .

"Don't give me drugs, I don't need any drugs I am not out of my mind, none of us here is."

"If you reject the drugs, you will have injections. You think you are all right, but we know you are not. So, just don't fuss, take the drugs and be a good girl."

The only two things that Clara had taken with her to hospital were her hand-made pure bristle hair-brush and the wooden comb, handcrafted for her by a Mexican comb maker.

- God was always in her presence, when she brushed and combed her long hair.

Even though her arms are arrested in a bent position and her hands quite stiff, she forces herself painfully to brush and comb her hair several times a day.

'Spinning Gold', her mother used to call it.

And Clara *was* spinning Gold, for she kept a spark of life alive inside her and that spirit of defiance, that was so important, so that the drugs could not ever again overpower her.

Brushing her hair, Clara mingles with God. One day, while brushing and combing her hair, she remembers the last dream she had had just before she was snatched away and brought here.

Vivid like an apparition, this dream suddenly stands in front of her:

I am standing in the circular opening of an autumnal woodland. I am wearing a beautiful full length brocade dress in gold and green. My hands are open-palmed, meeting at the triangle of my thighs. A man is beside me. I whisper: The Dark ONE. He is carving a wooden crown. He is carving around it the tree as it grows from the seed and in between, he is carving man and woman intertwined. The scene he is carving is like a ring-a-ring-around, like a dance. I am still and expectant. He puts the carved crown on my head and in the same instant I say, "O, my God, The Green Man, my Bridegroom."

Clara begs to go to Occupational Therapy. She needs to paint. It will also help her to get the use of her arms and hands back. She asks for large white sheets and as it is too difficult to hold the brush, she paints with her fingers.

She paints trees. Everyday, she paints trees. But with each new painting the actual tree shape becomes more and more a field of force and finally it becomes a cross. She writes over it: The Tree of Death - The Tree of Life.

Everyday, it's the cross. Stark, maybe, with straight vertical and straight horizontal. Then like a dance, maybe. Then with the four-petalled rose in the cross-point - the rose in the heart of the matter.

Matter-mater - Mutter-mother - Then like a candelabra, flames at top of the vertical and end of the horizontal. Then like a tree with roots and fruits.

Clara is deeply absorbed in her doing. And she feels a painful tearing away when the time has passed and she has to return up the endless metal steps to her imprisonment of the ward.

The energy that she receives while creating these tree images, is a most generating force that keeps the light going inside her and her connection with life.

And while lying sleepless at night, Clara dwells on The Dark ONE, The Green Man, the Bridegroom of her dream, that had let loose all these images in her. And she wonders at the meaning of his appearance and that of her being crowned with his carved wooden crown . . .

One morning, the cross-shape is seen as the letter T and Clara weaves into it the letters AOM to create the word ATOM, the O is drawn as a circle around creating thus a kind of Mandala. In the same way, she creates the word ATEM. Painting in this way, is like experiencing each letter in its innate being. Each being a force and together creating a living force: *A Word*.

The interweaving of letters, which is done in so many different ways, creates intricate patterns of triangular and circular fields, which create a new force and which, in great delight, Clara fills in with strong and bright colours.

So quickly, though, returning to the ward, Clara has to fight for breath in its stifling, heavy atmosphere of so many women's lives held down.

- Clara must get out of here. She must. Again and again, she has been asking for an appointment with the main Psychiatrist to review her position, but her name is never being called on his twice a week visit to the ward . . . She feels, that there is a conspiracy, that there are forces at work, that want to keep her in this place . . . for good, maybe . . .

What was she doing here . . . what was an absolutely sane life doing here . . . God help me, someone . . .

Help came somewhat and quite powerfully, when the cross became a woman as tree with branches, stem and roots like flames, but the woman-shape quite clearly there. While painting, still with her fingers, it was as though Clara was creating onto the piece of paper herself happening at the very moment: a marriage of forces to create the one force, the fire-force.

Stepping out of the spell-bound space in which the painting happened in very fast movements and looking at it, she sees in it, looking at her out of the flames, the now laughing face of The Dark ONE, The Green Man, the Bridegroom of the powerful dream . . . And she writes on the blank side:

Inner Marriage or Woman become Tree of Love.

On the same morning, Clara met Theo, a young out-patient. She had noticed him, his powerful head and huge shape, and had thought that he had put all that massive body weight around a being so sensitive and vulnerable to shield it.

He suddenly stood behind Clara and told her he had been aware of her but felt that she was too carried away in her painting to be disturbed - Clara was indeed glad that he hadn't made himself known before and glad that he appeared now, as she needed to share with a like mind what she had discovered through the paintings.

Theo seemed to be a most favoured outpatient and seemed to be able to come and go at his pleasure. And he commanded quite some authority, too, and was able to convince the ward sister, that Clara should be allowed out for a few hours occasionally.

They visited his home, where Theo introduced her to an amazing collection of stones, which he studied for their healing power. He was a geologist, but had always been much more attracted to the mystery that each stone is and the connection of the mineral world to all the other worlds and the planets and especially our lives. He allowed Clara to choose a stone and she chose a small Rose Quartz. It sprung at her, so to speak, and as soon as she held it in her hand, it was warmed through. It was her stone at this moment, Theo said, and she must carry it on her.

He introduced Clara to his writing, which was mostly poetry. But he was in a huge undertaking in writing a work, in which he hoped to reveal all the forces that had been instrumental through the centuries since the event of Christ, to bring about the evil as made manifest through Adolf Hitler . . . It was a mad thing to do, but then he was allowed to do mad things, as it was understood that he was mad.

Clara now looked even more forward to her occupational therapy time, as occasionally she was meeting Theo there. And the freedom he enjoyed in the hospital allowed him to bring in friends, painters, poets, writers and Clara was, for a few hours every week, in a lively exchange of thought and ideas. This helped her greatly not to lose her sense of the worth of life, which in the tight enclosure of the ward and its airlessness was always threatened.

But oh, how short the joy and enrichment of this intercourse.
On their last outing, Theo had taken Clara to a woman who lived like a hermit after an amazing life with the world and of the world.
She was the one who taught Theo the healing wisdom of the stones. She was of a great presence, strong and clear, and for Clara it was deeply moving and encouraging to encounter a beautiful woman who had lived a full life in the world and now was giving it in its fulfilled richness to those that sought her in their need.

Alas, Theo, so it turned out, had done terribly wrong in the eyes of whoever to have taken Clara to see the 'Witch'. - Neither Theo or Clara had spoken to anyone at the hospital about their visit - and yet from the moment it became known, Theo was forbidden to even speak to Clara, as this relationship was undermining her well being . . . He let Clara know all this in a forbidden note, which he dropped as he walked by her.
Not a word was ever said to Clara by anyone.

Clara was well neigh shattered by the way her freedom was once more abruptly cut by ignorance, and she was ever more determined to get out of hospital.
She had no one to turn to - Adam, she sensed, was part of the

plot to keep her in the hands of ignorance and well out of sight and sound.

She had to resort to her peasant cunning. And she did.

She was able to get hold of a phone, call a taxi known to her and slip out of the ward, when the main door was open for a moment. Her only luggage being her comb and her brush and wearing the morning gown she had arrived in, she would appear to everyone a patient just casually airing herself by the main entrance of the building.

What a relief, when she saw Alfi, her favourite taxi man, who had of course no idea that he was picking up a fugitive.

She found the front-door of her home wide open, was Adam back . . . Stepping into the living-room, she is being greeted from the top of a step-ladder in hostile astonishment, "What are you doing here, you were not supposed to come back, not ever. This is not your home anymore, Adam has given us the right to live here as long as we want to."

Clara had no money on her to pay Alfi and tried to write a cheque, her hands and arms, her whole being were in a frozen shock.

"Take your time, love, take your time," Alfi's warm heart-voice.

But the voice from the ladder said, "No use writing a cheque, Adam has arranged for you the need of a second signature to verify your cheques. Without that signature, your cheques have no value, they will bounce."

At this new shock, Clara lost not only her capacity to move, but her speech, too. There she stood, home in her own home, violently rejected, a stony broken pillar . . .

Alfi pressed her hands and holding back his tears, "I'll be looking in on you. Take care, my love, don't worry." - He had summed up the whole situation in one glance.

Tears were falling inside Clara and became ice-crystals on an inner window.

*   *   *   *

Adam! Adam! - The many splendoured thing that is love . . .

Alfi knew a load about life and love, he knew that the one is the breath of the other. He had been tried from his beginning, when as a baby he was part of his clan that was emigrating to the New World to a better life and became one of those chosen survivors of the fatal Titanic.

- When Alfi says 'my love', it is not merely an easy figure of speech.

Adam! Adam! How mean the heart that rejects life and starves itself of love in self pity and how dangerously convincing to all ears its velvet voice, that claims to be a victim.

O, love, dearest love, it was Clara's own daughter's family who had firmly been installed into her home and been promised a stay as long as they pleased. Indeed they should consider it theirs, as Clara was likely to be gone for a long time, if not for good.

And Adam's sweet tongue had been so clever in his telling, that he had been able to convince their young daughter, that her mother was heartless and loveless, violent and most seriously mentally ill . . .

In her own home, Clara was shunned by those next to her heart. She was indeed a fugitive. She lived - a recluse - in the smallest room in the house and slept in a bed, that was like an old, overworked donkey's back . . .

She had known loneliness. She is now learning it. And all the tears are inside her become pebbles - a load of pebbles.

She is too shattered and too stunned to weep the tears.

She is in the shock of bereavement. She had known what it

205

means to be abandoned, now she is learning it.

Where from the strength . . . Where the hand to hold . . . Where the heart to reach . . .

The only time she sees her daughter is the clock-time to take the drugs - instructions! The Drugs.

- Looking for meaning? Looking for meaning? You must be joking! Meaning, you fool!

With the eyes of her memory that are wide awake, Clara sees her daughter newly-born in the ancient family basket-cradle, lying in the gentle light of the veils of tender rose and heavenly blue, which are to create the tone of light in which, in an inner vision, Clara had seen her first-born - her son - held in, inside her womb. Clara sees her baby-daughter wide-eyed lying there listening, all of her small being listening, and her tiny hands moving in a rhythm of a music only she could hear . . . How heart-breakingly sensitive she had been to sound. And how inconsolable she was after a self-appointed apostle had come to the door shouting 'repent woman, repent, eer it's too late. The day of judgement is neigh!' . . . And how she had cried out again and again as if in pain that day after the young gypsy, who had come to the door braided with garlic down to his ankles, had cursed Clara, as he was convinced that she was a true Romany, but was ashamed of it and so refused to speak Romany now that she was living in a grand house.

His curse stuck like a blunt axe in Clara's neck.

It is some weeks, when Clara regains her speech, and the proper use of her limbs. And she acts at once and demands that the family return to their own home.

Once more, stone by stone, she is building her life. She takes the prescribed lithium, sees her GP regularly, but focuses deep innerly on the wholeness of her life.

Her gestures become prayers again, a tuning into the tune, a rhyming with the rhythm. Slowly, gradually, slowly, she is learning to see, to hear, to touch, to taste, to smell, to communicate and to commune.

But while the levelling-drug is levelling her functioning, she cannot truly recover her sensitivity, her capacity to experience. And that *is* after all the purpose of the drug: to keep level by all means. You cannot soar in lightfulness, you cannot fall in lightlessness. You do not live, you vegetate, you are manageable . . .

But in Clara is a mighty force of life, and it wants out. I tell you it wants out and it will out . . . Her life is not appointed to be a dead who buries the dead . . . far from it.

Her life is appointed to live.

To live!

I tell you once more, hear it, now that my voice has been returned to me:

My life is meant to live!

Shout it to the outgoing tide!
Shout it to the incoming tide!
Shout it to the sixteen corners of the wind!
    My life is to live and to love!

Clara is crazy. Of course she is crazy. Who wants to be sane . . .

The sane are embarrassed by life and by love and frightened of both. And they go about it nonchalantly in the name of defence and security and humanity and peace, above all peace, to kill life and murder love. And they speak about it like I might say I had bangers and mash for my breakfast this morning. Matter of fact like.

How much of true humanity, how much genius behind bars in prisons, and Lunatic Asylums and other securely locked-away institutions - and where and what are the law mongers and war mongers and money mongers and God mongers and moral mongers . . .

What of a world that is ruled by insanity and those with the spirit of adventure, vision, insight and foresight are filling Mental Hospitals and Prisons or are kept forcibly silent in other ways . . .

Tell me, someone, what is madness . . ?
Tell me, quick . . .
Tell me, someone, who is insane . . ?
Tell me, quick . . .

Clara has a wonderful dream.

I am standing outside my house looking to the south. The sky is one huge immensely black wall all the way from south-east to south-west. Suddenly, a sun appears in this black blackness. A radiant sun and it comes out of it towards me and it is my daughter in a sun-radiance. In a great radiant happiness, she stands in front of me irradiating me with joy.

Clara carries this dream through her days. It is like the far distance suddenly being here. A great happiness. It is like this great happiness to be has happened already there, where happenings have happened and are waiting to manifest in the moment of synchronicity: that which happened in the past and is happening now is already a potent cross-point in a future moment, which inevitably will be encountered.

One is, so it seems, happening all at once in a moment of now: long past, near past, past, tomorrow, time ahead, far ahead *are within one . . .*

Clara holds this dream in her heart. She needs to, it is like sustenance.

The dream is also like a call from the heart. Waken and open up the door and step out. The path of your heart lies before you. Trust!

Clara breaks tiny pieces off her lithium tablets, so reducing the daily amount. They are hindering every step of her becoming. But throwing them away all at once might deliver her again into the hands of self-styled, godful righteousness and she mustn't allow this to happen.

Adam announced his return. Clara makes the whole house festive and prepares a celebration meal. She is expectant like a child on Christmas Eve. She makes herself lovely. She stands outside the door long before he is to arrive. It is late in the year. Christmas is not far away, yet there are red roses still in the seafront garden. The day is mild. It is windstill, yet the sea is rippled. In the western sky, there are mackerel clouds. The rest of the sky is a tender blue. There are Curlews flying over, so many together, landwards, they are calling their magical liquid-sound that drop into one - deep - like heavenly elixir.

Time is a long time. You stand on one foot and then on the other.

He is here. She flies to the car, ready for his arms . . . they are full of things. A typewriter with lots of stuff on top. She shuts the door of the car. Adam returns to empty the boot of the car. A lot of stuff. She goes into the kitchen. She lifts the lids from the cooking pots and puts them back. She opens the oven-doors and closes them again.

A heart can vacate itself and in its place is a big gaping empty space . . . A heart can leap into your throat and throttle it . . . A heart can break . . .

On her summer-golden Greek gown, that falls like sun-lit water to her ankles, Clara had pinned a little delightful mosaic-heart, an early and treasured gift from Adam . . .

She fiddles round the sink. In her ears are voices. Her own voice, too. Many years ago. In Texas. A gathering in the gracious home of a Professor of German Literature. After dinner. Clara is telling of the life of a great visionary. She says, he died of a broken heart. They laugh. All these Professors crack up laughing. Did you hear that, this guy died of a broken heart. Hi, hi, hi, ha, ha, ha, ho, ho, ho . . .

Then silence.

A news flash. On the television: Death of a broken heart is now scientifically proved.

It is now a scientific fact.

Hi . . . Ha . . . Ho

Silence.

Dead silence.

Clara sings into the sink Humpty Dumpty sat on a wall, Humpty Dumpty had a great fall. All the King's Horses and all the King's Men couldn't put Humpty together again.

The table is singing with food. Festive. The candles are lit. Red candles. All the candles round the room are lit. Red candles all. Adam comes down the stairs. He is bathed. He is casually dressed. Silver grey sweater. Silver grey corduroys. They sit down.

"Clara, our relationship cannot work, unless you change. The way you go about your life throws us daily farther apart. As I say, unless you change drastically, there is no chance for our relationship to survive . . ."

A bit of food went down the wrong throat. Clara coughs. She coughs desperately.

The warm hands to pat her back . . . The warm voice to say 'throw up your arms, Clara, it will help the easing . . .'

The warm voice? The warm hands? The warm arms? The heart . . . O . . . The warm heart . . .

The days pass. Her nourishment is her trust. What is begun is begun. It is inevitable and must not be allowed to be threatened by anything.

I am on my path. I walk on. I do not look back. In trusting, I am held and guided. It is difficult. Terribly difficult.

I am alone. I am alone. In my aloneness I am.

The Dreams given are helpers: The sun out of the black blackness become my radiant daughter shining me, the great happiness. - The crowning by the Bridegroom - And yet another dream is given:

A vast and beautiful countryside. I stand and overlook it as though standing in the middle of it and being able, in turning, to see all the hills, lanes, valleys and brooks clearly.

People are gathering. Festive people garlanded with flowers. A wedding? My daughter Maya's wedding? There is no bridegroom, but there is no panic about it.

A wild honey-golden stallion appears. Maya catches him and tries to put a garland of flowers round his neck, but he shakes his mane and charges off. A younger, wilder stallion of the same beautiful honey-gold comes galloping along and Maya looking ever more lovely, calls joyously, 'That's him, that's him,' and throws the garland over his head.

And instantly, he changes into a princely young man and I realise at the same moment, that it is *my* wedding. There is a great procession of the many people.

The now-me is the sole onlooker and a much younger me is the celebrated bride leading the procession hand in hand with my bridegroom. We suddenly have to go down a rose overgrown and rose-fragrant passage. A very young man, dark in appearance but light in being, comes out of nowhere and races to the front of the procession that is now almost in complete darkness and he says, 'I'll give the lead!'

*   *   *   *

Clara wakes into a sun-rising morning with a pure hallelujah!

The week before Christmas is filled with the making of the Hearts. A delicate pastry, made with lots of sweet butter and pure freshly ground vanilla, is cut into hearts of various sizes and baked. Young mothers and children come to decorate them. Candied fruits of all kinds and colours and many other colourful sugar-things are laid in lovely patterns on the icing sugar, a gold-thread is drawn through a little hole so they can hang on the tree or on branches round the room.

On Christmas Eve, many of these delightful things are carried to lonely people around the village to gladden them. And everyone visiting round the festive time receives one and of course each mother and child carries a heart home too. Every day, the house is filled with festivity and laughter and gladness and joy.

The Christmas Eve feast starts well before midnight and flows into the early Christmas morning. There are many courses. This year the first course is fresh, grilled river-trout rubbed with sweet butter and drops of fresh lime and garnished on serving with water-cress.

Eight are known to partake at the feast and for the ninth, the unknown, the head of table is laid for Him who is always on the way on this Holy Eve and is bound to arrive just in time for the feast . . .

There are nine fish. - Nine red roses are woven into the evergreen at the ninth place. For the eight, there is one red rose each amidst the evergreens that are rich with red berries.

As Clara takes out of the oven the large tray with the ready fish, the door opens and the one to sit in the ninth place enters. It is Bessy, an old woman, her snow white hair a halo over her and within her the young and wild heart of a child, she comes in carrying a small home-made Christmas cake and a tin full of home-made mince-pies - and a small wreath of Christ-roses.

She is in a great and lovely surprise to be the expected

unknown guest and filled with joy to sit at the ninth place at the head of table made so specially festive with the nine fragrant red roses. Never in her long life had anything so wonderful happened to her to be thus received and honoured.

Bessy entertains the gathering and keeps everyone in laughter with her great gift of humour which turns the saddest story of her much tried and adventureful life into laughter.

For Clara, Bessy's coming, to share this most treasured evening of the whole year is the greatest Christmas gift. For here is a life that has been tried from its entry into this world and is still on trial, yet Bessy receives now and received then all that is given *as life* and transforms it with the power of her heart to become the ever growing tree of love that her life is.

Clara had asked for strength and a sign, a symbol for her own path - evermore, since Adam's return - Bessy is seen to be given as a shining light . . .

Clara wonders, every now and then, from what space inside Adam those words had come that he spoke on his arrival. And how there was no sign of warmth and tenderness then and since and a cold distance and matter of fact nearness as of one who had never, ever really been at home in Clara's life.

Where does love go, when it goes . . .
What *was*, if *it* never was . . .
For Clara it is that love cannot go, cannot vanish. There are aspects of love that come and go, maybe. *But love is love is* . . .

Every now and then, Clara wonders, too, what is it that I am supposed to change into . . . But after that one big statement from Adam, she encounters him only as a loaded silence inside which a kettle is boiling . . . the love out of the house.

. . . Finally, in whose Keeping am I, I ask you, but my own.

Adam went to bed early, even on this last night of the year; he needs his set hours of sleep. Clara and her friends are under the starlit sky in the seafront garden tossing a glass of champagne to the old year in thanksgiving for the whole lot of it, lock, stock and barrel that it had brought.

And on the crest of the New Year, Clara gives a toast: "Let's make all the shit of last year into the manure of this New One. A blessing on us all and on all, that is on the way for us all. Cheers! Happy New Year. Happy New Year!"

When, after the feast, the young people have gone to their various New Year parties, Clara sits alone in the candle light, musing . . . She sips Lacrimae Christi, the wine from the slopes of Vesuvius and muses . . . And she remembers the first hour of a New Year from her long past, when she sat thus with her Mother, drinking the same wine, and Mother musing on things past and future . . .

Clara and Adam share breakfast only on special occasions and New Year's morning is one of these. There hasn't been a year since their togetherness, that Adam didn't appear to wish a Happy New Year and have a main hand in preparing and making the celebratory breakfast. On this first morning of the year, Clara waits and waits. No Adam. Finally, she goes upstairs. He answers her knock with a "come in", and she enters and decides to say her Happy New Year in German: Ein glueckliches Neues Jahr. (The word gluecklich seems to her on this morning more of Glueck than happy of happiness . . .) She gets stuck on glueck . . . Adam sits like a stock. Adam does not get up from his low upholstered chair near the window with the vast sea-views. Adam does not look up. Adam does not greet Clara. Clara does not finish her wishing, it's stuck on glueck . . . Adam says, "By the way, Clara, on the 5th of January I shall move into a flat in town." . . . Ein glueckliches Neues Jahr, Clara . . . Happy New Year, Clara . . .

214

Joyeux année, Clara . . .

Clara is not made into pulp by this news.

Clara is not made into a scream by this news. You see, the lithium is there and does not allow the sensitivity to receive the news. They enter and go deep and are piled up and stored . . . for a later date.

A body on this drug is shielded from the true impact of anything, is made dumb, and you are in a kind of make-believe, except it is not you that does the make-believe it's done for you. As your sensitivity is wiped out to a high degree - all is brought to a nice level - you simply do not experience that which is happening to you.

But mind, it enters and goes deep and piles up and is stored. Clara having been given deep insight into her life and life as such, understands somewhere within her, that by all means and with all the will she can muster under the circumstances, she *must* keep a flame lit within her, however small a flame, for it is the very light of her life that is threatened by the drug.

At any one moment, Clara can see a long procession of mainly women whose light has been snuffed by one treatment or another they received to cure their minds and who are in a kind of zombyhood and kept there by fear, which is spread all around them in the name of 'it is for your own good', 'it is for your own protection . . . '

Clara sees herself as the unique one in countless many not so fortunate, who has been given insight and the strength, the will and the guardianship to take her life out of the hands of doctors and psychiatrists and put it into her own hands, where it truly belongs and where those lives of all those numberless women and men should be.

It is quite unfathomable to conceive what is done to Life by all those lives that are prevented from living . . . The greatest

215

pollution of our living-space is by fear and it reaches down into the bowels of the earth and out and up into space and spreads deep into time of future generations . . .

Everything we do, makes waves. Everything we think, makes waves.

And where is the Kingdom of Heaven but that it is in my own heart.

If I am not the House of God, who is? What is?

There is no God, but that He dwells in me.

For a moment a seeing: my life as a bright spinning multi-coloured Mandala . . . and gone.

For a moment a vision: a great deep darkness that is slowly through-lit and in it is as crystals shining my health, my sanity and my salvation - I am looking down into my unconscious, a world of litupness to be sought and gained.

Thus, every morning on waking, Clara receives a gift for the building of her life. Stone by stone by stone and each one is already hewn in such a way that it fits the one below and beside. Daily, the house of life is growing. And she does not feel lonely, abandoned and lost, on the contrary, rich and enriched by every moment of every new day.

Adam is gone. His rooms are empty. He left the large table. It was, Clara presumes, too cumbersome to transport. All the beautiful linen for the double-bed is gone. The best towels. Fine crockery. All the books, even some of Clara's personal library . . .

He is gone. Off to play the game of Dingley-Dong-Dong-Dong . . .

Who would abandon love - Love - for that game . . .

Clara wakes rich every morning. Gold pieces under her pillow one morning. Then the Three Golden Eggs one morning, then the

216

Golden Feather fluttering through her open window on sunrise one morning.

She builds Adam's two abandoned rooms into a shrine in celebration of life and love . . . A thousand and one small and beautiful handcrafted objects from time now, from time yesterday and long ago are displayed. Each is in its own potent presence like a prayer, like a song, like a thanksgiving.

They lie, they stand on a table cloth of finest linen grown on ancestral farms and spun and woven by women in the dark winter time of long, long ago. You touch this fine cloth, you see the field of flax, the blue of the flowers like a hush of dew. You see the women preparing the flax for the spinning, a long and patient work. You see them, a few together, spinning, gossiping, singing, telling stories . . . You see the one, alone, spinning and dreaming . . . I spring from a long line of dreamers.

Each object on the table sings. Each is chosen for its song: He who crafted it, made it in gladness, in joy. His life is in it. It sings. The whole table is a great jubilation and in its silence, its great deep silence, the heart renews, the soul renews, the body renews.

There is a power here. A might!

Imagine, in each object is the one who made it.

Imagine, the might of the hands that made the thousand and one things . . .

Enter the room, and you are irradiated . . . and you leave the room touched, penetrated and moved. And you walk home and you say Ah and Oh and the Ah and the Oh stays with you, it hides inside you and comes out at times and consoles you and heals you, maybe. Later, much later - and at odd times - the magical table appears in front of you and you say yes, I have seen it with my own eyes and it fills my eyes now as then with wonder and makes my heart glad, now as then. For as soon as you enter this space, that is now healed and made holy by the presence of these sacred objects, you are, as it were, received into the blessed hands of all the makers of these beautiful and enchanted things and you are held in a spell of love.

*　　*　　*　　*

k

Above the table, in the centre of the white wall, hangs a wooden cross of a great power. It was made by 'Big Bear', named thus by Clara on her first encounter with this giant of a heart-man. - Having amassed a huge fortune from doing a very creative and hugely lucrative job, his secretary looked up at him one day and said, "Man, tell me, why do you do what you are doing?" He looked down at her from his mighty six foot-plus-plus in astonishment and after a stunned silence said, "Well, honestly, I don't know."

He then and there gave his fortune away, became a recluse and started searching for the true face of Christ. He cut it in wood, he cut it in metal, he painted it, he carved it in stone and finally, after years, he created this crude wooden cross and in its centre painted The Face. This was it. This *was* Christ's true face. It had been given him into his hands. His agonised search of many years had ended.

Clara met Big Bear at this very moment, a man of pure light and the simple heart of a child. He entrusted his cross to Clara.

Possibly the oldest object on the sacred table is a small moss-green glazed clay-pipe, only some two inches long, but awe-inspiring in its beautifully crafted presence. And capable of quite a smoke! - It was found in Mexico on a huge ancient burial site by her then small five-year-old son Michael, who was fascinated by the story of this particular Indian tribe, that had died of starvation because their King had chosen Gold rather than the Seed of Corn also offered to him by the Gods.

On the wall to the right of the table hangs 'The Marriage', an ageless, archetypal couple in the gentle light of eight candles, that is like a halo all around their touching bodies and is as if emanating from their mingled souls. - A painting that grows on one and is ever more moving.

It is for Clara an icon, a sacred painting of the inner marriage. - A gift, so, so long ago, from the painter Satorsky to Clara and Adam.

*   *   *   *

218

On the wall between the two large windows facing out to sea, Clara hangs the Archangel Michael, a wood carving of ancient oak, carved by Adam, while Michael was growing in the womb and presented to Clara on his birth . . . Under the wooden cross stands the 'Lady from the Sea', carved by Adam a long loving age ago with longing hands from a piece of teak driftwood, fished out of St Ia's harbour. - This, too, is like an archetypal figure, an inner woman: the feminine as listening, as stillness.

The small room adjacent and entered through an arch has a small round leather topped Mexican table on which are many scallop-shells laid in a spiral pattern round a central small candle-stick in enamelled brass. They were, all together, thrown out by a huge wave that had fallen over Clara most unexpected, as she had stood, one evening, below the harbour wall watching the in-coming tide. Drenched and dripping, she gathered these fruits of the sea into her wide skirt - a gift, an omen: the shell symbol of femininity and love, Venus born from it . . . No two shells are alike and some of the smaller ones are like radiant rising suns in tender shades of yellow and rose and ochre.

A low, rush-seated, long-backed peasant chair from the Ticino stands in the corner by the window. - Ticino! the name enchants . . . the chair tells stories: remember . . . remember . . .
Pictures of enchanted times are thrown on the screen of memory: Clara in the very young morning dancing lightfully the meandering path-through the paradisiacal wilderness garden to the pool in the stream for her morning bath . . . Clara lying dreaming in the hammock slung between two large trees on a steep slope behind the cottage of magic and enchantment. In the hammock slung between heaven and heaven, Clara is dreaming. She is twenty. She is in love with love . . . Lago Maggiore lies in a vast silver slumber below . . . A golden early morning. Clara weightlessly floating up the endless steps to Madonna del Sasso above Locarno. The morning breeze carries a myriad of flower scents. The portal of Madonna del Sasso is wide open and sounds of heavenly music pour over Clara as she enters the church. No players are visible . . . Clara is carried away and forgets time and

place, and she receives the music as light and made light by it, flies away, out and up, and mingles with heavenly beings who chant: Son est Lumière . . . Son et Lumière . . .

Adam is gone.
No: Adieu.
No: au revoir.
No: so long.
No: good bye.
No: see you.
No: take care, my love . . .
No: farewell, dear heart . . .
Adam is gone.
To play the Big Boy's Game of Dingley-Dong-Dong-Dong. It's easily played. Needs only one other player. There are many such playmates to be found at any one moment of day and night to play the game of Dingley-Dong-Dong with . . .
Would you abandon love for this game?

Clara is building her life. Gloriously. O yes.
No less. Gloriously.
Clara makes Gold. She pours Gold, everywhere.
Shine life, Clara, and make it sing.
Shine life, Clara, as you shone the Blood-Ladle on Pig-Killing-Day when you were a small child. A most privileged and holy task: 'Look, Mother, look, I made the ladle shine like gold . . .'
Bring the light forth and let the light fall in.
Become a song!

Adam is gone. So, he is gone.
The light is falling into all the corners of the house . . . The spiders are spinning webs in front of the windows. The first morning rays play their light in these finest threads and each web becomes a dance of glittering diamonds.

Adam is gone. So, he is gone.
The days are long and deep and rich.

220

The days are mine.

Clara is rich. Her inner space grows. And she delves into it, down to the deep dark where the seed perishes into life. And she discovers the fire-force as light as colour as sound.

The openness. The glad openness.

Everything has to become itself.

For every gesture, there is the tool to fulfil itself.

What you wish, let it fully grow in the soil of your heart and you will be fulfilled.

O, the living moment lived!

I create myself, stone by living stone, moment by living moment, with the help of God.

And God is in my within.

I tune into my innermost, where God sings.

To live is to follow step by step the voice of your heart.

Every morning Clara wakes to find a gift of golden wisdom under her pillow.

Adam is gone. He has been gone for some time. He has been trying nasty tricks on Clara's life: to divorce her forcibly, to gain possession of the matrimonial home . . . to get her declared unfit to handle her life and affairs, so to be in need of legal guardianship . . . to have her declared incurably insane . . . All these failed. He did not reckon with Clara's clear and strong vision and sanity.

But he managed to totally alienate their daughter by scattering ill-begotten tales, which he disguised in the sweet cloak of saintliness, thrown over self-pity and guilt, and he did this with great success.

You reap eventually, do you not, what you sow . . ?

Was the noble man that he had been in Clara's eyes when they first fell on him a guise, too . . . or is the nasty one the underside . . . the shadow never acknowledged?

*   *   *   *

Love him, Clara, love him, do! More than ever it is clear, he needs your love.

- Fare well, dear man! Maybe this mischief that you are doing will, rather than undermine me, undermine you, and finally - eer it is too late - let you have the courage to look at yourself, right at and straight at, straight and clear and smile at what you see. May that be so! For what a pity, if you were a lesser man at the end of your life than at your gloriously gifted beginning. Fare well, dear man.

Later, much later, anger would come to the fore, dark anger, and Clara would make it into grief and put it under and deep down, where there was already a pile of it and, she would paint bright colours over and leave it there, until she *believed* that grief *was* her true inner state of being . . .

At this moment, farewell, dear man. Beloved. Farewell.

The inner space is growing. Space all around is growing. Light becomes lighter and from the silence that deepens, Clara receives, as if from a well, gifts of in-seeing and nourishing dreams.

I have, as it were, to prepare the house of me to receive myself in. I have to ready myself to receive my Self.

There is one person, so it seems, I made myself into to match the image that that dear man had of me and there is the other, the one I really am.

Among the objects on the celebratory table are many eggs. Some are real eggs exquisitely decorated in bright colours and with bright things as for Easter. Others are crafted elaborately in mother of pearl and silver filigree or cut of stone or of wood. All are, however simple, made in celebration of The Egg and in awe of its mystery. There are all sorts of seeds, too, some minute ones, barely visible to the naked eye. They make a splendour of shapes and colour. There is the eight-star, the wondrous seed of Bergamot, the scarlet Monarda, the tousled highly scented blossom and lovely leaves of which make the soothing and sleep inducing tea Oswego, that the American Indians still know. Holding any one of these seeds in the palm of her hand, Clara is holding the mystery of a new life, which, wonderfully, is in each as Geistkeim - the fire-kernel - the essential being of that which it is meant to become and be.

By perishing, by death, through chaos in the light-ful dark, in the hearth-womb of The Mother, the process of dividing, multiplying, twining, fusing happens endlessly. The five-star becomes. The rose-in-the-heart-of-the-matter becomes. Thus the dot - le point - der Punkt - this mighty power station of the spirit, of fire, when fired, when inspired, at that precise moment brings forth its transmuting energy of highest creative force. And each become new form is being gifted with the same energy and working in the same force-filled, transforming and transfiguring way, on and on, until the innate being is become.

Imagine this! See this! Holding the egg in the palm of your hand, holding the seed in the palm of your hand.

See your self thus become the seed, die the death, and from the substance of that death - the dot - the fire innate, rise, rise like Phoenix rose.

'Le point, ça c'est le point!' Zwei-Stein Einstein, my occasional one-minute-past-midnight-guest said smilingly one time, then vanished as He had come . . .

And it seemed to Clara after hearing this said, that all the scientists should become silence-ists: enter silence and dream.

Dream Le Point! Dream it in depth . . . Imagine! to have a whole house heated by this dot, bei einem Puenktchen . . . Imagine! this dot to be discovered at last as the greatest force of becoming and creating . . . Imagine! a whole world full of *human* beings, because this dot, this totally invisible dot, has revealed itself to the dreamers that the scientists now have become, as the mighty might of creativity: Love itself.

*   *   *   *

223

The blinders of their own brilliance have been removed and as dreamers they see, *see* how hellishly mistaken they have been to use this force in such a misunderstood way that it destroys.

O, scientists of the world, I call upon you, become Silence-ists! For in silence is that which makes the world go round and turns us and everything and all on.

Im Puenktchen ist's; in the dot!

Ah, ah, what a dreamer you are, Clara - ah, ah, but I tell you, it is in silence that The voice speaks and The Word is being heard . . .

It's in the egg, it's in the seed, where slumber dynamic worlds, which can only be awakened by the same force that brought them into being, the dynamic of dynamics which is Love.

The Dynamic of dynamics which is Love.

A dream is given: I am walking along in a pleasant country-side, idly, when out of the blue a loosely wrapped brown-paper parcel is flung at me and an urgent voice shouts, 'Catch it, it is the most precious thing and *you* have to bring it into safety!'

With that, I find myself instantly in the midst of a raging water clutching this stringless tatty parcel to me, getting to the shear rock side, which awaits me and which I have to scale, for behind me the turbulent waters roar.

With one hand I am clutching this parcel and the other helping myself up this vertical rock-face, where on top opens a sunlit lush green place and the precious thing in the parcel is revealed to me as 'The Last Shoot of Human Life . . . '

Clear thy mansion, Clara, make the rooms in it spacious, for there is someone ready to enter.

Adam is gone. He has been gone some long time.

You have done this thing, Adam, dear man. But let me remind

you, that any action finishes not at the moment it is acted, nor does thought at the moment it is thought, but they make echoes . . . echoes . . .

Clara makes her heart into a crown and puts it on her head every morning. - She pours her life into every moment.

Who said, Paradise is lost . . . look, you are standing in the middle of it.

Who said fear . . . look, I am holding and being held.

Who said the snake, the apple and The fall . . . look, I was blind and I can see now. Look, I was deaf and I can hear now.

It is not miracles that are happening, but that I am alive. Simply.

And that I love myself. Simply.

The one is with the other as breathing in and breathing out.

And flowers grow and flowers grow, where she walks.

I love myself: this immediately embraces you and you and you and God and all. It's a happening, an is-ing, and in all your doing you are transfigured into what you are doing, as you are doing it for the love of that which cannot be named, but is named God.

Imagine, to be thus transfigured into the bowl of cream of vegetable soup that you made to share with a friend or into the brocade slippers that you made for your true love . . .

No, I don't want to gain Paradise, nor eternal life, no, no, no. I want to make Paradise wherever I step and right here and now and live and live and live and make eternity in every living moment.

We have it in us. Each one. And woman has it in huge measure. We are made of infinite dots and each one a power station.

Beware! That day, when all these dots are let loose, this power of love let loose.

Beware! I say, of this Love, this pure energy that transmutes, transforms, transfigures and never ceases, endlessly flows . . .

Be aware! And tune in now, that you and you and you *are* this power-station, this Love. - Ha! and see the corn grow as golden as ever and children laughing and dancing in the streets and hearts opening everywhere.

Ha! Wait and see! When those dots are let loose and the Golden Calves in all the High Streets in every town and city everywhere, those money-palaces, will be turned into fun places, dance-halls and music-halls and theatres, for money will not be goods anymore, a substance that multiplies on its own, this evil aberration, but simply a means and all things will be in their right state, their right proportion and their clear being.

Great and unfathomable is the transforming power of the dot.

Mammon is blowing all over the streets, pieces of a burst balloon the children catch and play the game of farts with . . .

You have never heard such laughter . . .

And lo! The churches and cathedrals and chapels will not be market-places any more, where this creed or that creed is sold to the masses, this doctrine or that doctrine imposed upon the folk, this theology or that theology impressed upon the vulnerable to keep them ignorant. But rather will they be sanctuaries, where life and death are being celebrated with dance and music, feasts of loving and thanksgiving are being built and hymns sung for the small and great forgiveness.

For is not forgiveness the beginning of human love . . .

To for-give, is it not the fundament of loving . . .

You cannot build peace on an arsenal of lethal weapons nor on judgements of who is the good and who is the bad - for who is judging? - but from forgiveness grows peace as from rich soil, naturally.

And it starts with myself. - You do not condone what has been done, but by forgiving you step into the living moment and live: - I forgive myself and at once, in an instant, I create a field of light in me and around me. And wounds inflicted on my spirit are healed and a healing goes from me to you, and you are forgiven for what you have inflicted on me. The light-field grows. Light as love is innate in the gesture of forgiving.

And light like water finds ways of penetrating.

Nein, das Leben ist kein Jammertal!

Open your arms and receive yourself in.

Open your arms and lift your head and stand as to receive and give when you praise The Lord!

And praise Him! - Who wants to bend his head and mumble in his chest and get sore knees . . .

Praise Him wide-armed in a gesture of offering and receiving.

Joy living and *make* joy of living and thus make true that you are charged with the Grandeur of God.

Clara dreams.

Clara is dreaming.

Dreams are true. You look into a time not yet already happened.

And Clara remembers the dream given her of the tatty brown paper parcel containing the last shoot of human life and the urgency to bring it to safety . . . The urgency. The great urgent urgency to preserve life. And Clara breaks down and weeps for days.

- One time or another you must shed the tears unshed at the time of weeping.

*　　*　　*　　*

And then she dances.

She dances.

She dances.

Clara dances.

And into her vision come two black-gold dancers from the Gold Coast of Africa, one star-strewn night years ago, and a castle cum youth-hostel on a rocky hill-top somewhere in Wales.

A small patch of grass within a circle of rocks is the star-lit sanctum for this night of nights. The magical black eyes of the warden sparkle like jewels while he spellbinds the three young women's bodies into dance.

Wilder and wilder the music, wilder the dancing. On midnight, the swarthy fiddler, alight, turns his fiddle into a drum. And drums. Drums.

The two Black Diamonds from the Gold-Coast dance their Creation Dance. It begins slowly. So slowly, their movement is barely perceptible. Then faster and ever faster. Their bodies spin and are transformed.

They become The Dance, the force that pulls the sun over the horizon and brings the new day. At this moment, shouts and clapping of hands. The dancing slower and slower until they re-emerge into the first morning of creation: two golden shining creatures, themselves like new born suns.

They are standing there, deeply still, arms spread high and wide in the first rays of the risen sun. The drummer, flame now, takes the three women into his huge embrace and laughs and laughs and laughs, as God might have done on His first morning of Creation.

Clara dances.

She is interrupted a few times by young people who are in need of talking of their lives. By listening, she feels, she is allowing them to hear the answers within themselves. - Listening creates a spacious silence potent with news. And a word she may say, here and there, may fall like a seed into the desert of someone's heart and might lie there for years until, miraculously, another word like rain falls there.

A short while before she began her spell of dancing, a tall, elegantly dressed and well spoken man had addressed Clara just as she was walking through a crowded shop to reach the cafe behind. He told her, that his life was falling to pieces and that he needed help desperately.

Clara was on her way to meet Adam and was already late, so she wrote her address on a scrap of paper and hastened on.

In the later evening of that day, she had just sat down to dinner with friends, this man walked in and said how relieved he was to have found her. He joined in the dinner and briefly told of his plight.

Clara offered him spontaneously her cottage in the courtyard in the quiet of which he could sort himself out and told him, that he would only have to pay for the electricity used. There was one snag, that the cottage could only be reached by using the front-door of the double-fronted main house, which, however, was always left unlocked day and night, and by walking through its long corridor.

She almost immediately forgot about this 'lodger'. She never saw him go in or out, and he did not bother her.

Clara needs to dance.

And she dances. Dance creates a spacious silence potent with messages - it heals and makes waves. She does not eat, but drinks the healing water from Mont Blanc.

At dusk on the third day, through-lit and light-ful, she lights two three-branched candelabras and dances, one in each hand, the singing of Piaf.

However fast she moves, however brisk, the six candles burn gently on.

There is no time or place now, only dancing in celebration of life received.

She locks the front-door for the first time in all her life as a home owner.

The dancing, the singing, the light of the candles have created a sanctum she needs to be alone in.

The blind on the seafront window is pulled down.

Night has fallen.

There is a sharp rapping on the window. Clara dances towards it, the candelabras swaying in the movement of her dancing. Vaguely, she sees 'the lodger' outside pointing towards the front-door and making the motion of a key turning. Clara indicates that she must finish her dancing, then she will open the door.

No words are spoken only gestures made . . .

She immediately forgets the man and the locked door; She is wrapped in her dancing and Piafs singing.

There is a commotion in the courtyard. Voices. Lanterns. What could it be? There are very high walls there and no direct entrance from anywhere. Through the kitchen window she sees black-clad people coming over the north wall down a tall ladder. - What is all this . . . She dashes to the front door, opens it and finds an ambulance right in front of her. Turning back into the corridor she is being faced by two fully uniformed police men; one police woman, a well-dressed man who introduces himself as Dr So and So and the meek voice of a Social Worker.

*   *   *   *

"A man was violently threatened with burning candelabras; it is for your own protection that we have come. You will be taken to the Mental Hospital. Is there anything you need to pack . . ."

Clara has no chance of defence. Look, at the numbers that have turned up . . . This 'lodger', what is he? A front-man to lime her in? Put forward by Adam . . ? Had he not appeared at the very moment and in the very place where she had had a meeting with Adam?

Look! She had done him a great favour and look, what has he done, gone and called the police and accused her of having been threatened by her with burning candelabras . . . what humbug, what humbug . . .

Clara talks very quietly at first, then she screams: "You cannot take me away, I haven't done any harm to anyone and I am in no danger of harming myself. I am not mad! I was dancing for joy and in celebration. I locked the door to be alone. This man was outside my double-glazed window. I was inside, right here, in my living room."

"What are you doing here? How dare you come on my property the way you did . . ."

"I shall have to give you an injection if you don't calm down."

Clara was desperately outnumbered. And their greatest power was, of course, that she had a history of stays in the Lunatic Asylum.

She packed her hair brush and her comb and her toothbrush and a delightful handkerchief - to remind her of her Mother - and she stepped into the ambulance head high and bare-foot, clad in the gorgeous caftan she had danced in for three days and three nights.

It was her most beloved garment. She had made it from ancient hand-blocked Indian cloth bought in an antique-shop in Santa Fe, New Mexico, years earlier. She had lined the silk-fine cotton with as fine a geranium-red cotton matching the delicate patterns in red on the otherwise gold cloth. She thus had created a garment of elegance and beauty to at once enhance the inner and the outer.

The caftan was charged with the radiance of the cloth itself, the magical occasions it had been worn at and the many dream-filled days it had taken to hand-stitch it . . . and above all, Santa Fe, where she had had her first encounter with Navajo Indians.

'Our Sister,' they called her. And the most Ancient One - how deep his eyes - and did not life shine from him like suns and moons and stars, and was it not, being in his presence, like being in the presence of Love - put into Clara's hands a large uncut Turquoise and folding them, he held them and said:

"Now you will always be with us. Now we are always related. May you grow old. May your roads be filled. May you be blessed with life. To where the life-giving road of your sun-father comes out, may your life reach."

The kindly ambulance man, Fred, belted her into the seat, apologising for it, but that it was part of his duty.

The Social Worker sat stiffly.

The journey through the night into the night had begun.

How fateful a kindly gesture can be . . .

Fred clears his throat several times and fidgets, then he says, "We were supposed to be prepared to pick up a violent woman, but you are one of the nicest ladies I have met. I am really sorry to have to take you up there."

"It's all right, Fred. Some of us are put on trial again and again and at the time when it happens, we are not to know why. You look like a man who has seen an awful lot of life, you know how strange and wonderful its ways are."

Clara takes this chance to ask him to unbelt her for a moment. "I have a big pocket on the inside of my dress and there is something in it I'd like to take out."

232

From the big pocket, Clara brings out a golden cardboard heart - a recent gift from a child, it's hanging on an ordinary string and she puts it round her neck and wears it like a pendant.

Fred presses her hand and gives her a big warm smile.

The Social Worker sits without a word, stiff as a board.

Fred holds Clara's hand all the rest of the journey . . .

They arrive. Fred unbelts her and helps her out of the ambulance. It is pitch dark. The lights of the ambulance shine on to a grim looking building.

"Everything will be all right love," Fred and the driver say it together. The Social Worker and Fred take Clara up to the door.

Clara says anxiously, "But this is not the ward you had promised to take me to."

"O yes it is, it's the night entrance."

But Clara knew it was not.

A light is switched on. Keys are rattling. The door is opened. The three step in. The door is locked behind them. Endless winding metal stairs are confronting Clara. "You have lied to me, this is not the ward you promised you would take me to."

"Isn't it? Look, just don't start any trouble . . ."

Fred squeezes her hand. Dear man. Dear, dear man. But Clara's heart sinks terribly deep the higher they climb . . . what are they doing to her . . . is it an imprisonment.

Inside herself she calls out 'Oh, stand by me, stand by me heart of hearts, do not abandon me now. Keep me strong.'

Finally, they arrive at the door that leads into what . . .

Several nurses are there and a male nurse . . . so many . . . they are prepared for this violent woman . . . 'Fred, Fred, don't go . . . Fred . . . ' but the door has already been locked behind him . . .

"What's this place?"

"A closed ward for women."

"Here you are, take these tablets."

"No, don't give them to me, I am not sick, I am not violent. You have been wrongly informed. I have been dancing for joy

1

and suddenly these people appeared and took me away. I have done no harm to anyone. Look at me, do I look like someone who is crazy?"

"We know all about it. Come on, take these tablets, Doctor's orders."

"Please, please don't force them on me, I have been building up my life and I am very well. *Very well*. The drugs will crush me I know these drugs too well. Why do you want to take my life away .. ?"

"Come, come, its late, we haven't got all night, Doctor's orders is Doctor's orders!"

I say it all again. Then I shout it. Then I scream it, "Don't give them to me, don't give these drugs to me, they murder my spirit!"

At this moment, she is gotten hold of. She is being dragged into a small room and forced to lie down on a couch. "As you are refusing the drugs, we will have to inject you."

"Nooooooooooooooooooooooooooooooooooooooooooooooo"

"Listen! Hear me! Listen! I shall be crushed. I shall help myself, gently, gently."

The word gently was already suffocated by the weight of the nurses sitting on her, one on her face. And her own body now became the echo chamber and the screams volume became a monstrous force within her with no way out.

No way out.

The needle! Lightning fast! The brutal stab thrust deep into her buttock.

- The blood becomes salted. The breath snatched.
Light snuffed. Life cut.
They put a night-shirt on a leaden body.

Only moments before, Clara had been dancing lightly, wildly on a tight-rope high up in the air. Brutally, the rope was cut. No net to catch her falling. So she crashed to a horrible death of shattered and numbed senses, crushed mind, miserably bruised heart and battered soul.

And loud echoes are ringing inside her and outside her: is there a heart anywhere, a heart anywhere, a loving heart anywhere . . .

Every wall and ceiling inside and outside her an instrument tuned to playing this miserable chant louder and louder . . .

And then this solemn voice, '*The place of crucifixion is the place of rebirth . . .*'

When she woke, she didn't know who it was who woke.
She   didn't   know whoitwaswhowokewhoitwaswhowokewhoitwaswhowokewhoit-waswhowokewhoitwaswho . . .

Who woke? Who woke? Who was it that woke . . ?
A body that was mindless . . .
A mash . . .

It is days later when she starts to grasp where she is and that once more her life had been smashed.

She remembers her dancing and how light she had been and how through-lit. And how lightfully she had danced, for all fear had gone from her. How clear and bright her mind had been. How well it had been tuned to the sounds from the Earth and from Heaven. How at home she had felt in herself, how beloved to herself. How glad her gestures and how each word was that word spoken. There was no effort and such good measure in all her doing. And how rich the silence . . . There was weightlessness . . . does the earth ponder her weight . . . does heaven . . . do the planets . . .

There was weightlessness, a lovely equilibrium that was as light as radiance.

To be plucked out of this and smashed! What's behind it . . .

who wants her life out of the way . . . To whom is her life a threat when it is bright and strong and clear and whole . . . What are the forces that try again and again to wipe her life out . . . No doubt, Adam is at the bottom of it, but what is he trying to achieve, to gain . . .

Those words from that fatal night, those last ones before her mind was blacked out suddenly come to her tongue, and she says them inside herself:
'The place of crucifixion is the place of rebirth.' - Must she then be thankful to this undermining force from wherever it comes . . ?

A bit of light shines in, a bit of light shines out . . . Once more, she has to begin. As she recognises this, her limbs that had been arrested start moving again, and her speech that had been shattered is regained. And she says those words loud and clear:
The place of crucifixion is the place of rebirth.'

Her progress towards herself is fast and she is becoming aware of her surroundings. She is able to open her heart and let many of those other women come in that fill the ward. She listens to them. For a moment that is quickly lost, it makes them feel that someone cares and it helps Clara to rebuild her self-worth.

She finds, that they are all disconnected from their essential selves and that therefore there is no meaning in their lives. In all the stories Clara hears, guilt has become an unbearable load. A great wrong that they had done to themselves or allowed themselves to be done to. Wounds deep in their womanly selves self-inflicted or inflicted on them. Deep wounds. And unhealed. Clara sees them under the words that tell the stories. But the telling is separate from the one who tells.
The story lives an existence divorced from the woman it belongs to.

*　　*　　*　　*

The psychiatric treatment covers or even takes away from the patient the living field of emotions and the impulse to live and to cope and to muster the will to enliven themselves. In this confinement in the Lunatic Asylum there is no healing, on the contrary, that which wants out and to be laid bare is suppressed and covered up further. And what is left in the end is a body full of knots, often shapeless and hapless, talking and walking, but not inhabited by a lively, alive life. And in each one is a tithe barn full to overflowing of unthreshed emotions.

The life has been brought to a stand-still; *that* is understood to be the cure. In that motionless state, a life can be handled; it doesn't make any trouble for itself or anyone . . . What is not understood is, that this is murder. The real thing! And never named. Nor ever seen as the crime of crimes.

Someone's life is taken away, snatched away, and it is called cure! - There are many ways of murdering a life and never are these murders called by that name. But quietly they go on in families, in marriages, in institutions, in society at large . . . immensely quietly.

A great seeing is given to Clara. In the dormitory filled with many beds, her bed is nearest the door. As so often, Clara cannot sleep. She sits up in bed and lets her eyes roam and she wonders at each life lying there. Each so troubled, so lost and yet so rich with life if found or allowed to be discovered and lived.

Suddenly, the whole wall to the left becomes translucent with light and a wonderfully richly melodious humming as of many voices is heard, as into the room floats a ship made of light.

In it are lightful souls, egg-shaped luminous beings, their indescribable beauty is more deeply moving than that of a newly born child. Four of these wondrous light beings reveal themselves as the souls of beloved ones long departed. All together, and there are many in the ship, they sing in sounds not known to Clara, yet within her they immediately are translated into these words:

'We weave the same cloth, it is the cloth of life. We weave it in Heaven, you weave it on Earth. We weave all together the Cloth of Life. Life is in each moment. Fear not. Not ever more. We hold you. You hold us.

Together, we are one, in love.'

*   *   *   *

Clara is within their light, it is all around her, the room is it. She feels herself in a wonderful lightful embrace. Then, amidst the heavenly humming now become more voluminous, as if the air itself was it, the Divine Ship floats out.

Gentle, lovely sound and light linger a little. Then the room falls back to being the dormitory lit by minute piercing lights that pain.

Clara is filled with an immense beauty and joy which she cannot contain and she becomes a flood of tears of gladness.

Melinda, a fellow patient, comes up to Clara every day and touches her golden gown, and says, "You are like the Queen of Heaven," and pointing at her own heart-break-face, she adds, "I haven't got a face, see, I wiped my own face out."

Each time, she walks away hastily, then turns at a distance and putting both her hands over her face shouts through them, "I am faceless, see!"

Clara was without face, once, she had forgotten it. She had looked in the mirror and there was no face only a hand waving . . . She remembered the terror of the total isolation that gripped her and how she was ready to wipe all of herself out.

How did Melinda get to be on that brink . . .

Clara remembers, how Elisabeth helped her to find her face in her hands by moving her fingers over her face and discovering it bit by bit, until it was there in her hands. And how from that first gesture every gesture grew until her life was like a young growing tree.

Melinda has the palest blue eyes, the blue of the small butterflies of which there used to be clouds of at Midsummertime over puddles of clear water in secret country lanes. They are lightless in a colourless face. The face of a child that has witnessed horror

238

and stricken by it, froze. - But the heart- breaking beauty of it . . .

"I am a criminal. I shouldn't be here. I should be in the darkest dungeon of a prison . . ." Melinda says this one day, her eyes glazed as in a fever, and she holds on to Clara's gown and crumples it in her desperate fists.

Clara wraps her into her arms and folds her into the warmth of her body. And Melinda presses her head into Clara's breasts and into Clara's body are falling Melinda's words: "Queen of Heaven, that you are, forgive me, I have murdered. I allowed my child to be aborted."

The sobs of the two women mingle with their tears and the warmth of their close bodies.

And into Clara's closed eyes comes a vision of the healing force of touch. She sees a radiance of lightful rays flowing around the two closely held bodies; and just then Melinda whispers, "Your body is like a sun, hold me tight and do not let me go."

Love as touch creates a current, makes a flow. It undoes knots, makes connections where they have been severed, ties vital threads that have been torn. And the one who gives and the one who receives are the same movement, each becomes the healer of the other. And at once in each the source of healing is vitalised.

Thus, with hardly any words, by loving touch Melinda gradually opens herself to her Self.

It is a thawing process. The ice of her self-inflicted isolation has to be melted. The frozen inner, where to her Self she is this faceless woman who has committed this unforgivable sin, has to be penetrated with warmth.

She allowed this thing to happen.

Blackmailed by her husband, older than her own father, that he would kill himself if she went ahead with the pregnancy, friend-less and estranged from her parents because of her marriage to this much older man, she had no one to turn to. And too afraid to face life on her own, she had the abortion.

None of the doctors - all male - that her husband had arranged for her to see, asked, 'but how do you feel about this?' And in the Abortion Clinic the Surgeon's only words to her were, "So then, where is the envelope with the money . . ?"

The whole procedure was matter of fact. - There goes more compassion into plucking a chicken.

Her whole being froze at once. She could not function in any respect anymore. She was haunted. She was declared schizophrenic. Her husband didn't want to know her anymore and she was put in Mental Hospital, where she has undergone many treatments, including electric shock.

Clara knows in her depth that Melinda's life is meant to live. Melinda herself uncovered the vital spark. And in the warmth of their daily meeting the ice melteth . . .
Hand in hand they undertake this voyage of discovery in the dark underground that a psychosis (so called) must be understood to be and that there is a divine plan to it and that it *must* run its sacred course. Sacred, like the seasons of the year, and it must happen within the same divine laws by which the planets wander, the earth turns, the sun spins, the moon waxes and wanes.
Seen with the eyes of love - the only eyes that see truly - this voyage is an initiation into the life of my Self. Its passage is immanent in the sacred-being of this one unique individual life and seen thus, the healing process becomes a ritual.
By traversing the dark of myself, I become enriched with insights and once returned to the 'normal' world, I cannot, *can not* be the same as when I started out, for I now bear witness to the riches of life itself. It is vital, *vital*, that I am sustained and guided in my journeying, not hindered,blocked, suppressed.
For I am chosen to discover not just any life, but the unique life truly belonging to me and no other.

It was a wonderful, wonderful moment, when Clara heard Melinda say, "But I am not mad, Clara, I am on a journey!" And:

240

"Clara, you once said 'immediately on conceiving, the whole of a woman, mind, body, soul and heart, is flowing together to begin the building of this new life within her.'

"Well, Clara, all of me will need to flow together to build the new life that is to be mine. And I shall not only be the beautiful human being that I am but also the great musician that I am destined to be. It is in *my hands* and I have faith. Somewhere within me, it is already accomplished. Praise be!"

Melinda's affirmation of herself affirms Clara also. The one is a blessing to the other. Each one is destined to live and to love. Glory be!

Melinda meeting Clara - Clara meeting Melinda - and in the discovery of one another, they receive healing and a rich insight into their own lives.

They are in hospital. They receive treatment. But once you have found that Yes within you, you are free.

'With my music, I make love wherever I perform,
With my life, I make life . . .
Clara, Queen of Heaven,
      I love you.
        Melinda.'

A note from Melinda some years after their meeting in Mental Hospital.

This is Clara's destiny, too, now that her Self is born to herself from herself. Her musical instrument is love.

She makes love by living and lives by loving. She is in a readiness to receive life every day anew and to give it in vast gestures of love. By her loving, Love loves; by her living, Life lives. She is in a state of Grace.

*   *   *   *

Blow the horns!
Blow the horns!
Oh, blow them!
And tell it on the
Seven Mountains!
And Sing it!
Sing it!
Oh, sing it to the sixteen corners
of the wind.
And dance!
Dance!
Dance!

The work dress, worn and threadbare, had fallen off on its own unnoticed, and I find myself in the gold-threaded gown, ready. Ready for the dance.

Let's dance.

```
*********
*******
******
****
**
*

*
**
****
******
*******
*********
```

Clara's Dream. A Gift

I am swimming in a turbulent sea. I am swimming vigorously and wholly one with the element and right deep within it; and I am as one, also, with all manner of sea creatures that are moving under, over and around me. There is a symphony of magical sound. I come out on a shore, but I am compelled to leap back in, deep in, and I am so one, that I wonder which is me and which is sea. I float up and reach an island; standing on the shore's edge, bejewelled with bright drops of sea-water, a wild beautiful golden-brown horse comes galloping and, stopping still by me, presses his shining body against mine. I am caressing him and with each touch, there is a flash of golden light. And again this wondering: which is me, which is the horse, as energies flow from him to me, from me to him until we are not distinguishable, one from the other.

Being in this wonder and force of one with the sea and one with the horse and feeling myself to be alight, a might of lightful energy, there appears the figure of a Wise-Man, a radiant sunlike face. He gives me the gift of a Mandala, a wheel wrought of gold, most magically and beautifully crafted and composed in a splendid rhythm of forms, symbols, alike to Runes, and He says, 'This gift for you, Clara:

'The Letters of the Alphabet of Life. Listen, Clara, listen, The Wheel of Life is Sound.'

He shines my face with the light of His face and all is illumined by His presence! Continuously bowing towards me, walking backwards, He vanishes into the blue haze out of which He had appeared.

Clara is within a lit-up space of crystal sound.

Porth Enys, Day of Epiphany, 6th of January 1991.

The following are translations of poems printed in German within the text of *CLARA*. These have been kindly translated by the poet Philip Elston.

From page 94 of the book:

Home by Hoelderlin

And they who bestow us with heavenly fire,
The gods, with holy sorrow bequeath us too.
So be it, then. A son of Earth I
Seem: created to love, and to suffer.

Enlightenment by Friedrich Hebbel

In deep and immeasurable hours
Have you never in foreboding pain,
Perceived the spirit of the universe,
In your heart as a fading flame?

by Rilke

I have such a fear of the words of men.
Everything explained with their plain sounds:
and this they call house and that they call hound;
here is the beginning and there is the end.

From page 95 of the book:

The Observer by Rilke

What of the small things with which we struggle,
which struggle with us, and what of the large;
if, like objects, we allowed,
the great storm to conquer us,
we would become unnamed and vast.

In the Grass by Annette von Droste-Huelshoff

Heaven, I have this one request,
Only this: for each free bird's song
Which fills the skies of blue above,
A soul for it to trail along;
And for each sparse ray of the sun
My vivid outline shimmering,
For each warm hand the clutch of mine,
And for each happiness, my dream.

On The Tower by Annette von Droste-Huelshoff

I stand upon the tower's high balcony,
Shrieking starlings are brushing past me,
And I let a maenad run the fingers
Of the storm through my flying hair;
O rugged fellow, o wild jackanapes,
How I'd love to firmly embrace you
And sinew for sinew, two steps from the brink,
For death and for life I'd struggle.

From page 140 of the book:

From *The Secret Roses* by Christian Morgenstern

Oh, whoever knows all the roses,
which around the still garden grow -
oh, whoever knows all things, must
journey through their life in rapture.